RATCATCHER

ISBN-13: 978-1478298427

About the author

Tim Stevens was born in London and raised in Johannesburg. He lives in west Essex, England, with his wife and daughters, and works as a doctor on the National Health Service.

Ratcatcher is his debut novel. His other published works include the Cold War espionage novella **Reunion** and novelette **Snout**.

Delivering Caliban, the sequel to **Ratcatcher**, will be published in autumn 2012.

To Pippa

RATCATCHER

One

His world turned on its head for the second time at precisely ten eighteen p.m.

He'd been taken into custody a little under ninety minutes earlier, but that had nothing to do with it. They did the job efficiently, boxing him in, two in front and two behind. Four men, swift and grim, clearly plainclothes law enforcement officers.

One of the men in front of him stepped close, said something. He shook his head.

'Non parlo Croato. Solo Italiano.'

The man nodded as if unsurprised, tipped his head: *come with us*. He followed the front pair to the unmarked saloon parked up on the kerb ahead.

Before he got in the back he glimpsed the glitter of light off the restless water of the bay, the masts of the boats shifting in the embrace of the marina at the bottom of the hill. He glanced at his watch. Five past nine. Fifty-five minutes to go.

*

The room was a cliché: ivory linoleum curling at the edges, dusty fluorescent lighting strips with one bulb flickering like an eyelid with a tic, cheap wooden tabletop with metal legs bolted to the floor. The smell was of tobacco and sour sweat.

He sat facing the door, alone. After seventeen minutes, at nine forty-four by the clock on the wall, the door opened. A woman came in, dark-haired, with glasses like an owl's eyes. Two of the men who had picked him up followed her in. One seated himself in the chair. The other leaned against the wall, arms folded.

She stood across the table from him, his passport grasped loosely between her fingertips like a soiled rag. Without introduction she said, her Italian accented but fluent, 'Alberto Manta, of Lugano, Switzerland. Arrived in Zagreb on September second. Checked in at Hotel Neboder here in Rijeka the same day.' She paused. 'Why are you here?'

He said, 'I'd like to use my phone call now.'

'But you're not under arrest. Were you told that you were?'

She held up a finger. The man leaning against the wall came forward and handed her a folder from which she drew a sheaf of photographs. She dropped them on the table, fanned them across the surface. There were four, a series taken on a street with a long lens, showing him, neat goatee beard and hair a little longer than fashionable for a man of his age, grinning and slapping the back of a shorter man whose nose was distorted sideways.

'This man,' she said, tapping the top photo, which showed just the man with the deformed nose.

He said: 'Drazan Spiljak. A business associate. Imports and exports. I sell luxury hand-woven carpets, he's helping me break into the Croatian market.'

'He's a drug dealer. One of the big players here in Rijeka. Cocaine from Colombia, heroin from Afghanistan. Poison that ends up in the streets and the playgrounds of my country and yours, Mr Manta.'

He spread his hands. 'What can I say? Of course I condemn it. But Mr Spiljak is free, walking the streets. He runs a legitimate business. I can't turn my back on a good opportunity just because of some rumours about a man.'

'*Rumours*.' She half turned, looking down, then glanced up at him, eyes narrowed. 'You're looking at the clock, Mr Manta?'

Had he been? *Sloppy*. 'I'm late.'

'For what, might I ask?'

'A meeting.'

Nine fifty.

She paced, to her right and back, then placed her hands on the table top. She leaned forward and lowered her face to his.

'It would be better if you left, Mr Manta. Left Rijeka, and Croatia altogether. We have scum enough with Spiljak. We do not need any more.'

'I'm free to go?'

She straightened without a word and left. The men followed, one signalling him to remain seated. The door closed.

He kept his face impassive, aware of the spyhole in the door. Nine fifty-five, his watch told him.

Ten o'clock.

Time had run out.

At three minutes past ten the door opened and one of the men came in and tossed his phone and passport on the table. He stood, checking the display on the phone. Five missed calls. He followed the man out.

To a clerk at the reception desk he said, 'Taxi rank?'

'Turn right, then again after two blocks.'

He stepped out into the night, walked quickly but unhurriedly up the road, raising the phone to his ear. The first message had been left at nine thirty-two.

'Thought we said half past. He's here, they're having drinks on deck.'

Kendrick.

The next, at nine forty-six: *'They've gone inside now. Get a move on, sunshine.'*

He turned the corner and strode straight past the taxi rank, picking up the pace. The crowded streets would slow any taxi to a crawl. He'd get there more quickly on foot.

Message number three, at nine fifty: no words, just a muttered sigh.

Ten o'clock, and Kendrick again, a snarl: *'Where are you, for Christ's sake?'*

And at ten oh three: *'Fuck this. I'm going in.'*

Manta – whose real name was John Purkiss – closed his eyes for an instant. Then he began to run.

*

Purkiss had worked his way into Spiljak's confidence over the previous month. He wasn't, as it happened, particularly interested in Spiljak or his operation. The prize was instead one Nicholas Hoggart, retired officer of the British Secret Intelligence Service, who ran a private security firm in Rijeka. Suspicion had arisen that Hoggart was involved with Spiljak's outfit and was using to their mutual advantage the knowledge of the local criminal scene and of local law enforcement he had gathered while an active agent. Retired or not, Hoggart was an embarrassment to SIS. That was where Purkiss came in.

Purkiss had chosen the guise of an Italian Swiss, knowing Spiljak spoke the language, as did many Croatians in this part of the country. He'd presented himself as having access to Swiss bank accounts Spiljak couldn't afford. They had agreed on a deal granting Spiljak and his unnamed partner the use of these accounts in return for a cut of their profits. The unnamed partner was, of course, Hoggart, and Purkiss was supposed to meet them both on Spiljak's yacht tonight to seal the deal. It would be the only opportunity he'd have to get Spiljak and Hoggart in the same place together, and obtain recorded proof of Hoggart's involvement in criminal activity. Kendrick's role was to act as lookout, and to provide backup if needed.

The meeting was scheduled for ten p.m.

Thirteen minutes ago.

*

He was wearing a light linen suit, was towards the lower end of the normal weight range for his height, and hadn't smoked a cigarette in his life, yet Purkiss felt as though the marina was receding from him as quickly as he approached it. He sucked in the salt air coming off the bay and spewed it back harshly, the sweat slick on his face and sodden in the creases of his clothes where they bunched against the skin. He weaved and dodged and barged through the crowds filtering down the streets between the restaurants, trailing angry cries behind him.

The phone hummed against his hip. Purkiss slipped it out and glanced at the display as he ran. A text message, with an attached photo.

The message was from Vale: *Finish up and get back here ASAP. This picture was taken this morning.*

He looked at the picture.

Purkiss stopped running.

He was in the middle of the road and a car bore down in a yowl of brake and horn. He leaped forward onto the pavement.

He stood, staring at the picture, his thoughts cold as sweat.

Impossible.

The bustle around him took on a detached quality, as though he were the observer of a documentary film showing on a wrap-around screen.

Vale had it wrong.

At the top of the phone's screen the time display flicked to ten nineteen.

Purkiss drew a breath and closed his eyes. He shrank the picture and the thoughts and the feelings it evoked into a tiny box in his mind's eye. Then he sealed the box shut and buried it deep. He felt for the adrenaline wave in his blood, caught it and began to coast on it.

The final run to the water's edge, and the ground began to level out. Ahead he saw the pier and Spiljak's boat, a fifteen-metre German model, beginning its slow turn out of its berth towards the open sea.

Purkiss put everything he had into it, palms stiff and straight and arms whipping alternately past his sides and legs pumping, his mind already there and commanding his body to catch up. The end of the pier was twenty metres away, fifteen, five. The boat had turned its back on him and he could see the spume churning at its base. He reached the end and leapt, legs cycling at the air and arms lunging. For an instant he was suspended between pier and boat. Then his torso slammed against the fibreglass of the boat's stern and his palms slapped the slick surface. He began to slide but caught the upright of the rail, and he gripped it and and hauled himself up on to the deck.

*

Zagorec brought the gun up as Purkiss stepped through the doorway into the cabin. It was a VHS assault rifle, one of the ugliest weapons Purkiss knew. Beyond Zagorec stood Spiljak himself and another man in his fifties, squat and florid with a ginger tonsure clamped to the back of his head. The Englishman, Hoggart. Through the cabin at the top of the steps in the steering deck Purkiss spotted another of Spiljak's henchmen at the helm.

From a hook in the centre of the ceiling of the cabin hung a length of rope, the end of which was knotted in a hangman's noose around the neck of a fifth man. There was a slight slackness to the rope above his head. His hands and ankles were trussed and his feet teetered on a tiny stool. His lank hair and stubbled face were bloody.

'Where've you been?' said Spiljak.

'The police pulled me in. Showed me photos of us hanging out together, warned me to back off.'

'You're lucky.' Spiljak's distorted nose was the result of a knife wound. He had chosen not to have it fixed as a badge of distinction, he'd told Purkiss once. 'Zagorec saw you jumping after the boat and was going to pick you off in midair.'

Purkiss raised his eyebrows at the man at the end of the rope. 'Who's this?'

'We caught him trying to get close to the boat, just before we'd given up on you and were about to set off. He hasn't said anything yet.' Spiljak ran an eye down Purkiss. 'Know him?'

'Should I?'

'Your phone,' said Spiljak, arm extended. Purkiss took out his phone and handed it over, then raised his arms and let Spiljak frisk him. Previously the phone wouldn't have been an issue. Spiljak wouldn't have asked for it, and Purkiss would have used it to record their conversation surreptitiously. Now, Spiljak's suspicions were up.

The plan had been for Spiljak to introduce him to Hoggart with hearty endorsement. The dynamic was utterly different now. In the confined space he could taste the malice and mistrust. Spiljak had produced a handgun himself. It hung loose and ready by the side of his leg.

Purkiss moved close to the suspended man. 'He was approaching the boat?'

'Crouching by the side, looking for a way to get on board without being noticed,' said Spiljak. 'I was having a last look around when I spotted him.'

'Armed?'

'No. No ID on him either.'

Kendrick had done a crazy, foolhardy thing, but at least he'd left his ID behind. He'd been hit around the face and across the head. Otherwise he looked unharmed.

'You guys have no idea about interrogation. None whatsoever. What you do is, you hurt them badly, *first*, before you ask any questions. That removes all doubt from the word go.' Keeping his eyes on Kendrick, Purkiss reached his hand back. 'Give me a gun.'

Spiljak moved behind him and he felt the butt of a handgun slap into his palm. He hefted and glanced at it. A Bulgarian Arsenal, cheap and stubby.

Kendrick glared at his eyes but showed no recognition.

Purkiss stepped back, aimed straight-armed at Kendrick's left knee, and pulled the trigger.

The hammer cracked on an empty chamber. Purkiss turned, sighed. There was a shift in the atmosphere because he hadn't turned the gun on one of them as soon as he'd been given it, had instead fired at the prisoner whom they'd suspected of being in league with him. They were off-guard. It was the perfect time to make his move.

He transferred the Arsenal to his left hand and in a spinning backhand strike lashed Zagorec across the face with it. He felt the nose crack and Zagorec was down without a word. Purkiss completed the turn and used the momentum to bring his right leg snapping across in a roundhouse kick which caught Spiljak in the shoulder, sending him staggering back into Hoggart who had risen, his own gun emerging. Purkiss headbutted Hoggart between the eyes, hard frontal bone meeting bridge of nose. As he sagged, Purkiss seized his arm and twisted the gun free and fired at the steps where the helmsman had appeared, catching him in the chest and flinging him back. He crouched and sighted down the length of his arm at Spiljak, who was standing upright, his gun aimed at Purkiss, one foot propped on the stool on which Kendrick was balancing.

From across the water the shouting had started up.

Purkiss had time to notice the gun he'd taken off Hoggart, a Heckler & Koch P30. To Purkiss's right, on the steps leading up to the steering deck, the man he'd shot was groaning.

More shouting, and, distantly, sirens.

Over the guns, Spiljak's eyes mocked him. He tapped his foot on the stool, making the implication clear. *Shoot me, and I'll knock the chair away. Your friend will hang.*

Purkiss glanced up at the rope above Kendrick's head.

His first shot caught Spiljak in the right shoulder, jerking his arm upward so that his own shot would go high if it came, which it didn't. His second smashed into Spiljak's left knee. Spiljak dropped with a shriek.

And kicked the stool away with his other leg as he fell.

The rope snapped taut and Kendrick swung. Purkiss kicked the gun away from Spiljak's hand and caught Kendrick. He righted the stool, propped Kendrick's feet on it, and prised loose the noose around Kendrick's neck. Moving behind him he slipped out a Swiss Army knife, cut the cords binding his wrists and ankles.

Kendrick dropped off the stool, stumbling but keeping his feet. In a voice like a sheet of ice plummeting into an Arctic gorge he said: 'Bastard.'

'We're even. You shouldn't have gone in without me.' But by delaying the departure of the boat he'd allowed Purkiss to get aboard. There'd never been any danger of his neck breaking. Spiljak had committed the novice hangman's error of making the rope too short. In a few more seconds he'd have strangled to death, but Purkiss hadn't been planning on waiting that long.

Purkiss glanced out of the window. Flashing red and white lights were massing on the shore. Spiljak was rolling on the floor clutching his wrecked knee, too shocked to scream. On the steps the other thug Purkiss had shot was on his back, whimpering, his breathing not laboured.

He'd survive. On the floor of the cabin, Hoggart and Zagorec were out for the count.

Purkiss retrieved his phone from Spiljak's pocket and took the man's own handset. He thumbed through the various menus until he found what he wanted, then bent and grabbed Hoggart and hauled him so that he slumped against one of the cabin's seats. He twisted the man's ears until he howled awake, held up Spiljak's phone, played the recording.

Hoggart's eyes were slivers of white between the lids, his tongue lolling at the blood around his mouth. From the phone came snatches of English dialogue. Hoggart's voice, then Spiljak's, naming places, substances, prices. At the end Purkiss wrapped the phone in an oilskin bag and stowed it in his pocket.

He said, 'You insisted I surrender any recording devices I might have, but you didn't consider that your friend here might be keeping his own record for insurance purposes. Been a bit of a chump, haven't you?'

Purkiss straightened, looked down at Hoggart.

'Tell the police whatever you like. They might charge you and Spiljak and the rest of this sorry crew with disturbing the peace or whatever. Or, you might escape without a blemish on your name. I couldn't care less. But understand this, Hoggart. You're finished. Crawl away and bury yourself where nobody can see you. SIS doesn't need its dirty knickers washed in public. But you've let the side down. And the side won't forget. If you're heard from again, anywhere in the world, the Service will put an end to you.'

The sirens were getting louder. The police boats were close enough that their lights were strobing against the cabin's walls. Purkiss said to Kendrick, 'Time we were off.'

They clambered over the moaning man on the stairs and ran at a crouch across the deck towards the rail. Then they were airborne. Purkiss felt the shock of the water, surfaced, and glanced back to see the boats swarming round the yacht, the men crowding aboard. He located Kendrick's head a few metres away. They struck out for the shore.

*

Kendrick's car was in a side street just off the marina. They reached it by stealth, two sodden figures skulking through the alleyways. In the boot were enough dry clothes for both of them.

Purkiss climbed into the passenger seat. Kendrick started the engine but didn't move off. After a moment he said, 'That gun.'

'Yes.'

'It felt lighter than it should've. That's why you took a chance and pretended to shoot my leg.'

'Yes.'

'And you were certain the magazine was empty. Rather than just not completely full.'

Purkiss, one of whose guiding principles was that you could never be certain of anything, said, 'Yes.'

'Fuck off, Purkiss.'

*

Purkiss leaned his head back, closed his eyes, breathed deeply while Kendrick drove, letting his body find its own way down from the heightened level of alertness at which it had been cruising. Then he fumbled out his phone and looked at the impossible picture Vale had sent him.

It was a three-quarter view of a man's head and shoulders, taken in the glare of morning sunlight. The man was squinting against the light. There was no mistaking him.

The face belonged to a man named Fallon. It wasn't in itself especially memorable, but Purkiss would never forget it. The reason the photograph was impossible was that Fallon was serving a life sentence in Belmarsh prison.

The reason Purkiss would never forget the face was that four years earlier Fallon had murdered Purkiss's fiancée. Purkiss had seen him do it.

Two

All the Jacobin had wanted to do was ask the man a few questions. Was he photographing those people in particular, or did they happen to be standing in shot at the time? Was he freelance or part of an organisation? And why had he appeared now, an apparent complication when there weren't supposed to be complications at this late stage?

The Jacobin hadn't meant to kill him.

The man was small and slight, with prematurely receding hair and goggling eyes. The fight he'd been able to put up had been revealing, had confirmed the Jacobin's earlier suspicions that there was more to him than his appearance implied.

He had opened the door readily. The moment the Jacobin saw the flare of recognition in his eyes the time for innocent questions was obviously past. The Jacobin moved in and kicked the door closed, bringing a sword hand against the man's throat. But he was fast, faster than he should have been and therefore a professional. He spun away and crouched. They faced each other across the carpet.

The man leaped backwards and sideways through a door off the entrance hall. The Jacobin followed. Inside the living room the man was at the mantelpiece, scooping a vase in his hand and swinging it. The Jacobin dodged, feeling the slipstream of the heavy ceramic sigh past and hearing the vase shatter against the wall behind, not taking an eye off the man because the vase was a distraction, intended to disorientate with pain and noise. The man lunged for a real weapon, a curved sword on the wall. Its blade gasped as he drew it from its scabbard.

Blades were a problem, more so than guns, as any experienced fighter knew. In the Jacobin's favour, the man didn't look like a trained swordsman. He gripped the weapon in two hands which left him with neither one free and with both elbows, those exquisite points of vulnerability, exposed.

The Jacobin's first kick cracked the head of the radius bone in the man's left elbow, an injury so painful that the involuntary opening of the hand was automatic. The second kick was more daring: still using the left leg as a pivot, the Jacobin snapped a toecap into the upright blade, lifting it spinning out of the man's right hand to clatter across the bare wooden boards across the room.

Clutching his elbow, the man feinted to his right and darted left. The Jacobin didn't move. It was a battle of morale, now, one the man couldn't win. The Jacobin indicated one of the armchairs. The man didn't sit.

From inside the man's pocket a phone began to ring. They watched each other's eyes through one ring, two. The man reached into his pocket with the hand on his good arm.

'No,' said the Jacobin, voice soft, and moved in, a quick fist punching the man's ruined elbow provoking a yell, the other jamming up under the man's breastbone so that he rocked back and slumped down the wall.

The Jacobin dragged him to the centre of the living room, checked his phone. He hadn't had a chance to answer, and the call was denoted as 'missed'. The number was prefixed with the international dialling code for the United Kingdom. Pocketing the phone, the Jacobin propped him into a sitting position on the rug and knelt behind him. Sliding an arm across his throat, the Jacobin applied gentle pressure.

'How did you know me just now?'

No reply.

'Why the photographs?'

Still nothing. The pressure wasn't enough to be preventing him from speaking. The Jacobin applied fingertips to points in the neck, harmless but agonising. The man hissed rapidly between clenched teeth, his body shuddering.

He would have to die now, there was no question about that. The question was whether he was likely to divulge anything useful first.

Clearly he was trained to stand up to interrogation, to lie convincingly under duress.

In the event the Jacobin's hand was forced. The man made a last desperate effort, an extended-knuckle punch with his good arm behind him which connected with the kidney area. The Jacobin swallowed against the roiling pain and flexed the arm across the man's throat until he sagged. Not wanting to take any chances, the Jacobin gripped the pale, high head between the heels of both palms, and with a quick twist dislocated the vertebrae of the man's neck.

*

The Jacobin sat on the rug for a minute, eyes closed, finding calm. It wasn't formal meditation of any kind, but rather a necessary process of reestablishing equilibrium after the taking of another human being's life. For the dead man himself, the Jacobin felt nothing. For the fact of having killed – again – there was disquiet, a feeling that was growing, not diminishing, with each such episode. A limb that was beginning to rot with gangrene could be salvaged by the excision of the corrupted matter. Did the same apply to a soul? Could it?

In the passage by the front door, the Jacobin retrieved the small grip dropped there on entry. Inside was the equipment that, given more time, the Jacobin would have installed at leisure after first establishing that the man wasn't at home.

The man's body would have to be hidden within the flat. The smell would attract attention in a few days, of course, but by that time it would all be over.

Spreading the contents of the grip across the dining table, the Jacobin set to work.

*

Vale was a motionless silhouette against the cold morning sky. Purkiss parked in the dirt semicircle at the bottom of the track and made his way up through the light ground fog towards the churchyard. It was Vale's way, always had been. Remote locations for meetings to minimise the risk of surveillance. Purkiss had no idea where Vale's office was, or if he even had one.

They'd arrived back from Zagreb mid-morning. To be on the safe side Purkiss had packed Kendrick off to see a doctor about the strangulation injury. He had freshened up, then phoned Vale for a rendezvous.

Driving out into the Hertfordshire countryside, Purkiss let his thoughts drift back four years. He'd replayed those events many times but there had always been the imperative to look forward, not to wallow. There was nothing more that could be done, and justice of a sort had been achieved. Now, that justice seemed ephemeral, like a software programme whose licence had expired.

*

He'd met Claire Stirling at a consulate bash when he was stationed in Marseille, and he'd immediately recognised her as SIS, like him at the time. The service disapproved of office relationships but with discretion Purkiss and Claire managed it. They were spies, after all. After a few months they were engaged.

A field agent of five years' standing, Purkiss's work in Marseille involved the study of immigration patterns into the city from Middle Eastern countries and the application of closer scrutiny when anybody suspicious arrived. Someone, for instance, whose name had come up before in connection with a Service operation elsewhere. Claire's work was to all appearances more humdrum, monitoring radio traffic between the various embassies. They both enjoyed their work, they socialised mainly with diplomatic staff, and they loved together passionately, the clandestine nature of their union adding to the thrill.

The change came with the death of Behrouz Asgari. An Iranian-born businessman who had made Marseille his home for the previous twenty years, he was also a philanthropist whose investment in local infrastructure had lifted thousands of residents out of slum tenements. Asgari was openly opposed to the incumbent American and British governments and a devout Shi'a Muslim. He'd been extensively investigated, of course – Purkiss had done a lot of the work himself – and came up clean, with no links to hostile activity against the West.

One evening, while Asgari had been strolling along the waterfront with his wife, a lone motorcyclist had ridden up and shot him dead. The hit was a professional one, a double tap to the head using modified hollow-point nine-millimetre rounds. Asgari had been a personable, well-liked man, but he had business rivals aplenty, and the police investigation, such as it was, concluded that some unnamed competitor was responsible.

Two weeks after the murder, Claire had come round one evening to Purkiss's flat – circumstances dictated that they live separately – in an odd mood, silent and brooding. He'd gone easy, coaxing gently but knowing when to back off. At last over a glass of Beaujolais she'd told him. For the last six months she had been investigating her immediate superior, Donal Fallon, for corruption. She suspected he was the person who'd carried out the hit on Asgari.

Fallon was a legend, an Anglo-Irish agent only half a decade older than Purkiss and Claire but a veteran of numerous high-intensity arenas, including Islamabad and Damascus. Purkiss had met Fallon many times through Claire, had been impressed by the man's wit, his intellectual nimbleness, had liked his obvious gentleness and his affection for Claire. The three of them had become a trio, Fallon conniving at their affair with a twinkle.

Slowly, Claire had begun to detect irregularities in his working patterns, in what he did with the information she supplied him. She had started to pay closer attention, working off her own bat, relaying her suspicions to nobody. She amassed circumstantial evidence, unexpected blips in Fallon's bank account, little more, and she was about to give up the search when Fallon asked her to post surveillance on Asgari without giving her a satisfactory explanation. He'd received without comment the intelligence she gathered for him, though she sensed he was looking for connections to radical Islamist groups, the kind of thing Purkiss himself had investigated.

Then the hit took place, at a time when Fallon was allegedly on a solitary hiking holiday in the Scottish Highlands.

'It wasn't business related. It was political.' Purkiss had let her talk without interruption, the flow becoming a surge under the influence of the wine and of her agitation. 'Fallon saw Asgari as a potential threat to us, couldn't pin anything on him, and decided to take him out pre-emptively.'

She fell silent and he said, 'A one-man death squad.'

There'd been rumours, for at least as long as he'd been with the Service, but most people considered them to be urban legends.

She looked straight at him for the first time. 'The trouble is, I don't know if it's just one man.'

He understood then why she'd kept her fears to herself, why she hadn't taken her suspicions over Fallon's head the moment she'd been sure. If there were others working with him, they might be senior to her.

They talked past the dawn. Purkiss wanted her to back off, thought she was in far too deeply. Claire countered that she had come too far to quit. Besides, she was certain Fallon didn't know she was on to him. They reached a compromise. Purkiss would take over the active role, surveilling Fallon. Claire would provide logistical support. They would involve nobody else for the time being.

Two evenings later Purkiss let himself into Claire's flat, arms laden with groceries for their meal. In the second before he was able to react, he saw Claire arched backwards, her feet off the floor, Fallon behind her with an arm across her throat and a knee in her lower back.

Purkiss yelled, the primal roar of a berserker, and covered the distance between them even as Claire dropped away, dead weight. Fallon met Purkiss with a speed and grace Purkiss would have marvelled at under other circumstances, a kick to the face, another to the knee, felling him. Purkiss clawed at his foot and almost got a hold, but Fallon was at the door and was gone.

There was no question of going after him, of leaving her. Purkiss crouched with Claire's head between his palms and her lifeless, bruised eyes staring past him. He gave vent to a stream of nonsense words he could no longer remember. Later he recalled begging the paramedic to keep trying to revive her, not to let her down as he, Purkiss, had let her down by not overriding her decision to keep after Fallon, by not being there with her when Fallon paid a visit, by being so *stupid* as not to realise Fallon, the master spy, would have noticed he was under scrutiny.

Purkiss wasn't a believer in the idea of repressed emotions, the notion that feelings could actually exist as entities in their own right, simmering under the surface whether or not you were aware of them. But, fists white on the wheel, he understood the appeal of the concept. The fury, the anguish, had returned to him now in so whole and so familiar a form that it was easy to believe they'd never gone away.

Purkiss had missed the opportunity to mete out his own punishment to Fallon at the site of Claire's murder. Although there would have been ways to get at him after his imprisonment – there were always ways, even in an environment as hermetic as Belmarsh – Purkiss had found the idea of cold revenge wearying, depressing even. Now, though, if there was any substance to the intelligence Vale had forwarded to him, any possibility at all that Fallon was on the loose –

This time, he thought, *you don't get away*.

Three

Vale's overcoat shrouded his tall, rawboned frame like a cloak against the autumn chill. He was a black man in his sixties with salted hair and the beginnings of a stoop. Under the roving of his yellow eyes, Purkiss felt as though he were being measured for a coffin. Vale raised a thumb and fingertips to his lips and drew on his cigarette and from his nostrils blew scythes of smoke.

With two movements of his head – a nod and a tilt – he conveyed a greeting and a request to walk. They headed across the lawn to the graveyard.

'Hoggart pose any problems?' Vale had a habit of speaking in a virtual monotone which led people to assume he was on some kind of medication.

'No. He's small fry. It's the end of him.'

'Clean job?' He meant had Purkiss been discreet, left any traces of himself.

'The Rijeka police have me on camera with Spiljak. That's about it. No names.'

Vale nodded again. He stopped at an ancient gravestone and scuffed at the moss with his toe, crouching to peer at what was carved underneath. It wasn't his way to look someone in the face when delivering difficult information.

'The photo was taken yesterday morning in Tallinn, Estonia, by a contact of mine who lives in the city and who spotted Fallon in a market square. I called him, of course. He said he'd tried to follow Fallon but lost him.' He glanced up at Purkiss. 'He had no doubt it was him, even if you think that picture might have caught a lookalike.'

'How?' Purkiss meant, *how was it possible? Fallon, outside?*

Vale straightened. 'I rang the Home Office, got stonewalled. Tried Little Sister, same there. Eventually a friend in Big Sister came through.'

Little and Big Sisters were respectively SIS and the Security Service, or Six and Five. The adjectives referred to the sizes of their personnel lists.

'And?' Vale had started walking again and Purkiss kept pace.

'Donal Fallon was released from prison on February eighteenth last year.'

'Hang on.' Purkiss stopped, Vale turning to face him. 'Released?'

'Yes, it would seem so. I'm waiting for more details but it could only have been an amnesty granted by the Home Secretary.'

Disorientation set in. Purkiss had been expecting a narrative about an audacious escape from Belmarsh and an embarrassed cover up. Not this.

'He'd served two years.'

'Slightly less than.'

'The *tariff* was ten years.'

'I know.'

Purkiss fought the urge to gabble. 'For God's sake, Quentin.'

'It turns the stomach, doesn't it.' Vale paced. 'And it gets worse. Once I'd established that he'd been released, I went back to my Little Sister contacts and confronted them. Lots of awkward coughs and shuffling of feet, and they admitted that Fallon had started working for them again. A brilliant agent, guilty of a terrible crime but given a last shot at redemption, so forth. Then, after a fortnight, he vanished.'

'Vanished.'

'Before he'd even been briefed on his new mission. Took off without trace. They pulled out all the stops to find him, at first, but after a while they gave up. He was too good an agent to let himself be found, and chances were they'd never hear from him again. Better to avoid a scandal, put the whole sorry matter to bed.'

Purkiss walked away from Vale, making his way rapidly between the headstones. The hills, the grey sweep of the sky didn't seem vast enough to contain what he was experiencing within. His jaw muscles felt locked.

In time he walked back. Vale hadn't moved, had had the good grace not to watch him.

'Who's your contact in Tallinn?'

'A former Service chap, Estonian but one of us. Jaak Seppo. I've known him ten years. He does a bit of freelance work for me now and then, keeps me in the picture.' Vale thumbed his phone. 'I'm texting you his number and address. I've already told him you're coming.'

A connection fired in Purkiss's mind. 'Tallinn.'

Vale gave a faint nod. 'Yes. Quite.'

'When is it happening, again?'

'October the thirteenth. The day after tomorrow.'

'You think Fallon's got something planned?'

Vale fired up another cigarette. 'I know precisely as much as you do. But... I have a feeling.'

*

Abby's office, or "command centre" as she was pleased to call it, was a basement flat in Whitechapel which had been converted into one large room with a kitchenette, miniature bathroom and shower and fold-out bed. Two L-shaped desks dominated the floor, straining under an assortment of desktop computers, laptops, printers and scanners in various states of physical integrity. A gigantic plasma screen television had conquered one wall and was tuned to a news channel Purkiss didn't recognise. A pile of lesser TV sets in the corner displayed a cornucopia of what Purkiss assumed was real-time footage of mundane scenes: empty streets, the interior of a shopping centre, a busy motorway.

She had met him at the door with a screwdriver in one hand and a motherboard in the other, dark and untidy, a tiny pixie with a wild mess of hair.

'Hi, boss.' Her accent was broad Lancashire, unleavened after five years in London.

'I wish you wouldn't call me that. It makes me feel old.'

'You are old, Mr Purkiss, sir.' She stood aside for him. 'You've shaved off the goatee. Pity. I rather liked it.'

He declined her offer of tea – there'd been semi-dried paint in the mug once before – and dumped a sprawl of papers on the floor to make some room on one of the armchairs. Purkiss nodded at the pile of TV screens. 'That looks a bit dodgy, legally speaking.'

'Testing out some new surveillance gear. For professional use only.' She gazed at the images, rapt. 'Beautiful, isn't it? The resolution.'

'I won't ask where you got this stuff.'

'Best not, no.'

He employed Abby as both researcher and technological wizard. She had done the background work for Purkiss on the Rijeka case, tracking down Hoggart's address, rooting out the intelligence on Spiljak and his crew, even producing false credentials for Purkiss which were accurate down to the minutest detail. One of the things she did was generate a constant supply of fake passports for use at short notice.

She handed him a couple and he studied them, marvelling. They even smelled used. He chose a British identity: Martin Hughes. In the picture he was clean shaven, slightly amused looking. *Affable* was the word he'd most often heard used to describe his features. Even Claire had used it, among many others besides.

'Good choice,' she said. 'The alias all the best-disguised spies are using this year.'

'Stop calling me a spy.'

'Will sir be requiring any accessories? A driver's licence?' She handed him a plastic card. 'No endorsements – you've been a good boy.'

He pocketed passport and licence. 'The flight –'

'Booked for quarter past two, Stansted. You'd better get a move on.'

Purkiss planted a kiss on her cheek. 'Abby, you're a diamond.'

'Tallinn. That's where that meeting's taking place, isn't it?'

'Day after tomorrow.'

'Is your trip anything to do –'

He made a zipping motion at his mouth and she held up her hands in defeat. 'Anything else?'

'Be on standby. I might need your help later.' He headed for the door, then paused. 'Oh. Check on Kendrick, would you?'

'I already gave him a ring. He's back at home, they didn't keep him in. I gave him your best wishes.'

'And?'

'Apart from his usual dismal takeoff of my accent, he said, "Tell him to stick his best wishes in his arse, and I hope the corners hurt."' Her eyes were huge, her smile bright.

*

By the time he reached the airport his spirits had sunk again and he'd begun to brood. The last time he'd seen Fallon was in the courtroom receiving his life sentence. He'd been caught four days after Claire's murder coming off a chartered flight in Hamburg; his trial had been fast-tracked and swiftly conducted. After the judge had pronounced, Fallon had looked over at Purkiss, briefly, but there'd been nothing in his expression; no arrogance but no contrition either. The perfect agent, hidden, inscrutable.

And now a string of cockups and unanswered questions. The cynicism involved in his release was breathtaking but Purkiss found, unsettlingly, that he wasn't surprised. Fallon was a superb agent and the Service had obviously had big plans for him at the time he murdered Claire. The fact that he had pleaded guilty was no doubt considered in mitigation. He'd denied involvement in the Asgari killing but had confessed to corruption, on which charge he received a concurrent sentence of twelve years.

Vale had said: 'Of course it's personal for you. But you have to look on this as a job, if not quite like any other then one with the same principles at stake. He's a rogue agent who's somewhere we don't want him to be, less than forty-eight hours before an event of immense political significance.' The subtext was, *keep it professional*, though Vale didn't have to spell it out.

He'd cut it fine and the gate for his flight was already open when he got through the scanner. With him he had a shoulder bag with two days' worth of clothes, nothing more. After leaving Abby's he'd rung the number Vale had given him for the Tallinn contact, Seppo. The call had gone to voicemail. He hadn't left a message. Striding towards the gate now he tried again. Six rings, then the beep. He cut the connection.

Vale had said Seppo was awaiting his call. While one failure to answer could be overlooked, two couldn't. Once more he dialled.

'Vale.'

'Seppo hasn't answered the phone. Twice.'

Silence for a second. 'That's not like him.'

'I'm ditching the phone. If he rings you, tell him I'm going straight to his address.' He rang off, ducked into the last set of public toilets before the gate, deleted the call history on the phone and tucked it behind the cistern in the furthest cubicle from the door. It might have been safe just to dump the handset in one of the bins but he wasn't going to give bad luck an edge, not now that his contact in Tallinn appeared to have been compromised.

*

On the monitor the tiny beacon pulsed by a quirk of synchronicity in time to the ringing of the phone. The Jacobin glanced at the display: the same number again, from Britain and more specifically, as the beacon on the monitor confirmed, from Stansted Airport.

The Jacobin had noticed that the dead man, Seppo, owned a deep freeze, and had transferred the microwave meals and bags of frozen vegetables to the refrigerator until there was enough room, hoisted the body in, and closed the lid. A search of the flat revealed a laptop on a coffee table in the living room, its contents password protected.

Installing the equipment took a matter of minutes. The Jacobin prowled the flat a last time and, satisfied, departed.

On the way back the Jacobin phoned the mobile phone networks in turn, found the correct one on the second attempt. There was coldness and a little bluster at first, but once the necessary calls had been made, the woman came back ingratiating and not a little frightened. By the time the Jacobin was seated with the desktop computer booted up, the tracking was underway.

The Jacobin called up the schedules for Stansted. There it was, a two-fifteen budget airline flight to Tallinn. It was four twenty-five in Tallinn now and the time difference was two hours. The GPS tracking of the phone was taking place in real time, but the beacon on the monitor wasn't moving. Either the owner of the phone hadn't taken that flight or the phone had been left behind.

When there was no movement after half an hour, the Jacobin made two calls. The first was to demand the passenger manifest for the Stansted to Tallinn flight.

The second was answered curtly.

'It's me,' the Jacobin said. 'I need surveillance at the airport, set up within two hours.'

'Who on?'

'I don't know yet.'

Four

The boy took his punishment in silence, flinching with each blow of the strap, at the last hissing between gnashed teeth. Afterwards he disappeared into his room.

A weak man would have avoided his wife's reproachful gaze. Venedikt looked Marta full in the face.

'You think it's overkill.'

She sighed.

'A lack of respect isn't a minor transgression. It's the root. Strangle it at source.' He was aware he was lapsing into the jargon he used with his men.

Yuri was fourteen, sullen but usually wise enough to stay on the right side of well mannered. Tonight, after arriving home an hour beyond supper time, his eyes had slid past his father's, and he'd met Venedikt's final warning growl with his back. He was a fine boy, fundamentally. He would learn, as Venedikt himself had.

Venedikt had never liked his own father, but had always respected him, all the more because the man had taught him that to be respected was more important than to be liked. His grandfather on the other hand he had loved, and still did, which was odd as he had never met the man. He knew Vasily Petrovich from the stories his grandmother had told of her late husband, from the sight and feel and smell of his exquisitely preserved uniform, the heft of the medals when he lifted them out of their box.

He sat in his study, tea at his elbow – he didn't drink, was opposed to all intoxicants – and awaited Dobrynin's phone call, the final confirmation that tomorrow was to go ahead. Gazing at the photographs arrayed on his desk and on the walls, he allowed his thoughts to wander.

His grandfather, his *dedushka*, Vasily Petrovich, had fallen in the Narva Offensive in the late winter of 1944, fighting with the Soviet Second Shock Army to liberate Estonia from the fascists and from its own collaborationist government. As the widow of a war hero his grandmother had been permitted to settle in Estonia after the war with her young son, Venedikt's father. She had embraced it as her homeland, as had her son and his.

From Vasily Petrovich, a hero whom he had never met, Venedikt had learned respect. Respect for one's people, and one's country, that was so unbending one would lay down one's life to keep it alive. It was because of an understanding of the value of respect that Venedikt had, after his national service, decided to join the Estonian defence forces. He had served the Ground Force, the Maavägi, with distinction, rising to the rank of ensign. In August 1991 Estonia declared its independence from the Soviet Union, and announced that neither people who had settled in the country after 1940 nor their descendants had any automatic right to citizenship.

He was twenty-seven years old, young enough for the betrayal to be his first. It burned him.

Venedikt had been brought up speaking Russian, as had his parents. He could get by in Estonian but was not fluent enough to have a hope of passing the strict new naturalisation exam. Languages were not his strong point and the chances of his mastering the second tongue did not seem high. As such, he could remain a resident of the country, could continue his career in the armed forces, but was not permitted to vote in national elections. He was effectively stateless.

His career hit a glass ceiling or, as a fellow ethnic Russian junior officer put it, he "got drowned in the river of piss from above". He failed to progress to junior lieutenant level while younger, less experienced men – native Estonians, of course – soared past him. Bright young professionals began the gentrification of Tallinn, pushing up property prices and forcing Venedikt and his parents into increasingly ghetto-like quarters on the outskirts.

In August 1994 the last Russian troops left the country. Venedikt stood in his uniform by the side of the road out of Paldiski, the barracks town west of Tallinn, and watched the military vehicles roll past. The crowds were sparse. Slow applause broke out, and went on for several minutes before Venedikt understood it was mocking in nature. Then the jeering began, a counterpoint to the clapping.

A young man next to Venedikt, a student of some sort, boozy-eyed and stinking, yelled, '*Vene sead.*' *Russian pigs.* Venedikt was not aware of his elbow jabbing into the boy's face, or the blows after that, but it didn't matter because the whole process was laid out in detail, injury by injury, in the courtroom. Venedikt received eighteen months in prison, of which he served eight. His career in the military was over.

The phone startled him out of his brooding. It wasn't Dobrynin. He listened, asked a few questions, then, when the other person had rung off, made a call of his own. Afterwards he sat back in his chair, the phone still in his hand. This was a possible complication.

Again the phone rang. This time it was Dobrynin.

'Contact made, and the rendezvous is confirmed. Two p.m.'

He allowed himself to breathe out, slowly. In his head he had divided the operation into steps, major and minor, though nothing had been written down. The rendezvous tomorrow would be step two. Step three, the climax, would follow the next day.

He would not sleep well that night, he knew, so there was no point in going to bed early. But there was a risk his thoughts would wander back down the bitter avenues of injustice from which he'd once thought he would never escape. Instead he closed his eyes and called up the memories of an earlier triumph: step one in the operation.

*

The heat from the five bodies in the van fogged the windows almost to their tops. The engine couldn't be turned on to clear the condensation because the exhaust fumes would betray their position. Venedikt was in the front passenger seat. Beside him the driver, Leok, one of them in spite of his Estonian name, rested his hands on the steering wheel, impassive, not a hint of nerves showing. The second van, commanded by Dobrynin, was back down the road, similarly buried between the trees.

In the back of Venedikt's van one of his men had an open notebook computer across his lap. He looked up and nodded to Venedikt; the target was on course. Venedikt gave an order and he and the others pulled the balaclavas down over their faces. The man with the computer raised his hand, balancing on a tense edge, then chopped it down and Venedikt shouted 'Go,' and the driver hit the ignition and gunned the engine and they surged forward on to the road. Yes, there was the first of the armoured vehicles cresting the hill and then stopping, stalled.

Leok spun the van so that it was side on to the vehicle. The door slid open and the man with the rocket launcher knelt and hefted the weapon and took aim. Venedikt saw the man in the passenger seat beside the vehicle's driver cringe behind the windscreen and mouth frantically to the driver but the driver was already through the door and rolling on the tarmac. From the back of the vehicle men spilled like ants from a hill, guards in body armour who pressed themselves against the sides of the vehicle but held fire because at this range their shotguns would be useless.

Venedikt's man with the launcher fired. The windscreen disappeared and from inside the cab the man in the passenger seat screamed an instant before the blast tore him apart and blew the doors off from the inside. The guards sprang away from the sides of the vehicle and the other two men in the back of Venedikt's van crawled out and opened fire with their rifles, Finnish Valmet Rk.62s that spewed over seven hundred rounds a minute and punched through the body armour of the guards and flung them jerking and bouncing across the tarmac.

Beyond the front vehicle Venedikt could see the second, slewed slightly to its left. Its own personnel were out on the road and disorientated, turning to face the van commanded by Dobrynin which had pulled out across the road behind them. Some of them had the good sense to crouch on the far side of their vehicle from Dobrynin and his men but then came the trump card, Venedikt's man from between the trees, emerging on one knee and raising an RPG-28, a launcher that dwarfed the one used to penetrate the windscreen of the front vehicle. The yells of the guards grew frantic and they began to disperse, not caring if they ran across the sightlines of the men bearing small arms.

The twelve-kilogram round from the rocket launcher slammed into the side of the front vehicle, rocking it on its wheels so that it tipped, though it stayed upright. The vehicle was customised with galvanised steel armour designed to withstand high-velocity rifle ammunition but stood no chance against a projectile that could penetrate almost forty inches of hardened metal. The vehicle rocked again as the round exploded, shuddering and lifting this time off its back wheels like a bucking horse. Venedikt and his men swarmed towards the ragged oval rip in the side of the vehicle. One of the fallen guards, legs mangled, performed a half situp and tried to level his shotgun, face contorted, but a burst from one of the Rk.62s threw his head back. At the second armoured van the guards were down, most dead but two kneeling with their hands behind their heads.

Venedikt gave his order and two of his men put single shots in the backs of the kneeling guards' heads. The man with the RPG-28 had moved across and reloaded. He yelled a warning and Venedikt's men stood clear as the second round punched the side open.

The noise would have been muffled by the dense surrounding forest, and along the road on either side bogus *Road Closed* signs had been set up to deter the sporadic traffic; but the guards would have notified the police as soon as the attack began, and speed was of the essence. Venedikt paced and gave orders as his men unloaded the contents from the wrecked transporters and filled the two vans. Here and there came a moan followed by a shot as one of his people walked round administering *coups de grace*. Dobrynin, his second in command, raised a hand.

'Yefimov.'

Venedikt walked across the wet tarmac to Dobrynin who stood and looked down at Yefimov: the driver of the first armoured van, Venedikt's man on the inside, the one who had supplied the intelligence about quantities and timing and guard numbers and vehicle specifications which had enabled the robbery to be planned with such precision. Yefimov, who had deliberately stalled the van to allow the trap to be sprung rather than taking the evasive action expected of the driver of a cash transporter. He'd been hit by a blast from one of the guards' shotguns, his lower abdomen a swamp beneath his clutching hands.

Venedikt squatted beside him, gripped his elbow.

'Pyotr Mikhailovich, you have served your country with great honour.'

The man's grimace widened. His eyes looked into Venedikt's.

Venedikt stood, drew his pistol from his belt holster. He thumbed off the safety and shot Yesimov in the forehead.

The vans' engines were running, exhaust fumes clouding the brittle September air, and the last of the steel boxes was loaded, like the others undamaged by the rounds from the rocket launcher. The front van swung so that its passenger door presented itself to Venedikt. He sprang in and they were away. There was no cheering in the van. Triumphalism might have made them careless, and there were still the police to be avoided, the money to be counted to confirm that they had not been duped. But although Venedikt sat in grim silence, exultation gripped his chest and throat so fiercely he felt faint.

For you, dedushka, he thought.

Five

Purkiss was at the taxi rank in the back of a cab when he changed his mind, got out and walked on to the bus stop. The taxi would have been quicker but, glancing in the wing mirror as he settled himself in the seat, he'd seen the man striding past, rangy and crop-headed, his nonchalance too studied. The man had been part of the small crowd in the arrivals hall just after the final customs check. Although Purkiss had lost him for a few minutes, he'd spotted him again near the exit, peering into a shop window.

If he took a cab the man would lose him. Purkiss didn't want that.

He approached a middle-aged couple in the queue at the bus stop and said, 'Do you speak English?'

The man rocked a palm from side to side.

'Do you know how much the shuttle costs? Into Tallinn?'

The man told him. Purkiss turned to raise eyebrows at the driver of the cab. He hoped his change of transport choice would appear to be about money. In any case the crop-headed man had walked on past the bus stop and turned on to a pedestrian crossing. Purkiss boarded the bus, watched the man disappear into a multi-storey car park, not looking behind him.

Purkiss held on to a support pole as the bus tried to sway him loose. He focused on the feeling that was tightening his chest, trying to give it a name and thereby reduce its grip. Apprehension? He'd failed to reach the contact, Seppo, even before entering the field of operations. From the moment he'd set foot in the field, he'd been identified. Somehow Fallon had been expecting him.

Not apprehension, no. *Fear*.

*

On the plane, with nothing to read or otherwise occupy his thoughts for three hours, Purkiss had given himself up to memory, promising himself it would be the last time for a while.

In his mind's eye was Fallon as he'd been four years earlier. Forty years old, average height, slim build, shortish brown hair. Nothing conventionally distinguished about his looks, but he had a smile that could charm the paint off a wall. He was erudite without being affected, a supremely self-confident Harrow and Oxford boy without a trace of arrogance. To the amusement of those who worked with him he always carried round a particular book as a kind of totem, a paperback copy of Burke's *Reflections on the Revolution in France*. Apparently he'd been reading it during the mission in which he'd most narrowly escaped death.

And, as it turned out, he was corrupt. Corrupt and corrupting, his taint seeping into the lives of other people, spoiling them irreversibly. Purkiss had left the Service after Claire's murder, and while his colleagues accepted tacitly that he'd done so because to remain would have been to be reminded daily of what and whom he'd lost, in his more honest moments Purkiss admitted to himself that it was Fallon's rottenness that had driven him out rather than the offer that Vale had subsequently made him. It was like refusing to live any longer in a house in which a body had been found walled up and decomposing into the stonework.

Vale had appeared out of nowhere during the trial, turning up every day and sitting in the same spot behind Purkiss. He was obviously Service or retired – the trial wasn't being conducted in public and the spectators were being vetted carefully – but it wasn't until Vale fell into step beside him after a long day in the courtroom and suggested they go for a bite to eat that Purkiss had any conversation with him. Purkiss's instinct was to decline the offer. His social life had dwindled to a minimum since he'd lost Claire, and he wasn't anxious to change that. But he was curious despite himself about this quiet, gloomy man, his Afro-Caribbean ethnicity unusual in a Service employee of his generation.

In the Italian restaurant, Vale told him he'd taken early retirement from the Service twelve years before, his story a familiar one of a former field agent unable to adjust to life in mothballs. In the seventies, he'd infiltrated Patrice Lumumba University in Moscow under the guise of a Tanzanian postgraduate exchange student, had his cover blown by a KGB *agent provocateur* and got out hidden in a freight train with a bullet in one lung. After that his deep-cover days were over. He spent the rest of the seventies and the eighties working the diplomatic circuit in southern Africa, in the thick of the proxy Cold War battles between the superpowers. The nineties brought him back to London and, essentially, desk work.

They traded war stories for a while, both aware that this was preamble. Over coffee Vale made his pitch.

'One searches for a less hackneyed expression than *the tip of the iceberg*, but that, really, is what Fallon is.' He shovelled sugar into his cup. Purkiss wondered how he stayed so gaunt, though he'd learn later about the sixty-a-day cigarette habit.

Purkiss stared down at his fists, flashing back to the man in the dock. 'He hasn't got a hope.'

'Oh, they'll convict him, all right. He'll get life. But that's because he got caught in the act. It was a stupid mistake he made, and his punishment isn't going to deter anybody else, because all it will teach others is that they have to be more careful than he was.' He steepled gnarled fingers. 'When an agent goes rogue, the Service would prefer to dispose of the problem quietly. In a case like this, the murder of an agent by a fellow agent witnessed by yet another agent, there's no question of any cover up. Justice has to be swift and merciless. But if Fallon had stopped short, been caught with nothing more than his fingers in the till... The top brass would have sacked him, yes, but might have bought his silence rather than prosecute him. The Service is still punch drunk after the Iraq inquiries and the catastrophic intelligence failures which were brought to light as a result. It can't afford any more scandal, least of all the public outing of criminals in its midst. What I'm saying, John – may I? – John, yes, is that if you're a member of the Service, whereas you might not quite be able to get away with murder, you can get away with pretty much anything short of that.'

'And you have examples of this happening?'

'Plenty. I've made it my business to seek them out. In effect, I've been doing what your fiancee was doing on a smaller scale in her investigation of one man.'

Purkiss studied Vale, trying to prise his way behind the gaze. 'So why don't you go public? Blow the lid off the whole thing? They'd threaten you with the Official Secrets Act, but you could find ways around it. Plant rumours, be ambiguous.'

Vale watched him in silence, his eyes and mouth serious. He reached across for the salt and pepper cellars and placed them a few inches apart.

'You were what, fourteen years old when the Wall came down? Sixteen when the Soviet Union folded. Too young to have had any strong views one way or the other on the nuclear disarmament debate. I was against unilateral disarmament myself. Still am. I believed in like for like, matching the enemy's destructive power with one's own. But while many of us, most of us, perhaps, in the multilateralist camp were putting our trust fervently in the idea of deterrence, believing that if deterrence failed then it really didn't matter who had more weapons, there were others who saw the annihilation of the human race in nuclear fire as not necessarily a bad thing, as long as the other side didn't win.' He tapped one of the cellars. 'Better dead than Red, better rubble than roubles. I've no doubt such people existed on the Soviet side as well. Ideologues who believed ideas could exist without a population of actual people alive to hold these ideas in their heads.'

Some of the salt had spilled. Purkiss swept it into his hand and disposed of it on his empty plate. Vale said: 'What I'm getting at, John, is that to *blow the lid off*, as you put it, corruption and crime within the Service is to take the fanatic's approach. Let the whole structure burn as long as it keeps its purity. I don't take this view. I believe in the Service. I want to save it from itself. But I don't want to destroy it in the process.'

Purkiss learned a great deal that night, which stretched on into the early hours. Vale had had his eye on Purkiss, and Claire too, for many months before the murder. The man knew almost more about Purkiss than he remembered himself, not only details of his degree at Cambridge and his prior upbringing as the son of a Suffolk farmer and landowner, but names of people from Purkiss's childhood whom he hadn't thought of for decades.

Purkiss learned about drug rings, national and intercontinental, in which Service personnel were suspected of having a hand. He learned of deals between Western oligarchs and foetid tinpot dictatorships brokered by British agents. He heard about terrorist atrocities the commission of which had been assisted by undercover operatives, who had walked away scot free because the outrages had taken place in impoverished third world areas which lacked the blessing of a large population of lawyers.

What Vale was proposing was that Purkiss leave the Service and work for him instead. Purkiss's role would be to track down and shut down the renegades, avoiding the ponderousness and potential for scandal which would attend the normal official investigative process.

'You'll be hated,' Vale said. 'Hated, and despised as a turncoat. But if we do this right, in time you'll become a legend. And we know the power legends exert, the atavistic awe they inspire. Awe enough, perhaps, on occasion to deter.'

Purkiss asked Vale for a week to think about it.

Five days later Fallon was convicted of murder. The next morning Purkiss resigned from the Service. By the river in sight of Legoland, the name by which insiders referred to the Service's headquarters at Vauxhall Cross, Purkiss shook Vale's bony hand. It was all the contract they'd ever have.

*

The Jacobin watched the monitor as the zoom on the camera was adjusted and the image sharpened. Kuznetsov's man had chosen well, a position in a coffee shop with a head-on unobstructed view of the arrivals corridor. The other two men were among the crowd lining the railing, one of them visible on the periphery of the camera's field.

Six minutes earlier the man had relayed back that the baggage was now at the carousels according to the information board, and now the first of the passengers from Stansted began trickling down the passage, led by an exhausted young backpacker with a wan smile for her waiting parents. As the video streamed through, the Jacobin's computer was recording it for playback later.

The voice of the man with the camera murmured through the phone link as though to himself: 'Fifteen.'

He was keeping a tally of the passengers. Good. They were arriving in clumps now. The passenger list had numbered one hundred and seventy-four, none of the names familiar. The Jacobin examined every face, discarding each one in turn.

Then it flared, the shock of recognition, and the Jacobin watched the figure stride down the corridor and emerge into the crowd and disappear from view. The Jacobin brought up the window with the recording of the footage, rewound it and played it again at half speed, then paused it when the face was turned straight towards the camera.

A tall man, lean. Hair dark and on the long side. Clean shaven. Blue shirt, khaki chinos, duffel coat, a shoulder bag.

'I've seen him,' said the Jacobin, and gave the description. The two men in the crowd were on the audio connection and acknowledged. The Jacobin kept watching the streaming feed in case a second familiar face appeared, but the crowd dispersed and the flow stopped. The Jacobin shut down the video feed but kept the audio connection with the two men.

'He's been to a cash machine. Heading for the taxi rank now.'

'He's a professional,' said the Jacobin. 'Use especial discretion.'

The instruction wasn't acknowledged. Probably there was a sneer on the man's lips. The Jacobin leaned back in the swivel chair and stared at the ceiling.

John Purkiss. Here in Tallinn, at this point in the game.

He was going to be a problem.

Six

He identified the second tag within two minutes of boarding the bus. The initial process was one of elimination: as a rule, discount people in groups, children or obvious teenagers, very old people, and the physically disabled. The bus was crowded, but he soon filtered out everyone except the middle-aged couple he'd approached in the queue, a young woman in a short skirt engrossed in text messaging, and a short man of about forty in a fedora which he kept on his head even in the humid press of the bus. The man had squeezed on at the last minute and shuffled his rump into a tiny space on one of the seats, provoking mutters of annoyance.

Purkiss let his gaze drift over the other passengers. Through the windows the last glimmers of coral had been sucked down past the horizon and darkness had settled, and with it the cold.

The girl in the skirt pushed the bell and got off. The female half of the couple sat down in her place. Purkiss didn't think they were the ones.

The man in the fedora murmured into a mobile phone, his voice inaudible. Purkiss let his stare settle on the man. He didn't look up.

That was unnatural. Purkiss knew he was the tag.

After five minutes the bus stopped again and the man got off. Purkiss peered through the window after him but he strode off without looking back.

The bus pulled into what was obviously the terminus and came to a stop. Purkiss stood aside, letting others pass until he was the last person on the bus, then stepped off himself. The road bustled with shops and early evening crowds. He took a moment to locate the man he was looking for, then spotted him walking away into the town: heavy set, bull necked. Purkiss half turned. There he was, the rangy man with the cropped hair from the airport, ten paces behind, his lips moving.

Purkiss understood how they'd done it. As soon as it was clear he was taking the bus, the crop-headed man had gone to get his car and had driven here to the town gate to wait for him. In the mean time the man with the fedora had got on the bus to make sure they didn't lose him. When he realised Purkiss had made him, he'd rung ahead and got off at a designated stop, and been replaced immediately by the bull-necked man Purkiss had seen lumber aboard and who was now disappearing ahead.

So, they knew he'd spotted the one in the fedora. Did they realise he'd identified his current tags? It was a classic box formation, one ahead and one behind, except that for it to work the person being followed shouldn't be aware of either component.

Two followers were going to be difficult. If he could isolate one, lose him and then turn the tables and track him, it could lead him to valuable information. Throwing off two tags was possible, but usually involved breaking cover and running, which tended to make it harder to pick up the trail again afterwards. The answer was probably going to be to get behind the rear tag without appearing to be evading pursuit.

Disorientated by the complete unfamiliarity of his surroundings, Purkiss dropped back a pace, letting the bull-necked man round a corner ahead. He glanced across at a mirrored shop window and saw that his plan was going to need radical revision because the crop-headed man had changed tactics and was closing on him fast.

*

'He's made us. Both of us.'

The Jacobin stood and paced, the handset perched on the desk and switched to speakerphone. *I told you, damn it.* 'What's he doing?'

'Trying to subvert the situation.'

They'd never get back on to Purkiss if he turned the tables. 'Listen to me. If you lose him now we may never find him again. I want you to move in and apprehend him. Non-lethal force only.'

'Understood.'

'How public are you?'

'Very.'

'No police.'

'Of course.'

The Jacobin stood still, breathing slowly, frustrated at the lack of visual contact.

Purkiss, gone from the Service for four years. What the hell was he doing here now?

*

He looked back and there was no pretence now, a direct hard stare as the crop-haired man bore down. The street was crowded but not enough that an attack would go unnoticed in a press of bodies.

Unless the man had something in his – He reacted even before the thought was fully formed as the man lunged, a fluid sweep of his arm which Purkiss sidestepped feeling like he was defending himself against a fencing sword, except that protruding from the man's fist was no blade but a needle so tiny that it barely produced a glint. For an instant the man was off balance. Purkiss tried to swat at his back to tip him past his centre of gravity, but he sprang forward and righted himself and stepped aside. He glared at Purkiss across the pavement.

Nobody else seemed to have noticed. It was some sort of tranquilliser, Purkiss assumed, designed for quick action so that he'd go down and the man would support him, full of concern, explaining to the passersby that he was a friend. Then he would hustle him away to whatever fate was planned for him.

The man up ahead, the bull-necked one, would be either on his way back or staying put waiting for his friend to drive Purkiss towards him and so to try to keep the odds as they currently stood. Purkiss backed under the awning of a shop and elbowed open the door and stepped inside, letting the door swing shut. It was a bookshop, deeper than it was wide, not crowded but with a few customers browsing unhurriedly enough that it didn't seem about to close. Purkiss sidled down the centre aisle, keeping his eye on the door. It opened and the crop-headed man came through. He held back, standing near the door, watching Purkiss, waiting. Again his lips were moving. Purkiss knew he was summoning his colleague. There wasn't much time.

The fire door was down a passage on the other side of the service counter. Two women sat at the tills, one young, the other possibly her mother. Neither had looked up when the man came in. Purkiss walked to the counter. 'Excuse me, do you speak English?'

The younger woman said, 'Little.'

'Sorry to have to tell you, but I just saw that man near the door put a book in his pocket.'

The girl's eyes widened and she glanced past him. The other woman muttered a question and she answered and the older woman came out from behind the counter and called down the length of the shop at the man, her tone pleasant but assertive.

The man's stare flicked from Purkiss to the advancing woman, calculating. Then Purkiss was vaulting over the counter and as the young woman screamed he was down the passage and pushing the fire door open. He found himself in an alley, dark and murky.

The other man was there. He must have doubled back earlier and been lurking nearby. He saw Purkiss and ran the short distance towards him, quick for such a thick-set man. Purkiss was off running in the opposite direction but his foot slid on a slick of wet cardboard. He stayed upright but lost a second. The man bore down.

Purkiss turned and the man's forearm drove off his shoulder. In the man's fist he saw the flash of a needle – *he's got one too* – and he pivoted on one foot and brought an extended-knuckle strike against the man's neck. There wasn't much of a neck to aim at and he got the side of the man's jaw. He bellowed and punched Purkiss in the chest, slamming him back against the wall of the alley, winding him. There was no time to make a fuss about not being able to draw breath properly because the fist with the syringe was stabbing at his thigh. Purkiss twisted his hips, felt a sting in his upper thigh. He pistoned his leg side-on into the man's abdomen, the syringe spinning high with a liquid streak spilling from the needle's tip.

The man staggered back and Purkiss swept at his shins with a foot, bringing him down hard.

Ten feet away the fire door barged open and the crop-headed man came through. Purkiss felt it then, the leadenness in his limbs and his eyes as though the earth's gravitational pull had suddenly been doubled. He thought that while most of the contents of the syringe hadn't gone in, a fair amount had. Even his thoughts were heavy.

There was no chance of taking the other man down now. There was no option but to run, *run…*

*

'Talk to me.'

'Stefan's down, out of action. He got him with the needle first. He's running, but he's slowed down.' The man sounded out of breath.

'Stop him.'

The Jacobin kept the line open and picked up another phone and dialled.

Kuznetsov answered at once.

'I need more men. Near the bus station.' The Jacobin gave a quick summary.

'There's no-one else in the area at the moment. By the time I can get anybody down there it will probably be too late.'

'Send them anyway. Your man might already have him by then.'

'Who is this person?' said Kuznetsov.

'I'll explain later. Someone I know. Someone very dangerous.'

*

The wall toppled towards him and he recoiled and the opposite one slammed into his shoulder. One foot in front of the other, like a marathon runner on his last legs, like a baby taking its first steps. Where was the other man? He didn't dare look round in case the rotational movement dropped him.

A sense of proximity warned him at the last second and he summoned all his reserves and jerked his elbow back, connecting with something soft, a face. The cry receded behind him which meant the man had dropped back, even if for only an instant. Purkiss clasped the wall and swung round a corner. There ahead was a main street again, its lights harsh but welcome as the sun. He loped along the side of the building until he reached the main road. He turned, allowing himself a glance back.

The man was coming after him, closer than he'd hoped, darkness at his nose and streaked on his cheek, his eyes shadowed under the neon glare. Purkiss set off into the pedestrian traffic on the pavement, was immediately buffeted. He stumbled to his knees, hauling himself up amid angry mutters which he couldn't understand but took to mean *look at him, bloody drunk.* It wasn't a clever move being in a crowd because it would be so much easier now for the man to close in and slip in the needle, and this time depress the plunger all the way. What he needed was adrenaline to counter the sluggishness. If you couldn't get an adrenaline fix from running for your life where could you get it?

Then he knew.

Purkiss lurched towards the kerb, bouncing off a lamppost, and stepped into the road. For an instant he felt as if he were actually viewing his surroundings upside down, so dislocating was the chaos of sensation on all sides, the rushing of headlights and the fury of horns and the tiny faces on the pavement and behind windscreens. The razor squeal of tyres seemed to slash at his legs as a wing mirror clipped his hip and sent him to his knees again, another set of wheels missing his fingertips by an inch.

His pulse drilled in his chest. He lifted his head and saw the front grille of a car halted a foot from his face. He tried to stand but his limbs were nailed to the road surface. Then there were hands on his upper arm hauling him up and a face looking into his in sympathy and helping him back on to the pavement. A familiar face.

No, something wrong there. The face had blood on it and it wasn't expressing sympathy. It was the man with the cropped head.

Others clustered round. Purkiss saw the man's other hand come out of his pocket. As it moved between them Purkiss grabbed the wrist and twisted it and jammed the needle in up to the hilt and forced the weight of his thigh against the plunger, driving it into the man's groin. Purkiss smelt the bloodied breath through the man's nose as his eyes turned up. Purkiss let him fall, watched his head bounce off the pavement.

There was no time to go through his pockets because the growing crowd had shrunk back in a communal gasp. Shouting, there came the older woman from the bookshop. Was that where he was? He'd come full circle.

All he could do was push his way loose and, again, run.

Seven

After the call to Kuznetsov to tell him – *your other man's down, the target's free* – the Jacobin went for a walk in the Old Town. The conical turrets were blacker against the backdrop of the newly darkened sky. By the clock on the tower of the Holy Spirit Church it was half past eight. In thirty-six hours' time it would be over.

Purkiss. He was troubling in himself, but so were the implications of his presence in the city. The Jacobin hadn't yet explained to Kuznetsov who Purkiss was, but would have to soon, even though Kuznetsov would reasonably blame the presence of a former SIS officer on poor security on the Jacobin's part.

There was no point in conducting an intensive manhunt. Tallinn was a small city but not that small, and the manpower available to Kuznetsov wasn't unlimited. The Jacobin assumed Purkiss was still operational, so there would be little gained in checking the hospitals. He would have to be ignored for now, until he showed his hand again.

The Jacobin watched a British stag party posing crudely for photographs on the Town Hall Square, and was put in mind of the small man,

Seppo, and his camera that morning. Like Purkiss, he was another loose end unsatisfactorily tied off. Too much was unexplained at this late stage.

Unless –

Seppo and Purkiss.

Of course. The connection was not only possible but seemed likely.

With a renewed lift of spirits the Jacobin left the square.

*

Purkiss passed between the twin mediaeval towers of the Viru Gate into the Old Town at eight fifty-five by his watch. He'd assumed it was hours later, his sense of time having slowed along with his reactions. After lurching round corner after corner he'd finally stopped, hands braced on thighs, fighting the urge to vomit. For the first time he noticed that he'd dropped his shoulder bag at some point and had no spare clothes. The weight in his limbs was beginning to lift, but his eyelids still felt sodden.

A street newspaper vendor sold him a guidebook and map. From another vendor he bought a pay-as-you-go phone. He tried Seppo again, got no response, binned the phone and bought another from a different shop. He called Vale, surprised to find that his tongue and jaws worked well enough that he could make himself understood.

'I'm compromised.'

He told him about the surveillance from the airport, the chase.

'Fallon must have got on to Seppo.' Purkiss could hear cellophane being stripped off a fresh pack of cigarettes. 'Obtained your name and arrival time. I'm sorry.'

'Not your fault. Everyone breaks if the pressure's extreme enough. And Fallon's a professional, he'd have known if Seppo was trying to feed him disinformation.'

Down the line Vale drew deeply, exhaled through his nose. 'Do you want to come back?'

Purkiss ignored that. 'I'm going to Seppo's flat.'

'That's highly dangerous.'

'It's the only way.'

He rang off and dialled again. Abby answered after two rings.

'Abby, it's me. Sorry to wake you.'

'You didn't. It's a quarter to seven.'

He looked at his watch. 'Sorry, yes. Bit disorientated.'

'How's Tallinn?'

'Friendly people. Can you get a GPS fix on this phone?'

'I can do anything, Mr Purkiss.'

'If I don't ring you back in two hours, locate me and phone this number.' He gave her Vale's number. The two of them had never met; Vale provided the funding and some very basic logistical support but was otherwise content to leave Purkiss to hire his own help on a freelance basis. If she had to contact Vale it would mean Purkiss was fatally compromised.

With the help of the map he found himself on the outskirts of the Old Town, picture-postcard red roofs clustered on the far side of a busy main road. He crossed unsteadily, the blare of traffic making him flash back to the recent past. For a moment he wondered if there'd been some kind of hallucinogen in the syringe, but concluded that the stress of the last hour was still gnawing at him.

He walked cobbled streets, modern shopping facades kept discreet amongst the splendour of the mediaeval buildings. The aroma of roasting meat assailed him from restaurant doorways. He realised he hadn't eaten since grabbing a bite on the way to see Vale that morning. There was no time to stop. On the other hand he was weak, needed protein and carbohydrates. He stepped into a square, the cobbled pavement of which sloped alarmingly, bought a steak sandwich and a litre bottle of water from a vending wagon, and sat on a stone bollard to eat. He felt his blood glucose levels rise immediately. As if in tandem a memory surfaced for the first time.

After he'd dropped the bull-headed man and was staggering away with the tranquilliser starting to spread through him, the other man had been close enough behind him that he'd heard him muttering into his phone in Russian. The content wasn't particularly revealing – *he's hit, I'm going after him,* or similar – but the throaty vowels were unmistakeable. Although there wasn't anything odd about the man's being a Russian speaker, ethnic Russians making up over a third of the city's population according to the guidebook he'd bought, it might be significant that Fallon was working with Russians.

*

Seppo's flat was in a residential area of Toompea Hill in the upper Old Town. Using the looming silhouette of the city's castle as a landmark, Purkiss strode up the hill, pausing once to look back at the view over the city below. The autumn chill had deepened, cooling the sweat he'd accumulated.

He reached the end of the street he wanted and looked up it. Rows of parked cars lined one side. At a crouch he crawled up the street beside the cars, keeping his head up enough that he could peer into each one. None looked occupied. Straining his eyes, he stared across the street and identified Seppo's block. From where he was, Purkiss couldn't tell which of the two first floor flats was Seppo's. Lights were showing from behind the drawn curtains in the windows of only one of them.

He watched the entrance to the block for ten minutes to see if anyone would emerge. There wasn't much point. The place would have been searched already, the trap set and waiting for him to spring it. They'd be either in the flat itself or in the lobby, most likely the first. In that case breaking in wasn't an option, even if he could make it up to the window somehow once he'd established which of the two flats it was, because he'd be heard. Short of waiting until whoever was in the flat finished his shift and was relieved – and who knew how long that would take – the only course was the direct one.

He crossed the road beneath the flood of the streetlights, feeling his back contract as it anticipated a bullet between the shoulder blades. He made it to the door. Seppo's number was unadorned by any name. He pressed the buzzer and waited. Nothing.

He tried again, twice. The response was the same. There were twenty-four call buttons. He pressed them in rapid succession. Within seconds the voices started coming through, short and rising into questions at the end. In Russian he muttered, 'Hi, it's me.'

Another Babel of monosyllables, then a sharp buzz and he pushed the door open. The lobby was dim and smelled of antiseptic. He mounted the stairs, saw that Seppo's flat was on the right, which meant it was the one without visible lights on from the street. At the door he paused. A booby trap? Breath held, he tried the handle. Locked. He got out a credit card and set to work.

He'd been half expecting a complicated system, given Seppo's past as an agent, but the lock yielded at once. He pushed gently and let the door swing open. No light greeted him. For an instant he felt the primal terror of stepping into the dark. He reached for a switch. The passage filled with light. With a vase he found on a table just inside the door, he propped the door ajar and, hugging the wall, he moved down the passage. He reached an open doorway into the living room and dived in, rolling on his shoulder and coming up at a crouch. There was nobody in the room.

He turned on the lights and did a quick survey. It was simply and tastefully decorated, like someone's home rather than a safe house. A sword, some kind of antique, hung on the wall. Otherwise there was little to give any impression of the occupier's personality. The surfaces were dust-free and clean, apart from the shadow of a scrubbed stain on the carpet by the fireplace.

Purkiss put his head into the kitchen. It too seemed in order. He had crossed the living room to explore the rest of the flat when the echo of footsteps rang up the stairs. He ducked back into the living room, but the front door was already swinging open.

Eight

'He didn't mention anything about a visitor.'

She was early thirties, Purkiss guessed. Light brown hair tied back, thin fawn pullover and suede jacket, jeans.

'He wouldn't have. He doesn't know I'm coming, it's a surprise.' He gestured about the room. 'To be honest I wasn't even sure he still lived here. Still wouldn't be if you hadn't confirmed it. It's a few years since I last heard from him.'

She glanced around. 'I've never been here either. We're friends at work, but not that close.'

'And he hasn't been in for – how long?'

'Three days. He isn't answering his phone either. Our boss is livid. I'm more worried than anything else.'

It seemed presumptuous for either of them to sit so they remained where they were.

He said, 'What work does he do?'

'We're a small English-language newspaper for expats. *Living Tallinn.*' She didn't look at him as though she expected him to have heard of it, or cared if he had or not. 'He's a photographer. *The* photographer, really.'

She was lying through her teeth, as he was, and they each knew the other was lying.

He scratched the back of his neck. 'It's a bit difficult for me. I don't know much about him, about his life here. Do you know where he might have got to?'

'No idea, I'm afraid.'

He'd spun the first threads in the web of lies: *I'm a friend of Jaak's, well, not a friend exactly. I met him when he was an exchange student at Cambridge with me fifteen years ago. I came up here and the door was open*. He didn't say how he'd got into the block of flats in the first place and she didn't ask. She countered with her *concerned work colleague* fable.

They stood with nothing more to say, two strangers with a tenuous link meeting in odd circumstances. He broke the moment.

'Well, as I say, I was in town anyway. I'll be off.' He hesitated, then said, 'Look, if you do hear from him in the next couple of days could you ask him to give me a ring?' He scribbled his name – Martin Hughes, the one on the passport – and a random seven-digit mobile phone number on a piece of notepaper from a pad on the table beside the landline phone near the door. She took the paper and glanced at it.

'Likewise, if he gets in touch with *you*, call me, okay?' She handed him a business card. She'd slipped up: why not just ask him to tell

Seppo to call the office? The name on the card was Elle Klavan, the logo that of *Living Tallinn*, and there were mobile and fax numbers and an email address.

At the door he said, 'You staying here?'

'Yes, I'll wait a bit, see if he comes back.' Her eyes were level.

Another mistake she'd made: she hadn't been sceptical enough about his explanation for his presence there.

Outside the building Purkiss turned left and walked down the hill. He crossed the road and sidled up again behind the row of cars and took up position between two closely parked saloons, where he squatted, watching the windows and the entrance.

There was occasional movement behind the curtains. The brightness increased a fraction, as though a light had been turned on elsewhere in the flat. After several minutes the lights snapped off without warning. Shortly afterwards she emerged from the building and headed down the hill.

Within a block the streets started to become more crowded, something for which Purkiss was thankful as it provided cover. He was able to stay well back, yet keep pace with her. She wasn't trying any counter-surveillance moves, which meant either that she wasn't aware that she was being tagged or that she wanted to be followed. She headed back down into the centre of the Old Town. Purkiss tracked her through the square where he'd sat earlier, then off in a direction he hadn't been before. She had the unhurried stride of somebody with things to do but no particularly pressing deadline to meet.

She'd spoken startled Estonian on seeing him, but he'd answered in English and she'd immediately replied in kind, her accent unambiguously Home Counties. *Klavan*. Was the name Estonian?

The trap, if it was one, puzzled him. It made sense that she should lead him into the lion's den, but she'd been alone at the flat – what if he'd attacked her? The risk seemed reckless. He needed to ask Vale a few questions, but didn't dare compose a text message while he was walking in case she made a sudden move and, distracted, he lost her.

Uphill again, through restaurant crowds thronging the pavements and blasts of music as bars swallowed and disgorged their patrons. Just beyond a Turkish bistro she stopped. Without a backward glance she opened a door and went through. Instead of approaching the door, Purkiss stood on the other side of the road and peered at the number of the building. It was a narrow three-storey affair with something he couldn't read stencilled on a glass panel in the door. The phone he'd bought was 3G enabled. He called up a search engine and entered "Living Tallinn". There it was, the address matching. When he clicked on the newspaper's website he got an error message. There were no other matches for the name.

He walked to a corner so that he could keep the door in view, punched buttons. When Vale answered Purkiss said, 'Ever heard of a female Service agent called Elle Klavan?' He spelled it and described her.

'Doesn't ring any bells. I'll do some checking.'

Purkiss brought him up to date. 'Also, *Living Tallinn*. It's almost certainly bogus, a front. Maybe one of your contacts knows something about it.'

'What are you going to do now?'

'Go back to Seppo's flat and search it properly.'

Getting back in would be more difficult, as he couldn't try the trick of pushing all the buzzers in the block again. On the way back up the hill he spotted something that would fit his purpose: a skip outside a shop. In the skip he found a dilapidated chest of drawers which he hefted with some awkwardness. He attracted a few curious looks on his way back to the flat, but no opposition.

Twenty minutes passed until the door buzzed open and a couple stepped out, dressed for a night on the town. The man held the door open automatically. Purkiss smiled his thanks and hauled the chest into the lobby. He thought: *taking advantage of simple human courtesy. What a life we lead.*

He worked quickly and methodically, starting with the living room and dining area – the stain on the carpet was damp, he noted – and moving on to the bedrooms. Two of them, men's clothes of different sizes in each. Vale hadn't mentioned anything about Seppo's having a flatmate, but perhaps he hadn't known.

In Seppo's room – Purkiss deduced it was his from the size of the clothes in the cupboard, Vale having described Seppo as a small man – he noticed the slightest protrusion of the lower of two drawers in the bedside table when he closed it. He lifted the drawer off its rollers and pulled it out. Taped to the back was a memory stick. He pocketed it and replaced the drawer.

The drawers in the other room, the mattress, yielded nothing. He peered behind the row of paperbacks on the room's only shelf, then glanced at the books themselves. Estonian titles, some of them translations of popular novels by British and American authors. He turned away before a delayed realisation caused his head to snap round again.

Wedged in between two doorstop novels, its spine furrowed through repeated use, was a paperback he recognised.

He pulled it down. *Reflections on the Revolution in France.* The same edition. He riffled the pages against his thumb and checked inside the covers. There were no identifying marks, but it was the one.

Fallon's totem.

Purkiss sagged on the bed, gripping the book in both hands, staring at the cover. The memories were rising.

Claire, in a montage of images and smells and tactile traces, vivid as phantom limbs. Looking back over her shoulder at him while she dressed, grey eyes mischievous and smile gently mocking. Walking towards him in the rain in her turtleneck and the boots he'd bought her which were ruined on the first day she'd worn them. Pressing her small head with its short blonde hair scented with her lemongrass shampoo back against his face on the balcony of the Marseilles flat, his arms around her from behind as they stood and drew on the heady tang of the sea. Arching her back beneath him as he pressed his mouth against the hot musk of her neck.

Dropping sack-like to the carpet, eyes suffused and starred crimson, tongue like lolling liver, neck efficiently dislocated.

Claire, dear sweet Jesus. Claire.

He turned the book over and found that his nails had driven deep crescents into the cover.

*

He held off calling Vale, because although the shaking in his hands had stopped he wasn't sure his voice would be as steady. Also, he needed some time to process the new information. Suddenly nothing made sense.

He used the time to work through the rest of the flat. The bathroom contained nothing of note. Last of all he went into the kitchen. Having checked the cupboards and the fridge, he opened the freezer.

*

The Jacobin leaned close to the monitor, trying to identify what was different. Purkiss had disappeared from view several minutes earlier, doubtless to search the rest of the flat, but when he returned there was a change in his posture, in his facial expression. A tightening, something suggestive of a coiled whip. Had he found something the Jacobin had missed?

He disappeared again in the direction of the kitchen and emerged in due course, his face betraying nothing. Purkiss had his phone in his hand and was thumbing a number in when he stopped, looked slowly around the room, at one point staring directly at the camera before his eyes roved away. Then he went out into the entrance passage, closing the door behind him.

Clearly he'd considered that the room might be wired. It didn't matter, because when the Jacobin opened the other window and saw the slow movement of the icon across the screen, it became clear that Purkiss had taken the bait.

Nine

'It doesn't make sense.'

'Tell me about it.'

He was on his way down the hill again, glad to be outside. Purkiss had seen death before, but the sight had unnerved him, coming as it had after his memories of Claire: the small frame cramped sideways on its bed of frozen goods, the face twisted up at an unnatural angle so that it seemed to peer at him through cracked eyes. He had hauled Seppo out, noting the absence of lividity and of ice formation as he turned him over. Less than six hours, he estimated. There was no wallet or phone. Purkiss hoisted him back into the freezer, closed the lid.

Vale said: 'Why would Fallon leave his book in Seppo's flat after killing him?'

'He didn't. I mean, he lives there too. That was his room I found the book in. The clothes in the cupboard are his size. Seppo and Fallon were sharing that flat.'

The silence grew. 'John, this has got me. I'll need to think about it.' The rustle, as always, of cigarette paper. 'I do have something for you, though. Elle Klavan. She's an active agent.'

'Doing what?'

'I haven't got that sort of information yet. All I have is confirmation that she's with Little Sister, as in not 'ex'. I can make discreet enquiries at the Embassy over there.'

'That's useful.' Most SIS personnel operated out of the embassies or consulates in the host country. He was walking fast to burn off adrenaline. 'What do you want me to do with the body?'

'Leave it. It'll keep for a few days.'

It made sense. Tipping off the police now could be awkward, especially as Purkiss's DNA was all over the flat.

'Also,' said Purkiss, 'there's video surveillance in the flat.' He'd spotted the tiny lens at the back of the fireplace just before leaving, hadn't seen it the first time he'd searched the place because he hadn't been looking for it. 'I'm assuming Fallon set it up to see who came looking for Seppo.'

He told Vale he'd call back later. After reaching the Old Town square, he spent a few minutes in the side streets, trying to find the internet café he'd spotted on his way earlier. Inside it smelled of coffee and tourists. When a machine was free he sat and slotted the memory stick into one of the ports. The box that came up told him the entire stick was password protected.

Purkiss bought a paper cup of coffee the size of a small bucket and left the warmth of the café. He phoned Abby.

'How soon can you get here?'

'There's a six a.m. flight, so, eleven tomorrow morning your time? I've already booked it.'

He shook his head. 'What if I hadn't needed you to come?'

'You always need me. Anyway, I'd have put the cancellation fee on expenses.' Her voice dropped a notch. 'Anything the matter, boss? You sound… I don't know.'

'I'm all right.' He checked his watch. Ten forty-five. 'Could you do something else for me?'

*

She called back within the hour. He'd wandered about the town, frustration gnawing at him, unease flickering on the periphery of his sensory fields. The face staring at him turned out to be somebody trying to read a restaurant menu near his head. The man who stumbled spraying red onto the cobbles hadn't been stabbed, but had simply spilled a bottle of red wine after a glass too many. When the phone vibrated he tensed.

'We're in luck. All the flats in the block are owned by the same landlord.' She gave a name and address. 'It's walking distance from where you are.'

'I don't suppose you found out if he's at home this evening, did you?'

She paused. 'No, but I –'

'Only joking. Great work, Abby.'

*

Over the chain stretched taut across the crack of the door the man's eyes were black and baleful. He was old, a dressing gown open over a grubby vest.

'Mr Väljas?'

The man's face clenched. Purkiss thought it was because he'd spoken Russian.

'Apologies for disturbing you so late.'

The man muttered something.

'Sorry, I have no Estonian.'

In Russian the old man said, 'It's nearly midnight.'

'Sorry again. I have a question about one of your tenants.'

'Who are you?'

He held up his open passport. 'My name's Hughes. I'm a debt collector.'

'English?' The man's tone softened, though he made no move to lift the chain.

'Yes. The tenant's Jaak Seppo. He owes tens of thousands in unpaid rent back in London. I traced him here but he's not at home. You're listed online as the landlord.'

The fury was back in the eyes. Purkiss realised it wasn't directed at him. The door closed, reopened with the chain off. Inside it stank of sweat and onions and fried meat.

The man was shaking his head. 'I knew he was up to no bloody good.'

'He's behind on the rent with you?'

'No. He's always been regular. Been there –'
He screwed up his face. 'Three years? No trouble
at all. Then, one day, I find he's got someone else
living there. A man. Not homosexual stuff, the
guy's got his own room. I tell Seppo I think he's
taken in a lodger. Subletting. He says no, the
man's his friend, staying a few months.'

Purkiss let some of his eagerness show
through. His pulse was hammering. 'Did you
meet this other man?'

'Sure. Pleasant enough fellow. Name of –' He
broke off, suspicious. 'Why do you ask?'

'Because Seppo had an associate in London,
who was also involved in fleecing the landlords.'

'Son of a bitch.' An elderly woman appeared
halfway down the stairs. He barked at her and
she fled. He picked his way across the cluttered
living room to a sideboard, rummaged in a
drawer, found a notepad. 'Julian Fisher.'

It meant nothing. 'What did he look like?'

'Forties. Average in everything. Friendly
smile.'

'Like that?' Purkiss had downloaded the
photo of Fallon to his new phone. The man
peered at it.

'That's him, yeah.'

'How long has he been staying in the flat?'

The man turned down the corners of his
mouth. 'Three, four months. Haven't seen either
of them for about a fortnight. Lots of properties to
keep an eye on.'

'And you said it was okay for this Fisher to stay?'

'Wasn't thrilled about it, but I'm a nice guy, and Seppo's been a good tenant over the years. You should see some of the arseholes I get. I asked his friend a bit about himself, what he did and so on. He was quite forthcoming. He's working his way around the Baltics, doing small jobs to pay his way while he travels. Seems a bit old to be doing that sort of thing, but hey, live and let live.'

'Did he say what work he was doing now?'

'Bartender at *Paradiis*. You know it? Shithole of a nightclub out east. Always in the news. Drug raids, stabbings, you name it. He'd stick out like a sore thumb there.'

Purkiss didn't think so. Fallon's unremarkable appearance meant he could adapt himself uncannily to any environment. He nodded.

'Mr Väljas, you've been a great help. Thanks.'

'You catch these guys, you cut their balls off for me, okay?'

*

Out east meant a couple of kilometres outside the Old Town. He flagged down a taxi, sat in the back and willed himself to relax without letting the fatigue overwhelm him. The driver navigated crowds of young whooping party animals. At one point Purkiss recognised the main road where the pursuit earlier had started and ended.

The entrance to the club was unprepossessing. A small pink neon sign flashed the name, *Paradiis*, over a blue martini glass. From across the street Purkiss could see a dark archway with steps leading up under an awning and two bouncers in the shadows at the top. People were streaming up there but there was no queue. It was too early for that, just after midnight. He walked up the steps. The door opened in a blast of bass-driven noise.

The bouncers were mirror-eyed walls of meat in tight, shiny black suits. They stared at Purkiss's rumpled jacket and shirt and chinos, and motioned for him to step aside. They frisked him, one taking the upper body and one the legs. He was a little rough round the edges after the chase earlier, so he supposed he looked as if he might cause trouble. The torso man found his wallet, held it up as if it were a weapon. Purkiss didn't want to draw attention by making a fuss. He made a show of sighing in resignation, peeled off a couple of notes. The bouncer grinned goldly and clapped him on the shoulder, jarring Purkiss's own teeth.

Inside it was the worst kind of place, the music so loud that the bass set up a vibration in the outer pinna of the ear rather than just the eardrum. It was industrial electronica and triggered a mild clench of nausea in Purkiss, whose musical tastes ran more to the classical. The air conditioning was fighting a losing battle against the humidity of sweaty flesh. On each of four podia spaced throughout the floor area a woman gyrated, clad in a bikini and what looked like a Second World War gas mask.

Purkiss chiselled his way through the layers of dancers towards the bar counter. He signalled the nearest bartender with a hundred-kroner note held up between two fingers. The man, shaven-headed and burly as the bouncers, his leather vest revealing a phantasmagoria of tattoos on his arms, leaned across, his ear close.

In Russian Purkiss shouted, 'I'm looking for this man.' He held up his phone with the picture of Fallon together with the caption he'd added: *Julian Fisher*.

The man was straightening, shaking his head almost as soon as he had glanced at the picture. Then he frowned at it again. Beckoning Purkiss closer he yelled, 'Englishman. He didn't turn up for his shifts last week, so everyone's assumed he's moved on.'

'How long was he working here?'

The man shrugged. 'Couple of months? Lyuba will know. I'll get her.'

He plucked the note from Purkiss's fingers without looking at it and moved down the bar and tapped the shoulder of one of the other bar staff, bending to her ear. She stared at Purkiss, a compact woman with short punky hair and similarly bared and tattooed arms. *Lyuba*: a Russian name. Only briefly taking her eyes off him, she finished serving her order and made her way down the counter. Purkiss produced another banknote between his knuckles and showed her the photo. She glanced at it, then back into his eyes. Up close her face was hard and angled and seamed. She was perhaps thirty but looked five years older.

'You know him?'

She put her lips to his ear, but the music changed to something even more frenetic. He shook his head. She cupped her hands around her mouth and shouted, 'This way,' and jerked her head. He followed her further down the bar, where she lifted a hatch, let him through and took him down a corridor to where the noise was merely intrusive. Arms folded, she faced him.

'Who are you?'

'A friend of Julian's from England. I can't find him.'

'He was here since February. Then last week – *poof*.' She splayed her hands. There was naked hostility in her glare. In a moment Purkiss got it.

'You were seeing each other?'

'The famous English chivalry. One minute he's all over me, talking about getting a place together. The next he's saying he needs to move on. He's not ready to settle down. *It's not me, it's him*.' She delivered the last in a wincingly accurate parody of a well-spoken Englishman's Russian. Her mouth twisted in bitterness.

Suddenly her eyes were calculating. 'And you can tell your whoreson *friend*, if you find him, that I haven't forgotten the money he owes me, nor have those friends of mine he met.'

'How much?'

'Six thousand *krooni*.' About four hundred pounds, Purkiss estimated. 'He was always short.'

'Perhaps we can help each other find him.'

She studied his eyes, said, 'I have to get back to work. My shift ends at one o'clock. Will you wait?'

'Yes.'

She hadn't taken the note he'd been holding. He made his way back into the heat and noise of the dance floor. At the bar he bought a bottle of water and a Diet Coke, after which he wormed his way over to one of the walls and leaned against it, wincing at the stickiness that tugged at the back of his jacket. Lyuba reappeared behind the bar. She and her fellow bartenders swarmed back and forth, keeping up with the demand. Purkiss checked his watch. Twelve thirty-five.

Fatigue was starting to tug at his eyes and limbs, brought on by the shortage of sleep he'd had the previous night on the way back from Rijeka, as well as the emotional grind of learning about Fallon's escape. The lingering effects of the chase earlier and the sedative his body had absorbed weren't helping either. He took a long draught of the soft drink, waited for the caffeine to kick in.

There was no pattern that he could discern. Fallon taking a flat with Seppo, who'd then reported his presence to Vale after several months. Fallon working in a dive of a club and taking up with an apparent street fighter of a woman, stringing her along and then ditching her without warning – and owing her money into the bargain. But in Purkiss's experience the attempt to fit facts to patterns was one of the great errors of which human beings were capable. Of more use was the notion of probability based on past experience. His experience of Fallon was that the man didn't get infatuated easily and didn't run short of cash. His relationship with the woman had to be cover of some sort.

The relentless assault of the music was getting to him, proving hypnotic in both the mesmerising and the soporific senses. He thought about waiting outside but decided that he might miss Lyuba at the end of her shift. Instead he headed for the restroom. As usual the queue for the ladies' was long, the one for the gents' non-existent. He shouldered through the swinging door and into the reek of urine and bleach. He edged past the row of men at the communal urinal, found a vacant sink and ran the cold tap, ladling water against his face before pooling it in his hands and gulping it down. It was surprisingly palatable for city water. In the brown flyblown glass his face was pale, full of dark scoops: under the eyes, below the cheekbones and nose.

Beside Purkiss a skinny man with a ravaged face held open a jacket lined inside with slender pill bottles and knuckly twists of hashish. Purkiss shook his head. He was turning to leave when he felt a vibration against his leg. He pulled out his phone. A missed call from five minutes earlier. Vale.

He stood outside the cubicles until one of the doors opened. A man lurched out fumbling up his trousers. Purkiss went in, grimaced at the stink and the swamp of urine and toilet paper on the floor, kept away from the edge of the toilet bowl. He lifted the phone to his ear to hear the voice message while he reached behind him to slide the latch across.

The door slammed open against his thumb and the man cannoned into him shoving him forward so that his shins connected with the toilet bowl. He heard the door bang shut as he fought to keep his balance. With awful speed the man's hands came down on either side of Purkiss's neck and he felt the bite of the garrotte.

Ten

It was the phone that saved him from immediate death. It was in his left hand because he'd been reaching back to latch the door with his right and hadn't had time to lower it completely. The garrotte caught across his watch but cut into his neck on the other side. He felt the wire tighten and crush the heel of his hand against the side of his jaw and he felt the closeness of the man behind him and the hot sourness of his breath against his right ear.

Purkiss shifted his head a fraction, all he could, to the right. At the far extreme of his vision was the shape of the other man's head and part of one fist where it bunched with its fellow at the back of Purkiss's neck, increasing the torque on the ends of the garrotte. Pain slashed through his neck and he felt the flesh bulging around the crevasse gouged by the wire. There was no blood yet, he was fairly sure of it. His right arm hung free.

Purkiss fought against the roil of nausea and tried for a backwards head butt with his occiput into his assailant's face, but the twist of the garrotte around his neck might as well have been a vice holding his head in place because there was almost no range of movement. The wave of nausea was turning into one of panic as his watch slipped partially free from the garrotte and the wire began tightening across his forearm.

He pivoted back from the hips. This shifted the man back slightly and Purkiss was able to get his right foot up and onto the edge of the toilet bowl. He shoved himself backwards, pistoning his leg, slamming the man back against the door. Purkiss pushed again and a third time, each time pounding the man into the door and shaking the entire cubicle. From outside a drunken voice laughed *what the fuck's going on in there* in Russian – *another Russian speaker, this was quite a Russian club, that might be significant* flitted through Purkiss's thoughts – and the man behind him gasped back, 'Leave us alone,' which was met with cheers and wolf whistles. Purkiss got his right arm up and grabbed a fistful of the man's hair and bent his head sideways. The angle was all wrong because his arm was flexed behind him and he was trying to exert force outwards, but the stretch on the man's neck was enough to make him hiss through clenched teeth and momentarily shift his grip on the ends of the garrotte to secure it more tightly. In that instant Purkiss let go of the hair and gripped his left fist in his right hand and pressed his left forearm against the wire, the separate pains in his arm and in the right side of his neck blinding but the manoeuvre succeeding in creating a little slack. He was able to turn his head a fraction to the right and whip it sideways and he felt his frontal bone just above and to the side of his right eye connect hard with the man's cheekbone and with a soft cry the man loosed his hold on one end of the garrotte. Purkiss spun to face him and the movement tore the garrotte free from the man's left hand. Purkiss closed in, striking with a half-fist at the side of the man's neck.

The blow to his cheekbone had been hard but the man recovered quickly and brought his arm up and deflected Purkiss's attack. The man countered with a two-fingered eye jab but the space was too confined, ridiculously so, and he didn't have the distance available to build up any momentum. Purkiss caught his hand and wrenched it around and down. With the edge of his other hand he struck at the man's exposed neck. The man did his best to avoid it but with his arm held twisted as it was there wasn't much he could do, and he sagged against Purkiss.

Purkiss let go of his wrist and caught him under the arms and supported the dead weight for a second, catching his breath, blinking until the ceiling stopped rocking, struggling not to topple over the toilet bowl pressed against the backs of his legs. There was a flicker at the man's eyelids and *he'd been bluffing* and Purkiss let go of him and brought his knee up just as the man brought both fists stabbing in at Purkiss's kidneys, an incapacitating blow if done right. Purkiss's knee into the man's abdomen as he dropped took some of the force out. Now the man had an arm around Purkiss's neck and with his other hand he was gouging at Purkiss's face. Purkiss seized the wrist in his hand and held it quivering. He stared into the man's face, so close to his, red and sweating, the eyes narrowed to slits and the breath wheezing hot against his face.

For a fraction of a second they held the position, taking stock. The man had his left arm around Purkiss's neck and his right in a claw near Purkiss's face. Purkiss gripped the man's right wrist in his left fist. His right hand was free and between them.

Purkiss brought his left hand up with the heel of the palm foremost and slammed it into the underside of the man's jaw with as much force as he could muster, which was less than it would have been a minute earlier because the pain and disorientation were taking their toll. *Still* the man managed to avoid the worst of the blow by turning his head and taking the brunt on the corner of his jaw. He loosened his arm further from Purkiss's neck and jabbed his stiffened fingers at the side of Purkiss's throat and Purkiss staggered, vision blurring. The thrash of the music was suddenly overwhelming and as if detached from his body he saw himself stumble over the toilet and the man shift position for the killing blow. From somewhere inside him Purkiss felt something building, a great dark shadow which couldn't be contained and which erupted from his chest and along his arm as he rammed the heel of his palm out again. This time he caught the man directly beneath the nose and snapped his head back. He dropped, finally, the nasal bones driven into the soft tissues of his brain, his knees sinking into the foetid mulch on the cubicle floor.

Purkiss reeled, gripping the cistern and heaving over the bowl, though nothing came out apart from a sour spew of half-digested soda. His foot slipped in the mess on the floor and the wall tilted towards him. He shoved down the lid of the toilet and slumped onto it and leaned forward, head in his hands.

*

When he opened his eyes, panic scrabbled at him because he thought he'd been out for hours; but by his watch, which was still functioning, barely five minutes had passed since he'd entered the cubicle. At his feet, pressing against his legs with genuine dead weight this time, the man half sat, half slumped, empty eyes turned turned to the ceiling. When he was confident he'd keep his balance Purkiss stood and let the man slide sideways so that his head fell alongside the root of the toilet bowl.

In the man's hip pocket he found a wallet with a driver's licence. He read the name – Abram Zhilin, Russian again – and address. The man had no phone on him. Purkiss bent to peer under the door of the cubicle. There were two pairs of feet at the urinal trough. Swiftly he opened the door and exited and pulled it shut and walked past the two men who didn't turn. He went to the basins. In the mirror his face was bone-sallow, the eyes grey bruises and not fully focused. There were angry red lines along his left forearm and the right side of his neck, seeping blood. He washed his arms and neck, cupped water over his face and between his lips, spitting and repeating.

There wasn't time to reflect on what had happened, because he had to see if the woman was still out there. It was ten to one and he hoped she hadn't left yet. He stepped out into the dizzying throb and sidled along the wall towards the bar. She looked up, Lyuba. In her face there was shock. Her glance darted across the floor and he followed it and saw, picked out intermittently in the strobes, the face of the man with the bull neck who'd been following him earlier, separated from him by a mass of clubbers.

He though about moving sideways towards the entrance, but saw her looking in that direction as well, and he understood there were others, probably guarding the fire exits too. He'd been set up, and he was now well and truly cornered.

*

Afterwards the Jacobin went for another walk, this time along Pikk, the Long Street, past the old guild houses towards St Olaf's Church. Not one but *two* more scars on the soul. The old woman had to die after she'd seen what happened to her husband, there was no question about it; but she was blameless, as indeed was the old man. They might even have been left to live if the Jacobin could have been sure Purkiss hadn't given the man his phone number and asked him to get in contact should anyone come asking.

The three-quarter moon perched on top of St Olaf's spire, at one time the tallest of its kind in the world. The Jacobin gazed up at it, breath pluming in the cold night air, and thought about human hubris. A year's meticulous planning, and Purkiss was trying to put a stop to it at this late hour.

On the worst nights – perhaps one in every ten – the Jacobin's dreams were painted in vast, terrible vistas of devastation: charnel pits engorged with the stick bodies of concentration camp inmates, strontium-blighted cityscapes of black ruin, fields of mud and blood and bone. The Jacobin would wake, sweat-slick, fist crammed into mouth, driving back a scream. The terror would ebb after a few minutes, but the shaking in the hands would persist. The Jacobin didn't mind; welcomed the dreams, in fact. When one had committed oneself to a refusal to give an inch, the dreams stiffened one's resolve.

The figures were burned in the Jacobin's mind. Two and a half thousand operational strategic warheads, two thousand operational tactical warheads, seven thousand stockpiled warheads of both varieties. It was the best estimate of the Russian nuclear arsenal, not at the height of the Cold War but today, more than two decades after the fall of the Soviet empire. There was no chance, none at all, that the growing economic and geopolitical resurgence of the old enemy would not be accompanied eventually by the flexing of its military muscles, whether directly or through terrorist proxies. And no chance that the nuclear stockpile would remain unused. Meanwhile the governments of the EU and the US were embracing *détente*, *rapprochement*, a host of French terms that failed to disguise the English one they were meant to replace: *appeasement*.

As the evidence of the country's growing aggression and arrogance had accumulated – the Litvinenko murder, the crushing of Georgia – there had been those within the Service who had pressed for a more assertive approach to the Russian Bear: greater numbers deployed in Moscow and Petersburg to bolster the existing networks there, targeted assassinations, pressure on the politicians to adopt a more publicly pugnacious stance. These courageous voices had been shouted down by others, less courageous. *Russia is an ally in the War on Terror. We rely on Gazprom's oil.* And, more honestly if hardly more excusably: *Look at the state of the economy. There's no money left.* The mealy-mouthed justifications nauseated the Jacobin.

After the morning of Saturday the fourteenth everything would be different. Within a week, within days, the Kremlin would have made its move, and the weasels in Whitehall and Washington would no longer be able to cower in their burrows. And leading the fightback would be the Service, reenergised, with a reacquired sense of purpose.

The old man, the landlord, had opened the door in a fury. His anger quickly dissolved into terror. By the end he was grovelling. He'd been useful, not for revealing where he'd sent Purkiss – this was already known to the Jacobin – but for what he'd said about the questions Purkiss had asked. The picture was becoming extremely complicated.

The call came from Kuznetsov. 'My men are in place. He's trapped.'

That was quick. The Jacobin was impressed, but didn't betray it. 'They underestimated him last time. Make sure it doesn't happen again.'

'You have my word.' Was there snideness in the tone? Kuznetsov's true attitude towards the Jacobin had become increasingly apparent in the last week.

'Non-lethal force only.'

Kuznetsov said nothing.

'I mean it, Kuznetsov.'

'It causes delay, and ties up my people who are needed elsewhere. A quick despatch is far more efficient.'

The Jacobin gripped the phone, fighting down the frustration. 'I told you, I need to extract information from him. Crucial information that could scupper the whole enterprise if we let it.'

'If he is as dangerous as you say, then we're better off with him dead.' The call was disconnected.

The Jacobin paced, channelling the anger, trying to divert it like lightning into the earth. The pig-headed idiot had ideas above his station, was going to let his ego wreck everything.

From across the nearby bay a horn sounded, low and prolonged like a moan.

Eleven

He'd identified four of them so far but suspected there were more. The bull-necked man was barrelling his way through the throng, hanging back when Purkiss changed direction so that he could track him. On either side of the entrance there were two of them, their stares like spotlights trained on a lone sprinter across a prison yard. And behind the bar the woman, Lyuba, was ignoring the shouts of drinkers trying to get her attention and stood with folded arms, her gaze naked as the others'.

He fished the card out of his breast pocket and read the number by the light of his phone.

It was going to be impossible to make himself heard over the cacophony. On the other hand, he couldn't risk heading back into the restrooms where it was marginally quieter, because he'd be trapping himself down a cul de sac. He thumbed in the text message and hit the *send* key.

The bull-necked man was trying to drive him towards the two at the entrance and he headed deep into the heaving mass of clubbers but it was hazardous because he didn't know how many of them would be waiting further back in the depths of the dance floor and if one of them had a syringe like earlier they could slip it in before he'd realised what was going on and he'd be down and then they'd have him. He felt himself borne along by the press of bodies. This, as well as the strobing lights and the endless grind of the music, triggered panic in his stomach. He thought about screaming. Nobody would notice, and it might offer him some release.

The phone in his pocket vibrated. He looked at the screen, saw the words: *On our way. Fifteen minutes.*

Our? There was no point dwelling on what this meant, because he had to concentrate on staying conscious and keeping his wits about him for a quarter of an hour. It was no time at all and yet an eternity.

There was another possibility to consider, a wild card he had no control over. The body might be found in the cubicle in the next fifteen minutes and the place locked down. It would reduce the immediate danger, but would generate problems of its own. His best bet was to make his way to one of the walls and keep against it, limit the directions from which the enemy could approach without restricting his potential escape routes. Purkiss squirmed his way over to the far wall. Once there he turned and took stock.

The bull-necked man was approaching, his progress remorseless through the sea of bodies. From over to the left, one of the men who'd been guarding the entrance was advancing, too, sidling along the wall. Purkiss eased to his left instinctively but ten feet or so in that direction was a corner and that was the last place he wanted to end up.

Purkiss breathed deeply, sucking reserve oxygen into his lungs and his bloodstream. He flexed his limbs, bounced on his toes, preparing himself. Two of them at close quarters, in his weakened state, were going to be a problem, to say the least. If they had syringes they wouldn't even necessarily be filled with a sedative, as before. The man in the toilet cubicle had been trying not to subdue him but to kill him.

It murmured through the crowd like a ripple or a Mexican wave, a word he didn't recognise at first until he realised another word was filtering through in counterpoint, this one in Russian: *police*. The collective mood of the crowd shifted, most people continuing their frenetic leaping but considerable numbers moving fast towards the restrooms, the back of the dance floor, the fire exits. Near him a boy swallowed painfully, forcing down whatever had to be hidden. Another hopped on one foot, trying to stuff the illicit goods into his other shoe. The bull-necked man and his colleague halted their advance, looking about and then craning back towards the entrance.

Purkiss ran, diving into the crowd and not caring that he was treading on feet and elbowing chests, somebody yelling in his ear *hey, man, don't panic, they'll notice you*. She was there inside the

115

entrance, Elle Klavan, with another man, and they were holding up ID of some sort while one of the bar staff stood nearby frowning in bewilderment. Purkiss stopped short. She shouted in Estonian and he turned. The bartender he'd first spoken to when he arrived got him in a bear hug from behind. Purkiss kicked and struggled, but not too hard. Elle Klavan and the other man came forward, handguns drawn. Purkiss shouted in Russian 'Enough,' and the man released him. He raised his hands and let them turn and bundle him out the door, Klavan shouting instructions he couldn't understand over her shoulder.

*

She pulled up in a mews off the main street. The Turkish restaurant next door was closed and a few people milled on the streets, on their way to or from bars. They took the stairs to the first floor. Through an unmarked door a small office suite greeted him. The main open-plan section brimmed with computer equipment, less chaotically arranged than in Abby's basement.

'*Living Tallinn,*' she said drily.

She'd forced her way between the rows of taxis and parked right outside the club, swinging into the driver's seat. The man with her had opened the rear door and pushed Purkiss's head down as he clambered in, purely because that was what television had taught people to expect from police officers arresting a criminal, and got in beside him.

'Chris Teague,' said the man. He was late thirties, big through the shoulders like a former rugby player who'd kept in shape, fair hair short, mouth wry.

'John Purkiss.'

'We know.' Of course they did; they were SIS, and Klavan would have scoured their databases till she'd matched his face.

'You were quick.' She'd said *fifteen minutes* but it had been closer to ten.

'I happen to live round the corner. Stroke of luck.'

'Thanks.'

'Impersonating a police officer. That's a first for us, wouldn't you say?'

'Yes,' said Teague cheerfully.

Turning her head to address Purkiss she said, 'I expect you're wondering why we did it.'

'Because you want to know what I'm doing here.'

'Of course.'

He remembered the missed call from Vale earlier and said, 'Hang on a moment,' and put the phone to his ear, aware of the stinging of the laceration across his neck. The message was brief. Vale had established that Klavan was not working out of the embassy.

As if by unspoken consent they said no more on the journey. At one point a police car shot past, siren going. Clearly the body had been found in the toilet cubicle. Purkiss wondered how easy witnesses would find it to identify Klavan and Teague, given the darkness in the club. He himself was another matter: the bartender had got a good look at his face.

Another man was waiting in the office and stood as they entered. He was compact, several inches shorter than either Purkiss or Teague and perhaps in his late forties. Unlike his colleagues he was dressed in a suit, though the jacket was slung over the back of a chair and his sleeves were pushed up.

'Mr Purkiss. Richard Rossiter.'

There was an aura about him, a sense of tightly bound anger. Up close his pale eyes were like taut meniscuses barely holding back a flood of rage. He didn't offer his hand, just studied Purkiss's face before waving abruptly at a chair. Purkiss sat. Teague brought him a cup of water from a cooler in the corner and he gulped it. The others took seats themselves.

Rossiter said: 'No preamble. You, I assume, have worked out who we are. A Service cell, unofficial and operating covertly, without Embassy support. We of course know who you are. John Purkiss, Service until four years ago. We know why you left – rather, what had happened that might have prompted you to leave. You've left no trail since then, none that we can discern.'

There were two possibilities, Purkiss had decided. One was that they were who they said they were, and were unconnected to Fallon and

118

looking for him themselves. The other was that they were working with Fallon, that the rescue from the nightclub had been part of a ruse. Either way, there was little point withholding his reasons for being in the city.

He glanced at Klavan, who was leaning forward, elbows resting on her knees, watching him levelly; at Teague, who sat back with his arms spread across the back of his chair and his ankle propped on his knee, expansive as Rossiter was shut in and controlled.

'I'm here on personal business,' he said. 'Donal Fallon was photographed in Tallinn yesterday morning. He was released early from gaol, amnestied, and he's gone to ground.'

In Klavan's case it was the slightest hint of an exhalation, in Teague's a tilting back of the head. Rossiter blinked, once. Each of them, professionals though they were, betrayed their surprise. Now that was interesting, he thought.

Rossiter said: 'Personal business.'

'Yes. You know why I want Fallon.'

'You're not Service.'

'No. As you mentioned, I've left.' He took out his phone and brought up the photo of Fallon, watching their faces as they handed it round.

'Who took this picture?' It was Teague, sounding amicably interested.

'A contact of mine. I've kept some links going since I left.'

'Seppo,' said Klavan. 'And he wasn't there when you went to his flat.'

'Correct. Though I did find him later. In the deep freeze, with his neck broken.' Purkiss took the phone back and pocketed it. 'Now. Your turn'.

Rossiter's face worked. In a moment he said: 'We're here because of the summit. The Service's Embassy presence has been stepped up, of course, but there was felt to be a need for additional covert work, given the significance of the event.' He looked as if he wanted to stand and pace but was compressing himself into his seat. 'And perhaps your reasons for being here and ours aren't unconnected.'

'No.'

Another pause, then: 'So. In less than thirty-one hours' time, the Russian President is going to meet his Estonian counterpart here in the city in an historic gesture of reconciliation. We have to assume Fallon plans to scupper that.'

*

Coffee had been passed round. Rossiter stood at the flip chart like an incongruously fierce facilitator at a corporate away day.

'The Russian president arrives ten p.m. tomorrow at a private airfield, the whereabouts of which are unknown. There's a formal banquet with his Estonian opposite number, then an overnight stay at the official residence in Kadriorg. A working breakfast, then at seven a.m. both parties and their entourages set off to the Soviet War Memorial on the coast road. The handshake and the speeches are to take place there at eight.'

He moved over to a laminated map on the wall. 'The route is demarcated in red. Needless to say, we've gone over it countless times, looking for vantage points that might conceal a sniper. As have the local security forces. There's very little to find. A sniper would have to be armed with something more powerful than an ordinary rifle, in any case, because the cars are armour plated.'

'What about at the War Memorial itself?' said Purkiss.

'Again, not many places for a man with a gun to hide, and those there are will be heavily guarded. The crowds – and they'll be huge – will be kept well back, with sniffer dogs deployed in case anyone's planning to try the suicide bomb thing.' He paused for a beat. 'We're assuming Fallon plans to scupper the meeting. He might try to do that by other means – a terrorist outrage elsewhere in the city, for instance – but he'll know how much is riding on this summit, that it will go ahead anyway in defiance of any attempts to stop it, so we don't think that's a likely scenario.'

'The airfield where the Russian president's arriving?'

'As I said –' an edge crept into Rossiter's voice – 'it's a secret. But even if Fallon or anyone else has somehow found out where it is, the security there is likely to be impenetrable. The same goes for the banquet and the overnight accommodation.'

Elle took over. It was clear to Purkiss this discussion was one they'd had before. 'We're not going to work out how the attempt's going to be made, not with the information we've got at present. We'd be better served focusing on the lead we do now have, Fallon, and finding him before the event.'

Rossiter had come closer and stood looking down at Purkiss, hands folded before him as if he were anchoring them down. 'We work together on this. I'm not asking you to accept my command, but anything either you or we learn is shared. Are we agreed?'

Purkiss rocked his head from side to side. 'Possibly. Depends if I think it's worth sharing.'

Rossiter watched him, lips thinned whitely. 'If you're trying to get a rise out of me, Mr Purkiss, it's not going to work. I know you think you have the upper hand because you've given us the Fallon connection. Yes, it's an essential piece of intelligence. But we have the resources, the local connections, that you need. So be nice.'

It lasted barely a second, the quiver of tension between them. Then Purkiss said, 'Tell me how you got on to Seppo, how you found his flat.'

Twelve

'You need to speak to this woman, find out what she's not telling us.'

The Jacobin's voice was steady, grip on the handset loose.

'I have spoken to her already. She's hiding nothing.'

'This man she was sleeping with, this Fallon. Purkiss is desperate to find him and won't say why. He's got to be important in some way. We have to find out what the woman told him.'

'She told him nothing. She's rock solid, loyal beyond question.' Kuznetsov sounded offended.

'Kuznetsov, I don't think you really appreciate the seriousness of this. This man worked his way into the affections of clearly the weakest link in your outfit, then disappeared. Until we find him, we have to assume he has knowledge that could compromise us.'

'You speak to me like this, you impugn the character of one of my people. Yet you yourself keep this man Purkiss alive. You allow him access to your circle.'

'For your information, he's the best chance we have at the moment of finding this Fallon. I'm working on him, trying to persuade him to tell me why Fallon's of importance to him.' There was a tap at the door and the Jacobin opened it and held up a hand – *one minute* – and closed it again. 'We're going to have to bring the woman in. You need to make her aware of this, prepare her for interrogation.'

'No torture.'

'Of course.'

They spoke for another minute before ringing off. The Jacobin stood gazing through the window at the night, then went to find the others.

*

Purkiss had argued that there wasn't time to rest, but he'd been trying to persuade himself as much as them. In the end he lost the battle. Teague gave him the once over, applying antiseptic to the laceration from the garrotte. They had worked out a plan for the following morning, and it was agreed that Purkiss would crash out at the flat which Klavan and Teague shared. Rossiter was apparently staying behind at the base. Apart from individual offices off the central open-plan area, all of which were soundproofed, Purkiss noticed, there was a tiny bedroom and bathroom as well as a kitchenette.

In the car on the way back out of the Old Town Purkiss sat in the back again, with Klavan driving and Teague in the front passenger seat this time.

Purkiss said: 'Am I going to have a problem with your boss?'

'Rossiter?' Teague lifted a shoulder. 'No. He doesn't like you, mainly because he doesn't trust you. To him you're a rogue agent just like Fallon, even if your motives are more sympathetic. You have to admit, he has a point.'

Purkiss had told them Seppo was an old friend and colleague of his who'd sent him the photo of Fallon but then hadn't been contactable when he'd tried to ring him. He'd told them everything, essentially, apart from saying anything about Vale or Abby, and had admitted his bafflement at the signs of Fallon's presence in Seppo's flat.

'You think Seppo was setting you up? Luring you to the city?' Klavan asked.

'Possibly. But it doesn't explain how he ended up dead in the freezer, unless someone else sent the photo using his phone to lure me over here.'

For their part, Klavan and Rossiter had been taking coffee outside a café across from the Russian embassy on Pikk Street the previous morning when they'd noticed the small man, who turned out to be Seppo, taking photos apparently of the embassy building with his phone, trying to be surreptitious about it. Their curiosity piqued, they had spent the better part of the morning following him, and tracked him to his flat on the Toompea. They returned to the office to run a check on the address. Later, after she'd finished her day's routine work, Klavan went back to the flat, expecting Seppo to be at home, in which case she would have found a pretext to enter the flat and nose around. Instead she found Purkiss there.

'Your face was vaguely familiar, and became more so when I discovered you were English. I didn't spot you tagging me back to the office, though. That was good tradecraft.'

Purkiss didn't mention the memory stick he'd found at the back of Seppo's drawer. He supposed they had the equipment and possibly even the skills to override its password protection, but he decided this was something he'd keep to himself for the time being.

The coloured lights of stationary police vehicles daubed the streets around the nightclub. Klavan's and Teague's flat was two blocks away. They parked in the basement and took the lift. Inside it was comfortably furnished, a home rather than merely a place to sleep.

'How long have you been here?'

'We set up a year ago when the date for the summit became known,' said Klavan. She handed him a mug of tea and although caffeine wasn't what he needed now he took it gratefully, declining the offer of something to eat.

Teague threw a sheet and blanket on the couch. It was half-past two. They agreed on a seven a.m. start and Klavan and Teague disappeared. To separate rooms, Purkiss noted wryly.

He lay in the dark, feeling sleep and fatigue take gradual control. Rossiter didn't trust him. Nor, clearly, did the other two. That was fine, because he didn't trust any of them either.

His last thought before numbness overwhelmed him was of Claire, leaning on her elbows, supporting her frowning brow with her fingers and peering into a monitor, trying to solve some conundrum. He thought: *If you were here to help me now…*

But of course that wouldn't make sense.

*

Beside him his wife slept deeply, untroubled. Venedikt squinted at the bedside clock: two-thirty. He needed sleep for what was to come, but knew he wouldn't get it by forcing himself. Instead he rose, went into the living room, and turned on the television to a Russian-language twenty-four-hour news channel.

… will arrive in Tallinn tomorrow evening for a formal banquet…

… first official visit by a Russian premier since independence…

… historic signing of a friendship agreement…

The channel took great pride in what it called its political neutrality. Venedikt thought this a euphemism for cowardice, treacherousness even. Five years earlier he had been in the crowd protesting against the removal of the Bronze Soldier, the statue celebrating those like his grandfather who had fallen defending Estonia. Under cover of darkness the statue had been uprooted from its proud place in Tonismagi in the city centre and dumped in the wasteland of the Defence Forces Cemetery on the outskirts, along with the desecrated remains of Soviet heroes who were buried beneath it. Venedikt and his compatriots had vented their fury tirelessly, for two nights, during which one of their number had been shot dead, murdered, by the police. When he'd tried to explain to his son afterwards the importance of what had happened, the boy had shrugged and made to run outside. That had earned him a beating.

The ravaging of the statue was as nothing compared to what was planned for the day after tomorrow. The government had never admitted any intentional symbolism in the moving of the statue out of the city, even though nobody, not even those in favour of the act, had any illusions about why it was being done. But on October the thirteenth the Russian president was going to stand with his Estonian counterpart, the lickspittle of America and the West, and shake his hand, grinning, while behind them the memorial spire to the fallen of Mother Russia, not just those who died in the Great Patriotic War but all the others as well, was exploited for sickening political ends. The Estonian thinking was clear: *not only are we going to extort apologies and craven concessions from you, we are going to do so in the shadow of one of your most treasured icons.* Venedikt was not an especially imaginative man but he couldn't fail to see the metaphorical significance of the limp handshake in front of the proud spire, the suggestion of emasculation it brought to mind.

There was nothing symbolic in what Venedikt and his people were going to do. Nothing ambiguous at all.

He switched off the television and went to stare out of the window. It was far too early for daybreak, but the night seemed to have shed some of its darkness, as though conceding grudgingly that its allotted time was passing once more. Two dawns left, and on the second the sun would rise on a very different city. A different world.

The day had been a perfect one and had ended perfectly, with the news about the Englishman. He couldn't believe their luck. Nothing like this had even been considered when they'd first made their plans all those months earlier, yet the opportunity had fallen into their laps. Occurrences like this almost made Venedikt question his rejection of religious faith.

The excitement threatened to keep him further from sleep, so he went back to bed. In his mind he rehearsed the sequence of events over and over until it was smooth as a beach pebble.

Thirteen

Between finger and thumb Rossiter held up a SIM card.

'Tracker. We exchange it for the one in her phone while we interrogate her.'

They were back in the office. Purkiss, not by inclination an early riser, had taken his time responding to Klavan's gentle shake at seven. His eyes felt knotted and his neck and limbs ached as if he'd slept folded into a crate. Teague had gone out for coffee and hot rolls, and on his return he offered Purkiss a selection of his clothes. Purkiss chose loose ones for running in, chinos and a shirt that was a little big across the shoulders. In the shower he flexed and rolled, trying to work the tightness out of his muscles.

Teague and Klavan had been up early, working the Web and their phones. They'd achieved the breaks they'd wanted: they had the name of the woman in the nightclub, Lyuba Ilkun, as well as her home address. Teague had phoned the club and said he was a police officer investigating the two bogus detectives who had appeared the previous night and taken away the man suspected of leaving the body in the toilet cubicle.

'That took some nerve,' said Purkiss. 'Hats off.'

Klavan had checked the name of the man in the toilet cubicle, Abram Zhilin, and discovered that he'd had a military career, six years' service in the Ground Force, the Estonian equivalent of the Army, after his compulsory national service. She'd phoned a contact of hers in the Ground Force's records office who promised to look up Zhilin's file once he'd got into work.

Rossiter put the SIM card on the table. 'Two of us do the snatch, two the interrogation.' He looked at them in turn, pale eyes lingering on Purkiss. The anger was there still, livelier, as if sleep had rejuvenated it. 'You and Chris do the grab. Elle's an experienced interrogator, and a woman, which Ilkun will find disconcerting.'

Purkiss shook his head. 'No use my grabbing her. She'd recognise me. It's better not to let her know for sure who's got her, even if she suspects.'

'She wouldn't recognise you if you took her without her seeing you. There are ways, you know, using hoods.' Rossiter voice was thin, disparaging.

'No. Besides, I have to meet someone.'

Even Klavan and Teague stared at him. Rossiter became very still.

'Say again?'

'An associate of mine's arriving in the city this morning.' He stood. 'Oh, for goodness sake. I'm working with you but of course I'm not letting you in completely. I need insurance, some kind of backup in case things go wrong. You'd do the same.'

'And when's this... *associate* of yours expected?'

'Late morning.' Purkiss spread his palms. 'You lot take the woman – I take it you can do it without my help – and I'll meet you back here once you've got her and I've done my business.'

Rossiter's eyes moved, calculating; then he said, 'Fine. And if you're late, you won't mind if we start without you.'

*

Abby's text had arrived just after eight, minutes after the sun had come up: *I'm boarding now. See you half elevenish.*

Klavan and Teague offered him a lift to the airport on their way to Lyuba Ilkun's address and he sat in front this time. From the back Teague said, 'Pissed him off a bit there.'

'But he did understand.'

After a silence Teague said: 'He thinks you're the Ratcatcher, you know.'

'What?'

'The Ratcatcher. The outsider, tracks down Service personnel who've broken the rules. Emerged in the last few years.'

'Never heard of him, or her.' Purkiss shook his head. 'See, that's one of the reasons I'm glad I left the Service. It's such a hermetic world you end up losing perspective. Everyone's either with you or against you, an ally to be exploited or an enemy to be destroyed. Eventually you end up believing in fairy tales. Vast conspiracies, masked avengers smiting wrongdoers. It's insane. You go crazy.'

Klavan said, 'You've got to admit, though, that your story's an odd one. You turn up here on the trail of a renegade agent on the eve of an international summit. And yes, I know you have your personal reasons for wanting Fallon. But the part about this Seppo alerting you and then turning out to share a flat with Fallon... it doesn't ring true.' Her face in profile was amiable.

'It doesn't make sense to me either, as I've said. But you need my help, so you have to trust me up to a point.'

*

He was at the airport an hour and a half early and he used the time to carry out a complete counter-surveillance routine. He doubted the two agents would have bothered trying to keep tabs on him after dropping him off, but there was no harm in making sure. He booked a hire car at a kiosk, choosing a nondescript Toyota. Afterwards he ordered an enormous all-day breakfast at a restaurant in the arrivals hall, bearing in mind Kendrick's military dictum that when it wasn't clear how long it would be until your next meal, it was worth fuelling up when you could. He took his time eating, watching the boards.

Abby came through fifteen minutes after landing, dwarfed by the rucksack and suitcase she was lugging. He made sure nobody was observing her before catching up with her at the entrance.

'Hope you manage to find a fast enough connection with all this gear.'

She smiled up at him. 'It's one of the most wired cities in Europe.' Her face fell. 'You look *awful*, boss. What happened to your neck?'

'Nicked myself shaving.'

He helped her with the suitcase and they found the car he'd hired. Abby had booked a room at a chain hotel near the city centre and on the way he told her as much as she needed to know: about the SIS agents, and about Fallon and what they suspected his presence in the city meant. He described Fallon as impersonally as he was able, leaving out what he had done to Claire. As far as Purkiss knew, all Abby was aware of was that he'd lost a girlfriend many years ago just before leaving the Service.

She rummaged in her rucksack and took out a tiny object and handed it across. 'What you asked for.'

He took it and, still driving, glanced at it. It was the size of a pinhead, metallic with a row of minute hooks like an insect's bristles.

'Terrific.' In turn he fished out the memory stick he'd found in Seppo's flat. She slipped it in her pocket.

At the hotel he offered to help her to her room but she said, 'No, I'll manage. Go.'

'One more thing.'

'Sure.'

'There are three of them. The agents.'

'Yes, you said.'

'Two of us.'

She frowned for a second, then got it. 'Aha. Want to even things up?'

'Yes.'

'I'll ring him and make the arrangements.'

*

He was on his way back into the Old Town when the phone rang. He hit the speakerphone key. 'Yes.'

'Mr Purkiss, it's Klavan. We –'

'John.'

'John. We've got her.'

'Good. I'm nearly there.'

He parked several streets away and walked to the office. When he gave his name the door buzzed and he climbed the stairs.

Rossiter let him in, his expression stone. Neither Teague nor Klavan was in the main area.

'They've got her in my office.' He jerked his head. 'Took her two blocks from her flat.'

'She resist?'

'Like a cat in a sack. They're good, though. She didn't get hurt.' A flicker of pride in Rossiter's voice. Purkiss found himself liking the man for it.

'How did they get her up here in broad daylight?'

'There's a side entrance down the alley.'

Rossiter tapped on the door of his office. Teague emerged, and Rossiter went in and closed the door behind him. Teague nodded to Purkiss.

'We can watch and listen here.'

They moved behind a broad desk where on a computer monitor the woman sat, her head hidden by a canvas hood, on a swivel chair in front of a desk. Rossiter was perched on a corner of the desk, Klavan standing on the other side of the woman. Klavan reached out and pulled off the hood, and the woman's face worked as though the canvas had been stifling her. Her expression was hard, surly. Purkiss understood why they'd removed the hood, even though leaving it on would have had the advantage of increasing her disorientation and keeping their identities secret. Without being able to see her face they might not know if she was lying.

Klavan spoke first, her voice slightly tinny through the speakers. She used Russian, fluent though accented.

'We want information about the whereabouts of Julian Fisher, also known as Donal Fallon. We are prepared to use any means necessary to obtain this information, up to and including physical duress.' She sounded like a flight attendant reciting the safety drill.

The woman said nothing, sat with arms folded and feet hooked behind the castors of the chair, staring ahead.

Klavan bent forward, hands resting on her knees, and peered into the woman's face. 'No? All right.' She straightened, walked away; then half-turned.

'Sorry. I didn't make myself clear. I meant physical duress inflicted on your son.'

Lyuba Ilkun jerked erect, arms unfolding and hands moving to grip the seat as if to push herself up. Beside her Rossiter shook his head gently and put a hand on her shoulder to stop her.

'Ivan Andreyevich Ilkun. Seven, no, *six* years old. Lives with his grandmother because you can't handle the responsibilities of motherhood –'

'*That's a lie.*' The woman was up now and screaming. Rossiter too stood and laid a hand on her shoulder, all that was needed for the moment. Klavan faced her, hands in the pockets of her jacket.

'Where is he, Lyuba? Julian. The man we call Fallon.'

Purkiss leaned close to the monitor. The camera angle meant the woman's eyes were slightly averted as she stared at Klavan, her voice a whisper.

'For the love of God, I don't know. He disappeared a week ago without saying. I haven't heard from him since.'

Klavan watched her for a moment, then turned her back and faced the door. 'What did the two of you talk about?'

'Julian and me?' She seemed thrown by the sudden change in tack. 'How shit life was working in that club. How, once we'd saved enough, we were going on holiday together.' Her eyes drifted off into the corner.

Still presenting her back to the woman, Klavan said: 'Did he ask you about your background in the military?'

Purkiss glanced at Teague who nodded. 'Elle had an idea to check up on her, found she had a record. Same unit as the man who tried to garrotte you, at roughly the same time.'

The woman was looking at Klavan's back again. 'No. I mentioned it to him, of course, and he asked a few polite questions, but no more than that.'

'Lying,' said Teague. Purkiss had come to the same conclusion. And he'd thought – couldn't be sure, but had more than a notion – that she'd been lying when she'd sworn she didn't know where Fallon was.

*

It went on for half an hour, back and forth, leading and loaded questions dropped in among open ones: *how long have you known Fisher – three months – did he start asking you about your military career before or after you made plans to go on holiday*

– I told you, he didn't ask – what do you do when you're not working in the bar – I'm looking for work – did Fisher ask you about the work you do away from the bar – as I've said, I'm not doing any other work. Throughout, Klavan's tone was patient. Lyuba struggled to keep hers the same, exasperation creeping in when old ground was gone over. Once, Klavan alluded to her son, and again there was genuine fear in the response. Purkiss noted with interest the woman's posture. It wasn't hunched, defensive, the way most people's were under interrogation, particularly if they anticipated physical violence.

At last Klavan lifted her gaze to meet Rossiter's and he nodded, not having said a word. He tapped Lyuba on the shoulder and motioned for her to stand. Klavan fitted the canvas hood back over her head and said, 'Ms Ilkun, you won't realise it but you've been very helpful. We'll escort you to a place not far from your home.'

Klavan and Rossiter led the woman out of the room. Purkiss stepped forward and adjusted the hood where it was folded at the back of her head.

She said nothing, didn't ask who they were or why they'd questioned her. Teague placed her phone in her hand and, with a hand on each of the woman's forearms, he and Klavan walked her towards the fire exit.

Rossiter watched her go, and said into the silence: 'Not much.'

'Nothing, is how I'd put it.'

Rossiter glanced at him sharply. 'But we didn't expect much. The tracer's now in her phone, though.'

Purkiss was half listening, distracted by what his inner voice was telling him. Ilkun had sat there, almost relaxed, as though she'd been prepared for the questioning. Klavan's mention of her son had rattled her, admittedly. But even then, she had been able to lie. Almost as if she was confident that no threat against her or her son would be carried out.

It was as if she'd been primed. Someone had tipped her off that she was going to be interrogated, and about the line the questioning was going to take.

Rossiter stood, his back to Purkiss, working the computer that was going to be used to track Ilkun. Purkiss watched him.

It could only have been one of them, one of the three agents, who had primed her.

Fourteen

Once outside the Old Town he pulled over in an empty parking slot on a busy commercial street and sat in the car and waited for Abby's call. It came after a couple of minutes, on the phone she'd given him.

'Got it. Want to listen?'

'Yes please.'

Her voice was replaced with a burst of static which he realised was probably clothing brushing against the device. He'd slipped it under the collar of the woman's shirt when he'd fitted the hood over her head, its location making it less likely to be discovered but meaning that audibility might be reduced. The tiny, Velcro-like hooks were designed to attach to the fibres of clothes. It was an audio-monitoring device which was simultaneously trackable in real time using GPS. Abby was relaying the audio feed from her laptop to his phone while at the same time a pulsing beacon against a street map on her laptop indicated the location of the device.

After the static came a voice, distant but distinct: Elle Klavan's. 'Here's where you get out.'

Another harsher burst of interference and now Klavan's voice was clearer. The hood must have been taken off. 'Know where you are?'

'Yes.' The woman Lyuba Ilkun's voice, louder, closer by.

The slam of a door, then footsteps and a confusion of ambient street sounds.

Into the handset Purkiss said, 'Abby?'

'Hearing you.' Her voice cut across the feed from the listening device.

'That's great, works a charm. Can you identify my position in relation to hers?'

'Sure. Got a GPS track on your phone as well. You're half a kilometre away. I can guide you towards her if you want.'

'Not just yet. I need to make a call on the other phone. Could you mute the feed but keep my line to you open?'

'Done.'

With the other handset, the one he'd been using since buying it the previous evening, he called Klavan. She answered before the first ring had finished. 'John?'

'Just left the office. I'm going to stake out Ilkun's flat, see if she comes back and then tail her.' The lies flowed smoothly. 'There's no point relying on the substituted SIM card in her phone. She'll be wise to that and she'll ditch it.'

'How do you know?'

'Because you treated her with kid gloves in there. I'm not saying rough stuff would have got any more out of her, but it's what she would have been expecting. Her suspicions will be up:'

'I see. How did Rossiter react to your plan?'

'Hopping mad, as you might imagine.'

'So why are you phoning me?'

'To check if Rossiter's got a bead on the SIM card. I don't want to stake out her place if she's heading in the opposite direction.'

'Hang on.' Elle's voice faded to a murmur, then came back. 'Rossiter on the line to Teague. The signal from her phone has gone.'

'As I predicted. She's got rid of it.' He started the engine. 'I'll be in touch.'

He rang off, fitted the earpiece for the other phone and said, 'Abby, still there?'

'Right here.'

'I'm on the move.'

She began to direct him like a bizarre living satellite navigation system. He listened and took the turnings she advised. All the while he pondered the discovery he'd made: that one of the agents had tipped the woman off.

It was at least one of them, or possibly two, but not all three; he was fairly confident of that. If they were all involved then why would they have gone through the charade of the interrogation, just for his benefit? Why not simply say they hadn't been able to apprehend her? As to which of the three it was, he didn't think Klavan was likely. She after all was the one who'd responded to his distress call in the nightclub, when she could have ignored it and left him to the

Russians. Teague was a possibility. He'd come along for the ride with Klavan when she had rescued him from the club but might have done so to avoid making Klavan suspicious.

Rossiter was the one he favoured. Rossiter, who'd shown hostility and suspicion towards him from the outset, who'd almost flinched when he had mentioned Fallon's name. At the time Purkiss had assumed this was because of the ominousness of Fallon's presence in the city at this point, but now he wondered if it was the reaction of someone who had just felt the carefully constructed edifice of a plan tremble a fraction.

'Mr Purkiss.' Abby's voice cut across his thoughts. 'She's stopped moving and there's something coming through on the audio.'

He pulled over when he spotted a clear stretch of pavement and kept the engine running and listened. The scrabble of material against the bug again and a loud noise – another slammed car door – and then a man's voice in Russian.

'They hurt you?'

'No.' Even the suboptimal sound failed to disguise the fear in her voice. 'They knew about Ivan.'

'Your son is in no danger.' The voice was raspy, middle-aged. 'You told them nothing?'

There was a prolonged blast of static that made Purkiss wince, then a muffled rumbling. When it continued beyond ten seconds Purkiss said, 'Damn.'

Abby: 'It fell off.'

'Must have. It sounded like she got in a car. Her seatbelt probably pulled the bug off.'

'But it's still in the car. That sound is the rumble of the engine. And the signal's moving again, more quickly now.'

'Okay. Guide me again. And if there's a change in the audio, voices or anything, patch it through to me.'

*

It was more difficult this time because he was chasing an unseen target moving at a car's speed, with only Abby's directions to give him a sense of where to go. Always the other vehicle managed to stay several blocks ahead, so that he couldn't begin to work out which car it was.

'Hang on, they're stopping,' said Abby. 'Not a traffic light, I don't think. Halfway along the road.'

He put his foot down a touch and overshot before she could correct him and went round the block and she murmured, 'You should be nearing them just about now,' and then he saw her, Lyuba, standing talking through the open rear window of a black car by the kerb, a Lexus by the look of it. She straightened, nodded and walked away. The car pulled off.

'Got a visual,' he said to Abby.

'Are you going to follow her, or the car?'

'The car.'

Now it was easier because he could hang back a little, confident that if he lost visual contact Abby was still tracking the car. He couldn't be sure but it seemed there were two people in the Lexus: the driver, and the man in the back to whom Lyuba had been talking after she'd got out. The Lexus moved smoothly through the streets, heading north through the bustle of early afternoon commerce. Purkiss felt the first salt tang of sea air in his mouth.

The office blocks and arcades thinned out and finally yielded entirely. They were heading along a coast road, the sea shifting and glittering on the left. Ahead the Lexus was slowing and pulling on to the pavement. There wasn't any apparent reason for Purkiss to stop, so he drove past and turned off into a small parking lot on the edge of the water where people were unloading picnicking materials. He parked so that he could watch the Lexus in the rear-view mirror.

Another vehicle had been waiting where the Lexus had pulled in, a large four by four which looked bulkier than normal as though it had been customised, possibly with armour plating. A man emerged from the rear of the Lexus, large and blocky in build, hair in a military crop, perhaps fifty years old and dressed in a business suit. The distance was too great for any decent pictures but Purkiss lifted his phone to the window. He did what he could with the zoom function and took as many photographs as he could of the man before he climbed into the passenger side of the four by four, which began to turn on to the road back in the direction the Lexus had come. The Lexus pulled off in the opposite direction.

Purkiss considered the options for a second. The man in the four by four appeared to be in charge and was potentially a more valuable target, but the tracking device was in the Lexus. Plus, there was only the driver in the Lexus, which meant better odds in the event of a confrontation. He waited until the black car had passed, then reversed back on to the road and set off after it.

Ahead, inland to the right and set back from the road, Purkiss saw a stone spire which put him in mind of Cleopatra's Needle on the north bank of the Thames in London. The Soviet War Memorial. He knew this because it had featured heavily on the news in recent months, was the site at which the meeting was to take place between the Russian and Estonian leaders. As he passed it he saw the activity around the cordoned-off base. A couple of news crews were shooting footage and a chanting crowd brandishing placards was being kept back from the cordon by a thin film of uniformed police.

The Lexus turned off the coast road as the city began to coalesce into a discrete whole in the mirrors. Buildings started to become sparse and the aroma of pine began to supplant the sea air. Traffic was thinner here, too. Purkiss touched the brake to pull back.

'Abby?'

'Yes.'

'We're obviously heading away from the city. What's ahead?'

'Google Earth says forest, and plenty of it.'

'Okay. I'm going to keep well back. I might lose visual contact. Let me know if he turns off or does anything odd.'

*

The road began to wind and climb upwards. Pine and spruce soared on either side, blanketing the road in shadow, and the temperature was dropping noticeably. Purkiss had lost sight of the Lexus fifteen minutes earlier but took Abby's silence to mean that he was still keeping pace. They had taken a turnoff some way back when he'd still had the Lexus in view and were now on a single-lane road. Cars passed in the opposite direction at the rate of perhaps one every three minutes.

Abby's voice startled him. 'He's stopped.'

'All right.' Purkiss pulled off the road on to a pine-carpeted bank.

'Hang on. The sound's different. Listen.'

She patched through the audio feed. There was no longer the rumble of the engine. Instead there was silence, punctured by an intermittent undefinable scratching.

'He's killed the engine.' Purkiss put the car into gear. 'I'm going to drive past.'

'Careful, boss.'

The road ahead curved upwards and to the left. On the right the forest sloped downwards, the drop becoming sheerer as the road rose. Purkiss glanced out and down and felt a twinge of vertigo, the darkness of the depths accentuating the drop. Unbidden, the opening chords of Sibelius's *Tapiola* echoed in his head. *Wrong side of the Gulf,* he thought.

The curve was blind and he tensed, prepared to dodge a car speeding down towards him. None came. He kept up a steady speed, sensible but not excessively slow, to avoid giving the impression that he was on the lookout for something. After fifty feet or so the road curved again, this time to the right.

'Boss. You're right on top of him.'

The trees were packed tightly enough that there was no room for the Lexus to be hidden among them.

'You've passed him.'

Purkiss understood. The man had found the bug and ditched it.

The realisation caused him to slow a fraction. As he did so he caught sight of the nose of the Lexus around the curve.

The roar of the car's engine sounded off the forest wall and the shriek of tyres echoed like the cry of some unnatural woodland beast. The Lexus was bearing down on him from ahead, the driver's arm extended through the open window, his fist gripping something black and metallic.

Fifteen

Years earlier Purkiss had taken an amateur interest in the concept of time and the psychology of time perception. He'd concluded that it was all to do with attention. The more one concentrated on an experience, immersed oneself in it to the exclusion of all distractions, the more slowly time appeared to pass.

There were few experiences more likely to hold the attention than being fired upon by a man advancing in a car at high speed on the edge of a drop.

Purkiss's first instinct was to brake. Instead he gunned the engine. The Toyota jolted forward and at the same time he dipped his head. The first of the shots smashed a star into the windscreen and the bullet hit the headrest of the seat. His front nearside bumper caromed off the rear door of the Lexus on the driver's side, but the man kept control of the Lexus so that it didn't spin. Purkiss was past him and rounding the curve, but already the man was turning using the handbrake. He had the benefit of the more powerful engine and already he was gaining.

With the heel of his hand Purkiss did what he could to clear a hole in the sagging mesh of the windscreen. The cold air hit him hard and clear. In the side mirror he saw the man taking aim again. At the last minute Purkiss swerved into the oncoming lane, just for an instant to put the man off, and it worked because the bullet sang wild *but here was an oncoming car*. Purkiss jerked the wheel back just in time as the car blared past. The bumper of the Lexus grazed the back of the Toyota and then jarred it harder. Purkiss thought about slamming on the brakes, which would certainly stop the Lexus but would also send the Toyota over the side.

Another curve to the left, and when Purkiss saw the other lane was clear and the Lexus was a few feet back, readying itself for another shunt, he hauled on the handbrake and began the turn just as the Lexus surged forward again. Its bumper got the rear of the Toyota on the left in a spray of shattering rear- and brake lights. The impact helped Purkiss complete the spin through a little under one hundred and eighty degrees. He was facing in the opposite direction but the man was *fast* and as Purkiss passed him, his face close, he raised the gun and fired. Purkiss jerked his head back in time to feel the slipstream flick the pinna of his ear before the shot smashed out the passenger window.

The wrecked windscreen blasted his face with a funnel of cold air and petrol fumes and burnt rubber. He sucked it in, the smell of life in all its rawness. In the mirror the Lexus had turned again, of course, and was after him once more. A remote place in his consciousness registered the earpiece which had dropped out on to the seat, Abby's tiny voice piping from it.

He put his foot down, the speedometer barely visible under the coat of glass fragments. Eighty, eighty-five kilometres per hour. Instinct told him the next shot was coming and he ducked, hearing the ricochet sing off the tarmac. He understood the man was doing what Purkiss would have done from the start. He was aiming for the tyres.

Purkiss began to swerve like a slaloming skier, doing his best to stay within the lane because another car had shot past up the slope, the driver's face a confused smudge. Another shot flicked up from the road surface and this time clanged off the chassis somewhere. Purkiss checked the petrol gauge and the rest of the dials. Nothing crucial had been hit yet. He hadn't been counting the shots, but in any case the man might have another magazine, so it made no difference.

He realised suddenly that he needed to take the opposite tack to the one he'd tried previously. Instead of trying to outrun the Lexus, something he was never going to manage, he had to keep it close enough behind him that the man would struggle to hit his tyres. He jabbed the brake, *too hard, don't stall the damned thing*, and the Lexus bore down, but the man saw what he was doing and slowed himself. He hung well back so that the space between them grew, and in the mirror came the flash of the muzzle. With a sound that to Purkiss could have been a Zeppelin springing a leak the rear passenger tyre exploded. The Toyota slewed round so that Purkiss was presented side-on to the man. He braced himself for the next shot. It didn't come, because the Lexus was advancing again at speed. The man was going to ram him.

Purkiss spun the wheel into the direction in which the car was swerving, aware that he was straddling the road and an oncoming car wouldn't have time to brake. The front of the Toyota was close to the bank beyond which was the drop down into the forest, the darkness below looming like a living presence. The Lexus rammed him just behind the driver's door, the side of the Toyota buckling and compressing him and the impact shunting the Toyota so that its passenger side hung poised over the edge. The man's face was close again, separated from Purkiss's by the narrow gap between the opposite-facing cars. Teeth clenched, eyes narrowed, he raised the gun. Purkiss ducked but the shot didn't come. Instead he felt the Toyota rock as the Lexus disengaged. He knew the man was reversing, getting ready to ram him a final time and send him over the edge.

One chance.

He felt the revving of the Lexus's engine transmitted through the road and the chassis of his own car. When he judged it was almost on him he grabbed one of the phones from the passenger seat and straightened, took a split second to aim, and hurled it through the open window at the driver, a good solid shot that caught the man in one eye. Because the missile was coming in at an angle from the left the man flung up his left hand, which meant that his right hand dragged downward on the steering wheel, causing the Lexus to veer to the right. At the same time Purkiss floored the accelerator of the Toyota to try and pull it out of the path of the oncoming Lexus.

With two wheels over the edge of the drop, all the Toyota could manage was a couple of inches forward. The Lexus slammed into the Toyota behind the rear door, and in a grinding of chassis against rock the back of the car heaved over the edge.

Purkiss felt the jar of the seat against his back as he was flung against it and the world tilted crazily, the sky far above the treetops suddenly and incongruously in front of him through the mangled windscreen. The weight of the car bore down behind him. Helplessly he began to be dragged down with it. He turned his head to the left and saw the front of the Lexus tipping downwards, the chassis pivoting on a point just behind its centre. The phone he'd thrown had put the driver off his aim so that he'd rammed the Toyota just obliquely enough not to lose his own momentum, and he'd been unable to stop the

Lexus's front wheels from crossing the edge of the drop.

Purkiss groped with his left hand for the release button of the seatbelt and found it crushed by the impact, the clasp jamming the belt in place. Reaching across with his other hand he picked up the other phone from where it lay against the back of the passenger seat. The car continued its relentless grind backwards, and he transferred the phone across to his left hand and began to bash at the seatbelt clasp, feeling plastic splinter. Across from him through the open window of the driver's door he saw the face of the driver, florid and contorted, as he leaned forward against his own seatbelt.

As Purkiss watched, the man freed himself, the seatbelt rolling up with a snap. The man toppled forwards against his windscreen, and the movement was enough to push the Lexus the final few inches. With a groan it passed the point of no return and plunged out of sight, the man's scream drowned in the noise of smashing wood and rending foliage.

Something gave in the seatbelt clasp. With both hands Purkiss pulled the belt free and disentangled himself and jackknifed his body so that he was reaching up through the remains of the windscreen. He fell back, and the impact of doing so jarred the car so that it slipped down. He twisted his head round and, through the gap where the rear window had been, he saw that the back of the car was propped against the base of a pine trunk which protruded at an angle from the slope. It was a youngish tree, and even as he watched it was shifting, its movement accompanied by the graveyard sound of roots tearing through soil.

He faced the front again, drew breath, and expelled it as he jackknifed again, abdominal muscles on fire. This time he caught hold of an exposed root. He got his other hand round it and hauled, but it was giving way and so was the trunk behind and beneath the car. He got his feet against the back of the seat and pistoned his legs just as the loop of root broke free at one end and the car dropped away from him. For a moment he was hanging in mid-air from one end of the root, before he got a purchase on the slope with his other hand and pulled himself up. Behind him was the awful screech of metal against rock and ancient wood and a final plummeting grind punctuated by the smashing of glass.

Then, nothing but the hammering in his head and his chest.

Sixteen

He hung clutching at the slope for what seemed like an hour but was probably a minute. Then he clambered up over the edge. Crouching on the bank, he turned to look down the drop.

Far below, the only sign of it a hint of its buckled white door panels among the foliage, was the Toyota. It had turned sideways during its descent and had left a wake of smashed branches and fragments of glass. Closer by, ten feet below Purkiss, the Lexus was wedged nose-down in a fork created by the trunks of two huge trees. One of its rear wheels was twisted sideways, almost wrenched off the axle. From its engine came an occasional desultory tick. The smell of petrol swamped the pine scent.

Purkiss had had the presence of mind to turn off the ignition after the back of the Toyota had gone over the edge. He didn't know if the other man had done the same with the Lexus. Of the man there was no sign, and Purkiss wondered whether he'd fallen through the windscreen and dropped down into the forest, or whether he was still inside the car.

A car was approaching along the road. Purkiss debated for a moment but decided against flagging it down and crawled swiftly over the edge and squatted out of sight on the slope until it had passed. He moved, crabwalking, looking for the least treacherous way down, and began to make his way towards the Lexus, sliding on his bottom and gripping the roots and rock protrusions for support. Just above the car the slope dropped away, sheer. Vertigo made him reel and press himself against the slope. When it felt safe to look down again he peered straight through the rear window space of the car. He could see the dark shape of the man inside, folded against the windscreen, which hadn't entirely given way. There was no movement.

Purkiss turned onto his belly and sidled down the slope using his elbows until he felt his feet touch one of the trunks between which the car was jammed. He tested the strength of the trunk by stamping a little – it seemed solid enough – and reached out and took hold of the rear bumper of the car. He gave it an experimental shake. The metal protested against the trunk, and he felt the minutest shift. So it wasn't securely wedged; any significant weight would drive it through the other side and send it plummeting.

He knelt on the trunk and leaned over as far as he dared. Again dizziness took hold of him. The front end of the car hung below the trunks over a sheer drop of perhaps a hundred feet, a great cleft in the earth coated with trees. Secure though the trunk was, his movement on it produced further creaking from the car.

Craning his neck he peered through the driver's window just below the trunk. The driver was concertinaed against the webbed windscreen, his head locked in place by a branch that had been driven through the windscreen into his left eye socket. His mouth was agape.

He was in the way. Purkiss clambered back along the trunk to its base and moved across to the other trunk. This one did not feel as secure, and swayed palpably as Purkiss edged along it on his hands and knees. By lying along its length he was able to cling almost alongside it and look through the passenger window. On the dashboard he saw what he wanted. It appeared undamaged.

The problem was getting to it. He could climb into the car through the rear window or the passenger one, but that would certainly push the Lexus all the way through the fork and send it falling. His arm wasn't long enough to reach it from where he was clinging to the branch.

He hugged the trunk, and thought about Claire, and Fallon, and the three Service agents, one or more of whom were betraying him. And he thought about how the forest around him was darkening as the afternoon set in, and how this was the last afternoon before Fallon set in motion whatever he had planned for the morning.

He needed a way in, and urgently.

Purkiss shuffled up the trunk until he was directly over the passenger window and braced his hands on the trunk, testing the strength in his arms. He swung down so that once again he was hanging in the air, trying not to imagine the drop below him, the consequences of slipping and falling. He pressed his feet together and pushed them through the window hole, catching the back of the seat with his shoe as one of his hands slipped. He regained his grip but the nudge to the seat produced a terrible growl from the metal and it shifted against the ancient bark. The Lexus jolted a foot further through the wedge.

He had to withdraw his feet to steady himself. Once more he dangled, flailing. He tried again and this time he got one foot hooked around the back of the small box on the dashboard. Tongue between his teeth, he groped with the other foot, pressed it against the box and tugged gently, feeling it shift in its slot. In a second it was free. Gripping it between his feet, he withdrew it through the window. He hung for a moment, arms burning and the sweat in his palms slicking the bark. He could feel himself losing his grip, and every instinct screamed to let his legs kick and scrabble at the air, anything to help him regain purchase, but if he did so he'd drop the box. He kept his feet clamped together and instead tried to swing his arm further over the trunk in a movement like a swimmer's crawl stroke. As he did so his other hand gave way and he was falling.

Keep your feet locked together... With hands curved into hooks he caught the hub of the front passenger wheel and the jerk to his shoulders felt as if it had pulled them from their sockets. He hauled upwards with all his reserves, feeling the ton-and-a-half of vehicle begin its inexorable slide through the wedge, and now he was bracing his feet on the hub, awkwardly because of the prize still gripped between them. His hands were reaching up and getting hold of the trunk again and this time he didn't let go. He swung up and on to the trunk and *the box slipped from between his feet* but he reached back and caught it one-handed before it fell.

He scrambled to the base of the branch and leaped to the safety of the slope as the Lexus dropped in virtual silence through the space below and landed directly on to the Toyota. The driver hadn't killed the engine because the tanks went up in twin blasts that roared off the sides of the valley, the heat from the fireball sending up a shower of wood and rocks and spinning fragments of metal.

Purkiss lay prone on the slope, one arm shielding his head while he leaned on the other, staring at the box in his hand. A satellite navigation system, chipped and scuffed but in working order.

*

165

Behind the man the sea was wild, lashing ropes of spume against the rocks of the shore. He'd got there first and Venedikt didn't like that, although Venedikt himself was a little early. The man stood quite still beside his car, a top-range Mercedes. On either side of him were four other men in civilian clothes but with a bearing unmistakeably military. Most had the wiry build of the Special Forces soldier.

Venedikt emerged from his own car and approached, Leok remaining behind the wheel. Two others fell into step beside Venedikt, one of them Dobrynin, his deputy. Behind him and to his right the van lumbered forward and came to a stop, shuddering under its own bulk like some ungainly prehistoric behemoth.

Like Venedikt the man was wearing a suit. Counter to expectations he wasn't hiding his eyes behind a pair of dark glasses. Venedikt respected that, thought it showed the proper respect for him. The man was of medium height, far shorter than Venedikt, with a slight build. His pedigree was uncertain. His Russian was impeccable, down to the Muscovite accent, but he didn't look Slavic: his black hair and black eyes and burnished complexion suggested southern European or Middle Eastern origins. Yet he was said to speak English like an American.

Venedikt glanced about without moving his head. They were in a grassy depression half a kilometre across, lined on two sides by rocks, on one by the sea, in a peninsula jutting finger-like into the Baltic. A bank of clouds had dragged across the sun and from the rocks there came no tell-tale glints on metal. Venedikt's own snipers, two of them, were in position, invisible even to him. He assumed the same for the other man.

Venedikt stopped ten paces from the other man, refusing to do all the work. As if he sensed this the man gave a slight nod and stepped forward, his men keeping perfect time on either side. He extended his hand. Venedikt shook: it was dry, firm but not bone crushing.

'Let me show you.' The man's tone was pleasant, conversational. No names, no *hello, you must be*s. He gestured behind and to his left, towards the rocks.

Venedikt walked alongside the man up the slope, their respective people massing discreetly around and behind them. The man, the dealer, stepped up to the rocks first and offered down his hand. Venedikt accepted and was surprised at the strength with which the smaller man hauled at his arm.

He stood staring at what rested beyond for a long time. He felt the urge, overwhelming, immediate, to walk around it, touch it, but he had to maintain dignity. His elation squirmed as he fought it down.

'I'll need to check it. Verify its authenticity.'

'But of course.' The man called back over his shoulder and said to Venedikt, 'Come down. We'll bring it out for you.'

Dobrynin, the man with the nose for deception, stood by as the dealer's men brought the second part of the product down the slope. The authenticity of the larger component wasn't in doubt; it was visibly what it was. But when the second part was hefted down, exposed in its box, the frisson of excitement that rippled through Venedikt's group was unmistakeable. Dobrynin squatted beside the container and with eyes and hands began his examination.

Waiting in the van for the signal from Venedikt were two more of his people, their wrists chained to steel suitcases. Once Dobrynin was satisfied it would be the dealer's turn to carry out his own inspection. Perhaps he would demand a full count, in which case it would take a while, even though the money had been laundered from *krooni* into large-denomination euros.

Dobrynin muttered for assistance and two of the dealer's own men knelt and prised and lifted so that he could peer underneath. Venedikt tried not to hold his breath, tried to keep his back and neck from tensing in anticipation of the sign of a double cross, a movement on the part of the dealer or his men. Equally he tried to banish from his imagination the cry from the watchers, the massing of police cars and helicopters above the lip of the depression, the bullhorn commands to surrender. Beside him the dealer stood, feet slightly apart, hands folded neatly before him, almost prim, watching Dobrynin with something that looked like genuine appreciation of his thoroughness.

Dobrynin straightened and brushed off his trousers and hands. He paused in front of Venedikt, looking up into his face, before giving a nod of triumph. Venedikt felt the tension leave him in a great funnelling of breath.

He glanced at his watch, then up at the sky, allowing his neck to flex luxuriously. Step two was complete.

Two o'clock. Eighteen hours to go.

Seventeen

'Boss.' The relief in the syllable was almost comical. 'Are you all right?'

'Bit of a scrape.'

'I heard gunshots.'

He thought about saying it had been a car backfiring, but couldn't do it. He slumped, weary, his forehead against the cool glass of the booth. 'It was a trap. The man chucked the bug out, then lay in wait. He's dead. I'm okay, but I'm without a car or a phone. I'm calling from a public box.'

'Where are you? I'll come and pick you up.'

'Too dangerous. They'll be looking for me. No point letting them catch us both. I'm making my way back to town.' A face appeared through the grimy glass inches from his own. Purkiss recoiled, but it was only a backpacker peering in. The adrenaline was dissipating but was still there, rendering him jumpy. He held up an index finger and the man stepped away, looking disgruntled.

'Can you look up an address for me? It's from the satnav in the man's car. It comes up time and again as the starting point of his journey.' He read it out, spelling each word, then said, 'I'll call you once I get a new phone.'

'One more thing. Kendrick's confirmed and is on his way. Same flight as you took yesterday. He should be here sevenish.'

He had made his way back towards the city with difficulty, keeping amongst the trees as much as possible to stay out of view of any search parties, but being forced back on to the road when the forest became impassable. He'd emerged at a bus stop just as a bus had come down the hill and had held up his hand hopefully. The driver hadn't even slowed. The knees of Purkiss's trousers were ripped and his face was pallid, and he supposed he would have been reluctant himself. Eventually a pick-up truck had stopped and the driver, with a good-humoured face beneath a peaked cap, had jerked his head at the back. Purkiss had climbed in and wedged himself between bundles of metal piping. When he'd spotted the phone booth on the outskirts he'd tapped the rear window of the cab and hopped off.

After his call to Abby he dialled again.

'Vale.'

'It's me.'

'Pay phone?'

'Lost my own.'

He brought Vale up to date, leaving one detail until last. He'd wondered whether to reveal it at all, then decided.

'At least one of the Service agents is working with Fallon.' He explained. Vale listened in silence. After Purkiss had finished the silence continued to the point at which he wondered if the connection had been lost.

Vale said: 'I'm pulling you out.'

'No.'

'You're compromised beyond anything I could reasonably expect you to cope with.'

'No.'

'John. Listen to me. This has gone beyond tracking down Fallon. An operation involving numerous locals, some with military backgrounds, as well as not one but two or even more rogue Service personnel – it's too big.'

'So what do you propose?'

'I'm going to make it official. Alert Century House.'

'Fallon and his people will just go underground.'

'If it means averting a disaster tomorrow –'

'By cancelling the summit? That's the point, isn't it? That's what Fallon wants.'

'We can't know that.'

'I've told you. The answer's no.'

'For God's sake, John. This is bigger than you and Fallon.'

'Nothing's bigger than that.' Purkiss touched the bar, about to cut off the call. He said: 'And if you bring the Service on board anyway, I'll certainly be dead. Whichever of the agents it is that's helping Fallon will panic and get rid of me post-haste.' He pressed down, listened to the dial tone, then hung up.

*

At a little after three thirty Purkiss found a tired-looking department store in the outer suburbs, where he replaced his torn and filthy clothes and bought a new smartphone. He'd memorised Klavan's number and those of the other two agents and added them to the contact list, then went outside and stood part-way down an alley where he could watch the street. He phoned Abby.

'Got a fix on that satnav address,' she said. 'It looks like some sort of farm. East of Tallinn, about fifty kilometres.'

East: that was approximately the direction the driver had been heading when Purkiss had followed him. Abby continued: 'You can see it for yourself on Google Earth, though you'll get a better view on my monitor.'

'Okay, thanks.'

'And that memory stick you gave me.'

'Yes.'

'It's proving really hard to crack. Sorry.'

'I have absolute faith in you, Abby.'

He punched in Teague's number. When the man answered he said, 'It's Purkiss. Are you with Elle?'

'Yes. Where are –'

'I'm on the outskirts of town. Fallon's people tried to run me off the road. I'll explain later.'

'Need us to pick you up?'

'If you would.' He gave the address. Teague rang off without comment. Purkiss pocketed his phone and stepped out into the sunlight.

He'd crossed a boundary, had never cut himself loose from Vale before. He wondered what the man would do. Vale would know there'd be no way of tracking Purkiss now, and wouldn't waste time and whatever resources he had trying to do so. Instead, he might make good on his threat and alert Service headquarters and the Embassy. And then what? A police dragnet, which would uncover nothing that the months of extensive footwork by the Estonian intelligence services and SIS itself in preparation for the summit hadn't already. Meanwhile, Rossiter and Teague and Klavan would be tipped off by the increased activity, and whichever of them was working with Fallon would either go to ground, as Purkiss had predicted, or would sit tighter than ever, not betraying themselves. Meanwhile the media would get hold of the story, no question. You couldn't shut down a city without someone noticing. Panic would be stoked. And even if the summit went ahead regardless, the hysteria would be a propaganda coup for those who were opposed to the whole thing.

Vale knew this, which was why Purkiss was banking on his holding back. He'd be exasperated, furious even, but he might give Purkiss the breathing space to find a way in.

*

'Sixteen hours left.' Rossiter paced, terse choppy steps in a stereotyped route across the office carpet. 'And nothing. No leads.'

Teague was perched languidly on the corner of a desk. Klavan stood, arms folded. Purkiss was the only one of them to have taken a chair.

He'd told them everything about his tracking of the car into the forest, the ambush and subsequent chase, and the death of the man over the edge. He left out the part about the satellite navigation unit. This time Rossiter hadn't reacted with fury at his independent action.

'I wouldn't say *no* leads,' said Purkiss. 'We have what you've discovered.'

In the car on the way back, after Purkiss had finished his account, Klavan and Teague filled him in on what they had unearthed in the mean time. Klavan's contact at the Ministry of Defence had told her that Abram Zhilin, the dead man from the toilet cubicle in the nightclub, had served in the same unit of the Scouts Battalion, part of the Estonian Maävagi or Ground Force, as Lyuba Ilkun. Ilkun and Zhilin hadn't been exact contemporaries – he was six years older than her – but their time in the unit had overlapped by a year or so. Neither of them had been especially distinguished soldiers but neither had attracted negative attention, there were no disciplinary offences on record. Interestingly, both had left at the same time, five years earlier.

'Of Ilkun there's no subsequent trace until she turned up in the club,' said Elle. 'But Zhilin went to work for a private security firm here in the city. My contact found a reference request. Not an uncommon career move after the army. The firm still exists.' She turned in her seat to face Purkiss. 'Here's where it gets interesting. The name of the firm is Rodina Security. *Rodina* is Russian for *motherland*. Their website is entirely in Russian, with no Estonian version.'

'And Zhilin is – was – an ethnic Russian,' said Teague. 'Plenty of businesses target a minority clientele, of course. It's just intriguing, given everything else.'

Elle: 'Rodina Security handles routine work, according to the site. Bodyguard jobs, patrolling of private and corporate residences, countersurveillance.'

'Any record of run-ins with the law?' asked Purkiss.

'We don't know yet.'

*

At the office Purkiss remembered something and asked to use one of the computers. He called up the website he used to store photographs and downloaded the shots he'd taken of the man who had got out of the car along the coast road, the man he'd taken to be the one debriefing Lyuba

Ilkun on Abby's audio feed. The other three peered at the monitor. The resolution was poor but in one or two pictures the man's face was clear: grim, set, the features of somebody with purpose.

'Looks military,' said Elle.

Rossiter: 'And, dare I say it, Slavic.'

Elle switched places with Purkiss and emailed copies of the pictures to her contact at the Ministry of Defence. Rossiter stood looking down at the desk for a moment, then said: 'All right. Are we agreed that for the moment our only lead, such as it is, is this security firm? Then we take a two-pronged approach. Two of us use every means at our disposal to find out what we can about the firm. History, personnel figures, finances, complaints, trouble with the police. The other two visit the firm's offices and try to get an audience with somebody senior, on the pretext of wanting to hire them.' He looked at them in turn, calmer, in charge once more. 'Purkiss, you visit the offices. If the firm itself is involved in all this, they'll know what each one of us looks like from the Ilkun woman, so it makes no difference which of us goes. But we have the local knowledge and contacts to do the financial and other searches. You don't.'

'Can't argue with that.' Purkiss stood and stretched, easing the stiffness that was beginning to creep back into his limbs. 'Who comes with me?'

'I will,' said Elle. The glances shot back and forth between the three agents, too quickly to be interpreted, but Purkiss thought he knew what they were thinking: whoever went with him would be running a risk. Rossiter nodded.

'Yes, it makes sense. A woman will be less immediately threatening.' He removed his tie and handed it to Purkiss. 'You'll need this. It's a bit late to get a suit.'

Elle's phone rang. She listened, murmured a question or two, then said to the others, 'My contact. The man in those pictures you took is Venedikt Kuznetsov. Former Scouts Battalion, same infantry company as the other two, but several years before either of them. Reached the rank of ensign, a junior officer, before being imprisoned following a court martial in 1994 for beating a civilian half to death.'

Rossiter said to Teague: 'Get on to him.'

'We've come across him already,' said Elle. 'He's named on the Rodina Security website as their managing director.'

*

In the lift down to the basement Elle said: 'If we don't make some progress soon, we're going to have to hand it over.'

'To the police? The Service people at the Embassy? No.'

'We might have no option –'

'If we do that, Fallon will get away. He'll go even further to ground than he has already. He's clever, he knows he won't be able to escape the combined resources of two countries' intelligence services while staying active in the field.'

'But is that so bad? If it aborts whatever he's got planned, keeps the summit alive, does it matter?'

'It'll only postpone his plans. And if he disappears now we may never have another chance to get him.'

'*You* may never.'

He stared ahead as the doors opened. 'If you like.'

She kept a pace behind him as he strode towards the car, then said quietly, 'I wasn't being snide. In your situation I imagine I'd do exactly the same.'

She pressed the remote control for the car's locks, swung into the driver's seat. Purkiss got in the passenger side. He pulled the door shut and then his head snapped round at her.

The gun must have been in some sort of holster on the side of her seat. She was left-handed and she held it low and pointing across her body at a slight angle upwards towards his head, the barrel grotesquely elongated by the silencer screwed to its end.

Eighteen

The word *silencer* was a misnomer when it came to guns. Nothing currently in existence would produce the tidy *quip* sound heard in the movies. *Suppressor* was more accurate: at best, the shot would be muffled so that the sound resembled a heavy book being slammed down on to a table.

The basement was almost empty and echoes were likely to carry, but with the car doors closed Purkiss didn't think a suppressed shot would be noticeable by Rossiter and Teague, two floors above. Which meant that she might risk one.

He stared past the muzzle at her eyes. They were steady, unreadable. Hazel, he decided, though he was generally hopeless at distinguishing shades of colour.

She was a trained agent and no doubt a fighter but the right side of her throat was exposed, the pulse beating steadily beneath the skin. He could immobilise her in less than a second, except that her index finger was tight across the trigger and he didn't think he'd have long enough.

A second passed. Two. She said nothing, made no gesture for him to get out. It was to be an execution, which meant there was nothing to lose by making a move.

Purkiss's instincts took over. He turned his head a fraction to the right because a shot to the face was likely to take out his frontal lobes. A shot to the head from the side would almost certainly kill him, too, but there was the minutest chance that the bullet would pass through another part of the brain, the occipital lobe perhaps, and blind him but allow him to continue functioning for long enough to take her down. The long muscles of his limbs tensed in readiness for action and to reduce the amount of his body available as a target. The trick was to act before the breathing rate increased, as it inevitably would, because that was a giveaway to one's opponent.

He brought the side of his left fist across in a hammer blow at Klavan's face while his right arm reached across to grip the wrist of her gun arm. It was a two-pronged attack intended both to incapacitate and to get the gun pointing elsewhere, because even in death the trigger finger was liable to twitch, and it would be embarrassing to go down in the annals as having been shot by a dead person. The gun arm was already gone and her right arm was up and his fist caught the side of her wrist. She gave a cry but managed to gasp, 'Wait,' and pointed the gun at the roof of the car . She jacked the magazine out into the footwell and ratcheted the remaining bullet out of the chamber so that it bounced off the dashboard.

He waited, tense, a moment longer. She was rubbing her wrist where his fist had connected. He sagged back into his seat, staring at her.

'I had to know,' she said.

'Know what?'

'That you didn't suspect me.'

He let the silence play out, his breathing slowing.

She raised her eyes. 'Of course I know what's going on. The woman, Ilkun, didn't get rid of her SIM card because of some vague suspicions about the delicacy of our interrogation. She did it because somebody tipped her off about it, alerted her beforehand about the interrogation and everything else. I knew you'd worked that out after you called me in the car. And assuming you yourself aren't the one who tipped off Ilkun –'

'Because that would make no sense at all –'

'It must be one of us. Richard, Chris or me. I assumed I was under suspicion just as much as the other two. But when you saw the gun just now you were genuinely surprised.'

He had been, she was right. The realisation unsettled him. Ruling her out entirely was dangerous, especially if he'd done it unconsciously.

'That wasn't very clever. I could have killed you.'

'No, you couldn't. You wouldn't have seen the shot coming.'

He pinched the bridge of his nose between thumb and forefinger. Too many shocks, too many adrenaline spikes. He'd read that repeated surges of stress hormones might contribute to the development of dementia in the long run. Perhaps it would come as a relief, no more memories.

'Your arm okay?'

'I'll live.' But she gripped the wheel more gingerly with the hand on the affected side. She hadn't started the engine yet.

'So if it's not you, which one is it?'

She shut her eyes. 'I've been thinking about that ever since I made the connection.'

'Naturally. And?'

She sighed. 'It must be Rossiter.'

'Why?'

'Mostly by elimination. Because it can't be Chris Teague.'

'You had a thing together.'

'You noticed. For a year. It's been over for six, seven months. We decided to keep sharing the same flat for convenience's sake.'

'Not wanting to sound cynical, but don't you think your judgement of him might be a bit clouded as a result?'

For the first time she looked at him. 'That's not it. For him to be involved with these people – this Kuznetsov, Fallon, whatever's going on – and not to let something slip, given how close we were and are, I mean literally, physically close… it's not possible. I'd have noticed something. And after I came to realise about the tipping off of the woman, obviously I started trawling through the events of the last year, trying to think of clues that weren't apparent at the time. There's nothing, John. It's impossible that Chris is the one.'

'Improbable, perhaps. Not impossible.'

*

Once they were clear of the exit ramp Purkiss said, 'Have you ever used it? The gun?'

'Fired it plenty of times.'

'That wasn't what I asked.'

'A question like that is like asking a lady's age. Downright rude.' She half smiled. 'As a matter of fact, no, I've never fired it in the line of duty.'

When he didn't respond she said, 'Why did you ask?'

'Just curious. As I am about a lot of things about you. All three of you, before you start getting any ideas.'

She shrugged. 'What do you want to know?'

'Your surname, for starters.'

'Klavan's an Estonian name. My father was born and bred in Tallinn, my mother's from darkest Buckinghamshire.'

'And you're English.'

'Grew up there, but I've been visiting Estonia since I was a child, since before the Soviets left. Joined the Security Service after university.'

'And then you were headhunted?'

'In a manner of speaking. Someone in Little Sister thought fluency in a Baltic language was wasted at home. I've been with them three years now.'

'This someone. Was it Rossiter?'

She glanced across. 'No. He was already here, an agent in place. Chris and I both worked from the Embassy until the summit was announced a year ago; then we were introduced to Richard. Good boss.'

'He strikes me as a bit tightly wrapped. Volatile.'

'He's like a lot of us. He becomes calmer, and functions most effectively, when the stress is extreme. You might have started to notice that with him.'

Purkiss nodded.

They had left the Old Town and were threading now through downtown streets populated with highrises and shopping malls. Something was different from before and in a moment Purkiss realised several streets were cordoned off and the traffic was being herded into more restricted routes. Behind the cordons police vehicles were backed up and uniformed officers were congregating and conferring. Overhead helicopters hung and flitted, their rotors like distant drills. All part of the security preparations for the summit, he assumed.

Elle said, 'I don't understand why.'

'Why what?'

'Why Richard would be working with Fallon. Assuming Fallon's planning on derailing the summit somehow, assassinating one or more of the parties involved.'

'Nobody really knows why anyone does anything, in my experience.'

'It's just –' She shook her head. 'Any bad blood between Estonia and Russia... it isn't Richard's fight. Richard is one of the most patriotic people I know. Not in some bigoted, jingoistic sense, but in that quiet way you sometimes see in the very best civil servants, you know? He loves his country with a commitment I've never seen in anyone else. Britain stands only to gain from good relations between Estonia and Russia. It's in all our interests, Richard's included, that the summit works.'

'The fallacy of motive,' said Purkiss.

'What?'

'In every crime novel you read, the detective invests heavily in trying to work out what motive each suspect might have had, and more often than not solves the crime based on his deductions in this regard. Speak to any real detective and they'll tell you that's not how they work. They go by evidence, pure and simple. There's less chance of being misled by wild speculation that way.'

'But you can't mean that people's motives are irrelevant.'

'Of course I don't. It's just that those motives can be figured out afterwards. All that matters when you're trying to find a perpetrator is evidence of his or her guilt.'

His or her. It hung between them like a trace of smoke from an illicit cigarette.

After a pause that seemed to last aeons Purkiss said, 'He'll have forewarned Rodina Security and Kuznetsov that we're coming. Rossiter, if he's the one.'

'Yes.'

'You're not worried.'

She shook her head. 'They won't harm us, not there. Richard – as you say, if it is him – knows you have another contact in the city, the person you met at the airport. He knows you'll have told them where you're going. If you disappeared on the premises of Rodina Security your contact would raise the alarm immediately.'

'Right.' He had in fact sent Abby a text message shortly before they'd set off, telling her where he was heading and asking her to dig up whatever she could on the security firm.

She said, 'But it also means we're not likely to get much out of them. They'll be shut up tighter than a clam.'

'Still worth a visit. It'll give us a feel for them. Numbers, whether or not the whole firm's involved, how jumpy they are.'

*

The offices of Rodina Security occupied the entire second floor of a block near what Elle informed Purkiss was the Central Bus Station. Behind the desk in the lobby the security guard looked bored beyond endurance.

Purkiss said in Russian: 'Second floor. Rodina.'

The guard pushed across a book with removable slips of paper. They filled in their names, Purkiss using the Martin Hughes alias from his passport. The guard tore out the slips, folded each into a plastic badge holder with a metal clasp on the back, and handed them across.

The lift opened on to a corridor with marble-effect walls and a maroon carpet. Glass doors led into a waiting room and a young woman behind a reception desk looked up: austere, hair pulled sharply back, pale lipstick.

'Good afternoon.' Purkiss took the lead. 'We're here to see Mr Kuznetsov.'

'Do you have an appointment?' Her Russian was that of a native speaker.

'No. But he'd want to see us. We have a business proposal he'd be very interested in.'

Her eyes and mouth were sceptical. 'Mr Kuznetsov isn't here now.'

'Where might he be contacted, please?'

'He's out of the country on business.'

Elle spoke: 'Is Mr Dobrynin available?' Dobrynin was named on the website as the deputy director of the company.

The receptionist hesitated a second and Purkiss pressed the advantage, leaning in a little. 'Please. Do us a big favour and bend the rules for us. Fifteen minutes of his time. He'll be grateful to you once he's heard what we're offering, believe me. *Very* grateful.'

She held his gaze and he was glad he hadn't offered a bribe. She looked as if she would take serious offence. He said, his voice low: 'Tell Mr Dobrynin it's about tomorrow.'

The receptionist sat back a little, her face betraying nothing. Keeping her eyes on him she picked up her phone and pressed a button and a man's voice came in a tinny syllable through the receiver: '*Da?*'

She turned away and, still maintaining eye contact with him, murmured quietly enough that Purkiss couldn't make out the words. After ten seconds she replaced the receiver and said, 'Please take a seat. Mr Dobrynin will see you shortly.'

They didn't sit, moving instead back towards the glass doors and out of earshot of the receptionist. Elle stepped in close and looked up at him, eyes taut. 'What's the plan?'

'Direct confrontation. There's no point pussyfooting. He knows who we are and that we know who he is. He'll deny it all, of course, but it'll spook him. It might shake them enough to make them slip up somewhere.'

'What if he doesn't deny it?'

'Then we won't walk out of here. But as you said before, that's unlikely to happen.'

A man appeared at the reception desk, mid-fifties, trim in a tailored but plain charcoal suit. 'Mr Hughes and Ms Klavan.'

They approached. In his gaze Purkiss saw a mild curiosity but otherwise almost friendliness. The man shook his hand. 'Anton Dobrynin.'

The hand felt odd, knuckly and too narrow, and as it was withdrawn Purkiss glanced at it and saw its deformity, one third of it missing including the ring and little fingers.

Dobrynin gestured for them to precede him down a corridor at the end of which a door stood ajar. Purkiss went through first, saw a medium-sized conference table, windows darkened by drawn blinds, a connecting door opposite the one by which they had entered. It wasn't until Dobrynin had closed the door behind them that the connecting one opened and two men in shirtsleeves came through, handguns drawn but held pointing down at their sides.

Dobrynin said, 'Sit.'

Nineteen

'A business deal.'

'Correct.'

Dobrynin watched him, seated opposite him at the table, the fingertips of his good hand supporting his chin. Elle sat beside Purkiss and the gunmen had taken up position on either side of Dobrynin, their pistols out of sight. They had frisked him and Elle thoroughly, had taken their phones from them and placed them in a small soundproofed safe in one wall. Clever, thought Purkiss, and professional.

'Mr Dobrynin,' Purkiss said, 'you'll have realised, of course, that we have insurance in place. If we don't leave here, unharmed, by five o'clock, my associates will blow the whistle and this place will be buried under so many layers of anti-terrorist police you won't be able to breathe.' He'd pulled the five o'clock part out of the air.

Dobrynin's expression remained mild.

Purkiss said, 'This is my offer. You tell us where we can find the Englishman, Fallon, and we'll walk out of here and leave you in peace.'

A frown of interest drew Dobrynin's brows together. 'Mr – Hughes, yes? There are two problems with what you say. The first is that I don't know what kind of a threat you believe yourself to be to me or my company, such that your leaving us in peace would be a blessing.' The affability hadn't left his manner. Over the edge of the table his mutilated right hand showed for an instant.

'You evidently see us as a threat.'

Dobrynin raised his eyebrows. 'The guns? Security, nothing more. You and your colleague arrive and demand an audience in a fairly threatening manner. It's natural we should be cautious. In our work we come up against men of violence all the time. Somebody whom we have previously upset might have sent you, for all I know.' He paused a beat. 'The second problem is that I don't know any Englishman called Fallon, or anyone else by that name, come to that.' Palm raised to the heavens, he smiled ruefully. 'So I'm afraid I can't help you.'

It was going to be a game of bluff, then. Fair enough. Purkiss said, 'Fine. But it's a pity. Because when Fallon goes down, you're going down with him, and it could have been avoided.' He stood up. Neither of the gunmen moved. Elle rose as well. Dobrynin watched Purkiss, his smile lingering.

'Sit, please, Mr Hughes. Coffee?'

'No.' They stayed on their feet.

'Perhaps my company can help you find this Fallon. We carry out investigations as well as performing security operations. Who is he?'

Again the interest in the narrowed eyes. Purkiss realised suddenly: *he doesn't know*. What did that mean?

'Former British Secret Service. Now a wanted criminal. A murderer.'

He leaned slightly forward as he said it and although the muscles of the man's face remained shaped in the same expression of polite attention, the change in Dobrynin's eyes was unmistakeable: a dilation in the pupils crowding out the surrounding grey irises, an almost imperceptible raising of the upper lids.

'I see.' For the second time Dobrynin's mangled right hand came into view as he massaged it with the other. Then it disappeared again as if he'd been caught out indulging a nervous mannerism. 'And what is he doing in Tallinn?'

'Conspiring. As you know perfectly well.'

'Conspiring to do what?' He spoke as if he hadn't heard the second part.

'To derail tomorrow's summit meeting.'

Dobrynin's stare lasted a full five seconds before he blinked and shook his head. 'Mr Hughes, I'm sorry, I really can't do business with you. Not to put too fine a point on it but you're a crank. If somebody you know is planning something as serious as you say, then it's the police you should be talking to.' He stood, as did his men. One of them waited for his nod, then went to retrieve their phones from the wall safe.

'Goodbye.' Dobrynin didn't offer his hand this time. Purkiss said nothing, trying to keep his churning thoughts in check long enough that he didn't mistake what he was seeing in Dobrynin's face. The two gunmen opened the door and gestured them through. At the last glimpse, the rest of his face neutral, Dobrynin's eyes were lit up with the unmistakeable fire of triumph.

*

They rode the lift in silence. Purkiss braced himself all the way for the sudden jolting halt, rough hands and gun butts taking over, but by the time they handed in their plastic visitors' badges to the guard at the front desk he realised they were in fact going to be allowed out.

On the street Elle let out her breath in a slow whistle.

'What the *hell* was that all about?'

'Three possibilities.' The car was parked two blocks away and as if they had communicated telepathically they began walking in the other direction to flush out tags. 'One, Dobrynin genuinely has nothing to do with any of this, it's all his boss Kuznetsov's operation.'

'Highly unlikely,' she said. 'He's a good liar but not that good.'

'You saw it?'

'The hand? Yes.' Dobrynin had kept his disfigured appendage out of sight beneath the desk except when he'd been saying he didn't know what kind of a threat they thought they posed to him and his firm. Unskilled liars will touch their faces during the act of lying, as though trying to keep the untruths from escaping their mouths. More accomplished ones usually still struggle to prevent their hands from beginning the movement.

They paused at a corner as if debating which way to go, and Purkiss did a quick check. Nobody obvious behind them. Turning left, he said, 'So. Possibility number two is that Fallon is working freelance. They've obviously come across him – he was sleeping with one of their number, Ilkun – but Dobrynin was genuinely surprised in there when I mentioned both that Fallon was former SIS and that he planned to scupper the summit.'

'So both Fallon and Kuznetsov's crew are working independently to achieve the same thing?'

'Doesn't seem credible, does it.' A car was crawling alongside them but it was just an elderly driver, peering at the street signs. 'Unless Fallon is trying to hijack their operation for his own ends. It's the only explanation that makes the remotest sense that I can think of.'

'That look on Dobrynin's face at the end,' she said. 'It was as if the penny had dropped. As if he understood that Fallon was in competition with them.'

'Yes.'

They had come almost full circle and the car was in sight.

'You said three possibilities.'

'The third is that we're completely wrong about the first two.'

*

At the car they took turns, one keeping watch for tags while the other ducked to peer under the chassis for tracking devices. They'd parked far enough away that it wasn't likely they had been spotted emerging from the vehicle but it was worth taking precautions.

He'd thought about telling her about the satnav he'd salvaged from the wreck of the car earlier, about what he had planned for that evening once dark had fallen. But he thought again of how he'd been caught off guard by his surprise when she'd pulled the gun.

No. It was best to trust only those you knew.

*

'Play it back.'

Venedikt had gone inside as soon as Dobrynin called. The noise of the men in the yard was distracting. He sat at the kitchen table and listened to the live feed, then to Dobrynin's voice directly into the mouthpiece: 'They've gone.'

He listened again, keeping his breathing even, trying not to let delight overwhelm him.

Afterwards he said, 'As we suspected.'

'Yes.'

'Our British friend has been lying to us.'

'It looks that way, Venedikt Vasilyevich.'

Venedikt sat staring at the flagstones, pondering. Then he said, 'Did you try to follow Purkiss?'

'It wasn't worth it. What staff aren't with you we needed to close the office down. We have to assume our British friend will keep track of him.'

'A big assumption. He's disappeared twice already.' Venedikt stood. 'But you're right. How's the shutdown progressing?'

'Just reception left, really.'

'Good.'

'A pity. Years of memories, Venedikt Vasilyevich.'

'It has to be. We can't turn back now.'

*

Unlike previously, Purkiss felt bad about giving her the slip. It seemed dishonest, and he had to admit he was rather enjoying her company. Nonetheless, the best time to do it was when she was least expecting it. As Elle started to pull away when a light turned green he said, 'Sorry about this,' and popped the door and swung out and slammed it shut. He took off across three lanes, weaving expertly through the blurt of horns and not looking back until he was lost in a warren of back alleys.

Police helicopters criss-crossed the darkening sky overhead. Assuming Elle wasn't the one working with the opposition, she'd be adrift now, with no leads to follow up on and a deadline that was drawing ever nearer. He appreciated the frustration she must be feeling.

As he strode the streets looking for what he needed, he made an effort to untangle the threads. Seppo had photographed Fallon and alerted Vale, but it seemed Fallon and Seppo were sharing a flat. Seppo had been murdered, almost certainly by Fallon, and Purkiss's phone call to Seppo's phone from London had been traced and watchers had been set on to Purkiss from the airport. Fallon had had a relationship with a member of Kuznetsov's crew, and when Purkiss had come around asking questions Kuznetsov's people had tried to kill him. One of the three British agents was working with Kuznetsov. Kuznetsov's second-in-command appeared astonished to discover that Fallon was ex-Service.

A snarl of ends, tangled like weeds and choking out coherent thought. All he had at the moment that seemed to hold out some promise was the address on the satnav. If it was a base of some sort then he might have a way in.

It took a frustratingly long time to find a car rental place and by the time he did it was a quarter to six. Once more he used the Hughes ID. It was a risk, but not a great one. There was one risk he wasn't going to take, however. Once behind the wheel of the car, a year-old Fiat, he slipped out his phone.

'Change of plan, Abby. Tell Kendrick to meet us at the hotel. The opposition might be watching the airport, so I need to keep well away.'

*

The Jacobin normally preferred being outdoors, finding the confines of a room, however large, unpleasantly claustrophobic after too long. This evening, though, the sky had a smothering aspect, pressing down like a cold shroud. There was no stillness on the streets. Even the tourists seemed to be affected by the sense of anticipation, even of awe, that the events of the next morning were kindling.

A quick stroll to calm the mind and stretch the legs. As if on cue the Jacobin's phone rang. Kuznetsov.

'You lied to me about this other man. Fallon.'

'I didn't lie. I just didn't give you the full facts. In any case, you've been lying to me all along. You know where he is.'

'No, I don't.' Kuznetsov's voice was thick with something – fury? 'But given what we've learned this afternoon, don't you think it might have been relevant to tell me earlier about his background?'

'As I say. I'll give you full disclosure when you afford me the same courtesy.'

This time the anger was unmistakeable. 'Don't fuck me on this. It's worked out well so far –'

'Agreed.'

'But I owe you nothing, beyond the protection we owe each other.'

'I have no quibble with you there. But remember this isn't over yet. Fourteen hours. A lot could go wrong.'

'Purkiss could destroy everything.'

'Yes.'

'He's killed two of my men.'

'I know.'

'Give him to me, damn it.'

'As soon as you give me Fallon.'

'I've told you, I don't know –'

'Then we've nothing more to talk about for the moment.'

The Jacobin folded away the phone and idled back down the street, expecting it to start ringing again. It didn't.

Purkiss's latest disappearance might be his last. Perhaps it was time to do as Kuznetsov asked, to hand Purkiss over or get rid of him. The longer he remained active, the likelier it was that he'd get lucky and find a way in.

And yet… and yet. Purkiss's fanatical need to find Fallon was driving the man, and he wouldn't stop until he was successful. Since Kuznetsov was being uncooperative there was no better way to locate Fallon than to follow where Purkiss led.

After that and only after that would it be safe to dispose of Purkiss.

No; not *only* after that. There was another circumstance in which Purkiss would need to be got rid of, and that was if he was in imminent danger of exposing and stopping the operation. Then he'd have to be despatched, and quickly.

Twenty

Abby had turned the cramped hotel room into a home from home. Two laptops sat opened on the writing desk, flanking an enormous flat-screen monitor. Across the carpet were arrayed a printer, scanner and shredder.

'Where did you get all the gear?' said Purkiss, seating himself in the room's only armchair.

'Some fantastic shops down the road. I told you it's one of the most wired cities on earth.' She gazed at the equipment with a mother's joy. 'Cheapish, as well. The expenses bill won't hurt you too badly.'

She'd been unusually downbeat when she opened the door to him. When he asked why, she said it was because she hadn't yet cracked the memory stick he'd found in Seppo's flat.

'It's the most diabolical protection system I've ever come across,' she said, staring at the tiny piece of plastic. 'Five hours, and a couple of promising-looking results, but still nothing.'

'I can give it to someone else,' he offered. She gave him a look that would have stopped a tank in its tracks.

Her phone went and she listened and said, 'Kendrick. He's coming up, says not to attack him when he knocks.'

Purkiss got the door. Kendrick was in cargo trousers and a bomber jacket. No jeans, which was sensible because Purkiss had said there might be outdoor work, and it looked like rain, and wet denim was terrible for mobility.

Kendrick pointed at his own chin. 'You've got rid of the facial hair. Wise move.'

'Really? I thought it made me look quite the part.'

'It made you look like a Cypriot whoremonger.'

The rope burn on his neck was red and raised, and Purkiss remembered with a sense of dislocation that less than forty-eight hours earlier they'd been on board the yacht in the Adriatic.

Kendrick saw him looking and ran a finger along the mark. 'Looks like you've seen a little action yourself.'

'Garrotte.'

'Ouch.' He nodded across at Abby. 'Don't fancy yours much.'

She ignored him and busied herself at her monitor.

Kendrick said, 'This has got something to do with the fun and games tomorrow, I take it.'

'Yes. Pull up a pew and I'll fill you in.'

'Got guns?'

'No.'

'You should have said. I'd have brought some.'

*

Kendrick was former Colour Sergeant Tony Kendrick, Second Parachute Battalion, or 2 Para. He'd been in 16th Air Assault Brigade during Operation Telic in Basra in the autumn of 2003, shortly after which Purkiss had met him for the first time when he himself was stationed in Iraq for six months, helping to establish the fledgling Service presence there. By the time Purkiss left the Service to work for Vale, Kendrick was already out on the street, drifting and kicking his heels. Both men had spotted an opportunity, and they had come to an arrangement that benefited them mutually: extremely hazardous freelance work in return for an exceptionally generous fee. Not that Kendrick would ever admit it was generous.

Purkiss brought them up to speed as they sipped Abby's venomously strong tea and the hard drives whirred, quietly busy. Outside the first rain began to spatter against the panes. It was the first time Abby had heard the full story, the part about Fallon in particular, and she said, genuine sympathy in her eyes, 'You poor man. If I'd known how personal it was…' She left the thought unfinished because there wasn't anything she could have done.

'Thanks,' said Purkiss, because there wasn't any more he could say.

'Jesus,' said Kendrick. He was sitting on the bed, booted feet propped on the stool at the dresser.

'What?'

'The man killed your girl.'

'Yes.'

'It was my girl, I'd be out there, mad as a snake, finding the bastard. Not sitting on my arse in some crappy hotel room.'

'I've been waiting for you.'

'Should've called me sooner.'

'I didn't know what this involved until this morning. This Kuznetsov... whatever his connection with Fallon, we're going to have to go through him first. And he's got his own private army.'

'Any idea of numbers?'

'Those British agents are delving into that,' Purkiss said. 'We can't know if everyone in Rodina Security is involved. My guess is that it's a select few, not the whole firm, though how many exactly is anybody's guess. Twenty? More, perhaps. Certainly I've had a whole load of them on my back.'

'The more the merrier.' Kendrick had his middle-distance stare on, was cracking his knuckles, grinding his teeth. Purkiss didn't want him to peak too soon.

He said, 'Here's the plan for this evening.'

*

The Jacobin sat at the computer, headphones on, listening to the dispatch from the SIS contact at the embassy in Moscow.

'Takeoff time's confirmed at twenty thirty-five hours. President and entourage en route to private airfield now. The usual one near Sheremetyevo.'

The Jacobin listened a while longer, then thanked the contact, ended the connection, turned to the other two at their desks and said, 'On schedule. President's expected to land just before ten p.m.'

'Anyone think the attack might come tonight?'

None of them did. The security was too tight, the landing zone outside Tallinn too closely guarded a secret. A late supper with the Estonian president was expected, again at an undisclosed location. No, the danger was going to present itself in public.

The Jacobin peeled off the headphones, ran a hand through tired hair, said, 'And where the hell is Purkiss?'

Neither of the others offered an opinion.

They rolled their chairs over to one of the computers to share information. The Jacobin listened as the facts and figures were rattled off, pretending that the information was new. Rodina

Security was a private concern with ambitions to go public. It was solvent, had survived an audit two years earlier by the tax authorities, and had no record of trouble with the law, if one discounted the fact that just under twenty per cent of its staff, including its managing director, had criminal records. It employed thirty-four people, twelve in administrative and clerical capacities and the rest as security personnel. All thirty-four were of ethnic Russian background.

On the screen Kuznetsov's face appeared alongside a potted biography. The Jacobin studied it. It was a face which the word *craggy* seemed to have been coined to describe. Dark eyes glowered from beneath a domed brow on which the hair had been cropped back; the mouth and jaw were set like a boxer's. A brutal face but not a stupid one. Kuznetsov wasn't stupid. He was boorish, crass even, but he was cunning as a whip.

The Jacobin was under no illusions as to Kuznetsov's intentions after the event. The man despised the English. He'd never pretended otherwise. The Jacobin would be caught up and swept away, drowned in the tide of history, as Kuznetsov would put it in one of the mangled, half-remembered Marxist platitudes he'd picked up from what passed for his reading. But the Jacobin too was making history, of a very different kind. And in it there would be no place for Kuznetsov and his ilk.

Kuznetsov hates the English. There was something relevant there, something that nagged at the Jacobin's attention but scurried away when focused upon. It would come in time. Of more immediate import was the question from earlier. *Where the hell was Purkiss?*

It was nearly eight o'clock by the Jacobin's watch. Two hours, and if Purkiss hadn't surfaced by then, it would be time for the trump card.

Twenty-One

'Looks like a farm to me.'

They were huddled in front of Abby's monitor. With the mouse she altered the view so that they were sweeping in almost horizontally, trees and buildings rendered in squat, distorted three-dimensional images.

'That was our impression,' said Purkiss.

The property covered ten acres, a curving driveway leading down from a gate set in a stone wall to a low but two-storied building which appeared to be the farmhouse. There were smaller buildings scattered about: stables, a couple of sheds, what looked like a garage for a tractor. The stone wall surrounded the entire property in an approximate rectangle. The gate was in the south wall, set back from the road, and the north of the property was carpeted in fields and woodland. A couple of cars were parked outside the farmhouse, but their details were obscured.

'How up to date are these pictures?' asked Purkiss.

'They were taken some time in the last three years,' said Abby.

Kendrick: 'This isn't real time?'

She shook her head. 'You'd need direct access to a satellite for that. The military, the CIA have that capability. I don't.'

'My three Service friends might,' said Purkiss.

'Want to ask them?'

'No.'

Purkiss stood and stretched. 'You brought what I asked for?'

'Yep.' Kendrick had brought a rucksack and he rummaged in it and pulled out two pairs of night-vision goggles.

'Okay, good.' He paced to get the blood flowing. 'We circle the wall, see if there are any other ways in. If not, we go over. Ideally we want to have a look in that farmhouse, but if we manage to take captive anyone there, quietly, that'll be good too. Abby, we'll stay in phone contact with you all the time. If you lose both of us, contact these people individually and tell them where we were.' He gave her the numbers of each of the three agents. 'It'll mean we've failed, but at least they'll be able to alert the police and have the farm raided.'

He paused, looked at them in turn, said: 'Ready?'

Kendrick shrugged on his jacket. 'Farms. I come all the way here on a city break and you want me to get my feet covered in cow shit.'

'The fresh air will do your complexion good.'

'It's all right for a swede basher like you. Some of us, the ones whose brothers aren't also their dads, prefer city life. You know, cities? Where people respect species boundaries.'

'He's been learning some big words lately,' remarked Abby as she opened the door for them. 'Now leave me alone so I can work on that memory stick.'

*

On every street it seemed there was the wash of police lights, the corralling of traffic into fewer lanes than usual. Purkiss spotted several shop fronts with blown-up pictures of the two presidents. Instead of using the satellite navigation system in the rental Fiat and running the risk of being directed up roads that had been newly cordoned off, he headed for the familiarity of the coast road. Here too he was struck by the security presence. Police not only swarmed over the road and pavements but cruised the dark, glittering bay in small tugs. Packs of sniffer dogs rooted around by the side of the road.

*

Purkiss pointed to the Soviet War Memorial. 'That's where it's happening. The handshake.' As he'd expected a wide area around the base of the needle was cordoned off and men with bomb-sweeping equipment roved about.

Kendrick said, 'You think it's going to be a bomb?'

Purkiss shook his head. 'No. Security's too tight.'

'A rifle?'

'More likely, but again I doubt it. There's no real vantage point. And the crowds are going to be kept right back, there'll be no plunging in for a grip and grin session at the end, so a handgun wouldn't get close enough.'

'So...' Kendrick frowned out the window. 'A full-frontal attack by this Kuznakov's –'

'Kuznetsov's.'

'Kuznetsov's private army? Some kind of suicide attack?'

'It'd be suicidal, all right, but it wouldn't achieve much else. Say he's got twenty people. With the numbers of police and probably military there are going to be on the streets tomorrow, they'd be cut down before they got within half a mile.'

The needle and the mass of activity beneath it dwindled in the mirror.

Kendrick said, 'This Fallon geezer.'

'Yes.'

'You think he's acting on his own.'

After a pause Purkiss said, 'I don't know. I think he's connected to the Kuznetsov crew but not in a way they're fully aware of. I believe he's hijacking their operation in some way, letting them do all the hard work and then planning to, I don't know, take the credit for it, add a twist of his own. Something.' He rubbed his eyes in frustration. 'Ten minutes with him. All I need.'

'You'll need longer than that if he's as hard a nut as you say.'

'Ten minutes.'

Kendrick grinned sourly. 'The bedwetting bleeding-heart liberal I know. Gone in forty-eight hours.'

Purkiss said nothing, fists tightening on the wheel.

Kendrick said: 'So how long are we going to leave it to find Fallon before we hand everything over to the coppers?'

'As soon as we get him, SIS and the police get everything else. The location of the farm, Kuznetsov's involvement, all of it. That's their business, not mine, beyond how it helps me to find Fallon.'

'That wasn't my question.'

'It'll take as long as it takes.' He glanced over at Kendrick. 'Getting hanged hasn't softened you up, has it?'

Kendrick chuckled. 'No, mate. Just wondered if you were planning on chickening out early.'

*

The roads were less familiar in the darkness and after a time Purkiss punched in the address of the farmhouse so as not to get lost. At one point he saw the strobing of emergency service lights through the trees ahead. As they rounded a curve, the place where he and the other man had gone over the edge earlier that afternoon came into view. A makeshift barrier had been constructed and clusters of police remained, waving traffic past.

After that there were no lights for miles. They seemed to be tunnelling into the forest, its massive presence almost mountainous around them. A few miles on, the foliage began to thin out, the odd field to appear. The satnav indicated their destination was five kilometres ahead.

Two kilometres short he pulled in at a layby. He killed the engine and the lights. Purkiss thumbed Abby's number into the phone, heard it ring and then cut out. He looked at the display.

'Damn it.'

'What?'

'No signal.'

'Told you. The trees. I hate the countryside.' Kendrick checked his phone. 'Mine's no good either.'

'Let's walk.'

They moved down the road, keeping on the left hand side where the forest was, ready to duck between the trunks at the sound of an approaching vehicle. After a while Purkiss stopped and tried the phone again. This time he got Abby.

'Signal's not brilliant out here.'

Kendrick got out his phone and they linked up in conference call mode, both men putting their earpieces in. Presently they came to a wall, hand-built from stone. It wasn't the one, yet. They moved along it. More forest, and then another wall, this one reinforced with concrete and curving away from the road, a recess and gates visible along its length.

'This is it.'

Dull light rose from behind the wall, but the trees blotted out what illumination came from the moon, which was obscured anyway for the most part by clouds. They fitted on the night vision goggles. They were fairly basic first generation pieces of equipment, providing amplification of ambient light up to about two hundred times, too crude for precision work such as sniper activity but enough to show up the presence of an enemy in the vicinity, and portable as well.

They flattened themselves against the wall and moved along it towards the gate, Purkiss in front. As he crept nearer he heard a cough, saw the glow of a cigarette tip beyond the gate just as the smoke reached his nostrils.

'Other way,' he whispered.

They retraced their path along the wall until they came to the corner at which they had started, then followed the wall to the right. The forest had been cut back from the wall far enough that no branches were within leaping distance from the top. Purkiss chose a particularly stout looking fir tree and began to climb up the trunk,

Kendrick following suit on the other side. They reached eye level with the top of the wall and hauled themselves a couple of metres higher and peered across.

As the Google Earth images had shown, the farmhouse lay at the end of the drive sweeping down from the gate. The windows of the farmhouse were lit up and the brightness shifted with movement inside. Smaller lights burned here and there in the yard.

'What the hell's that?' said Kendrick.

Some distance behind the farmhouse was a huge wooden building, a great sprawling barn of some kind, floodlights rigged to illuminate its front and men, four or five, moving back and forth through its doors. Their voices were too low and distant to be made out in any detail.

'It wasn't in the pictures.'

'No.' Purkiss muttered down the line to Abby, describing what they were looking at.

In a moment she said, 'Checked again. It's definitely not on Google Earth. Must be new, or newish. As I said, the pictures can be up to three years out of date.'

They clambered down and set off along the wall once more. Further down they shimmied up another tree. They had come a longer distance than Purkiss had estimated and the buildings were behind them now, the view directly across the wall one of fields and copses.

Kendrick was tapping his arm and when he looked he noticed it. Just visible within the perimeter, thirty metres away, a man's shape was making its way on foot along the wall. Before he disappeared from view Purkiss saw he was carrying something in both hands, pointing downwards: a rifle.

Unless the man had some kind of night-vision viewing capability himself he wouldn't have seen them. They climbed down anyway. Faintly, from the other side of the wall, they heard the rasp of static from a walkie-talkie, a low murmur in reply fading as the man moved on.

So there were guards patrolling the perimeter, perhaps more of them at the rear where the tree cover was dense inside and outside the wall and intruders would be likeliest to attempt entry. As silently as they could Purkiss and Kendrick continued along the wall, eventually reaching the next corner and turning in so that they were following the rear wall.

Again they crept up a tree and looked over. On the other side was a copse, the gleam of the farmhouse and the barn barely visible in the distance through the layers of fir. Purkiss scanned from left to right and back with the goggles. No signs of life. He indicated with two fingers and Kendrick nodded. To Abby he murmured, 'We're going over the wall.'

There was no reply and he glanced at the screen again. The signal was gone.

The wall was of varying height, the ground uneven along its length. At its lowest it was perhaps three metres high. Kendrick squatted and interlocked his fingers. Purkiss used it as a step and pistoned himself up so that his hands grappled with the top of the wall. His toes found a purchase and he hauled himself to the top and looked down. No movement on the other side. He braced himself and reached down for Kendrick's hand and helped pull him up. They dropped on to the carpet of fir needles at the foot of the wall.

Moving apart a little they passed between the trees at a crouch. From far ahead beyond where the fields sloped upwards they heard the voices of the men moving in and out of the barn, the words still unintelligible. The wind had come up and overhead the clouds were being dragged free of the moon until it loomed, three-quarters full, bathing the fields in pale yellow light.

They'd be plainly visible if they tried to cross directly over the fields. On the other hand, the wall was painted light grey on its inner aspect, almost white, and they would stand out if they traced the perimeter. Purkiss held up a hand. They would wait in the copse until the cloud cover was back in place before making their way across the fields, using the low stone walls between the fields to duck beside when the moon emerged again.

'We're waiting for a bit of darkness, then heading up to the barn,' he said to Abby. He shook his head when there was no reply.

At his elbow Kendrick muttered, 'That's weird. My phone says I've got a signal.'

Purkiss glanced at the display on Kendrick's phone, then at his own. It showed the same, a strong signal, three bars.

He said, 'Abby?'

*

Venedikt was alone at the kitchen table, finishing a hasty meal and a mug of tea, all he was permitting himself that night, when his phone rang. The rustic-looking clock on the wall said it was ten past ten. His work was done and he needed to get some rest. The men were applying the final touches in the barn, most of which involved cleaning and polishing, and there was nothing left that he could contribute. Still, he knew he would sleep very little that night. He had considered going home but decided to use one of the bedrooms in the farmhouse instead, wanting to be near his acquisition as if it were a loved one, his own limb.

He looked at the caller ID, said: 'Yes?'

'We have a problem. Purkiss is somewhere on the grounds of the farm.'

Venedikt took a moment to react, disorientated. 'Here?'

'If you're on the farm now, yes. He's said he's just waiting for darkness and is then going to head for the barn.'

'How do you know –'

'I heard him say it a minute ago. You need to get on top of this, Kuznetsov.'

Venedikt rose slowly, eyes straining to see through the window into the darkness. 'No problem.'

'And forget non-lethal force. It's beyond that. You have to –'

'I don't need you to tell me that.' He was reaching for his shoulder holster and pistol even as the phone was dropping into his pocket.

*

There was no shouting, very little noise at all to begin with, just the almost surreal sight of dark humanoid figures emerging and massing quietly in the yard between the farmhouse and the barn. Ten men, a dozen perhaps. As Purkiss and Kendrick ducked lower between the trees, the silence on either side of them began to be punctured by static stabs from walkie talkies. Black apparitions peeled away from distant points along the wall and broke into trots, each one carrying something slung low before it.

Then the relative quiet was torn to shreds. Purkiss felt coldness fill his chest and spill through his limbs as there rose towards the naked moon like smoke from a sacrificial fire the manic baying of dogs.

Twenty-Two

There were four, Purkiss noticed, in the instant after blind panic had immobilised him. Four small shapes, coloured green by the goggles, hurtling across the fields like ground-hugging guided missiles, yelping and screaming in harmonies that broke and formed and broke again. The rectangle of the farm was at its longest from north to south, from the gate end to the rear wall, which meant five hundred metres or so between Purkiss and Kendrick on one hand and the dogs on the other. A distance that was closing rapidly.

In the copse they were protected from the men on either side of them, who were unlikely to attempt a shot given the density of the trees. But the dogs would be upon them soon, and if they ran back to the wall and tried to climb over they might as well daub bullseyes on their backs.

Beside him Kendrick gripped a low branch, braced both feet on the trunk of the fir, and heaved until the branch peeled away enough that he could wrench the rest off. He broke the other end and stripped it to form a point. Purkiss lifted a fallen branch, heavier than Kendrick's, and hefted it.

The baying was becoming more frenzied and the blood lust seemed to have affected the pack of men behind the dogs, who were shouting unintelligibly. By now Purkiss recognised the skinny bodies and streamlined snouts of Dobermann Pinschers.

He tore off the night-vision goggles – they were unnecessary now – and signalled Kendrick with a jerk of his head. They moved sideways towards the rim of the copse. Through the trees they saw a man waiting, rifle raised to chest height. If they separated and rushed him far enough apart he might be able to hit only one of them, but one down would worsen the odds exponentially.

They pressed themselves agains the widest tree they could find. With his mouth close to Kendrick's ear, Purkiss told him what he wanted him to do.

The dogs were on the final approach now, two of them well in the lead, hurling themselves across the final hundred-metre stretch of field towards the copse, almost sobbing, moonlight flashing in the ropes of froth slavering from their maws. Purkiss counted down with his fingers and shouted 'Go,' and Kendrick emerged from the side of the tree. He lobbed his phone high and arcing and the man raised the gun to take aim at Kendrick, looked up, and for a second lifted the gun higher as if participating in an absurd clay-pigeon shoot.

He took several trotting steps back, half-taken in, and before he could register fully that it wasn't a grenade Purkiss hurled the club of wood so that it spun through the six or seven metres separating them and caught the man in the mouth. He staggered and Purkiss and Kendrick had already broken cover and Purkiss dived the last distance, low to the ground, and caught the man around the legs as he was trying to bring the rifle down again.

The butt of the rifle glanced off Purkiss's head, bringing tears to his nose, but he hung on. Above him Kendrick brought the man down with a blow to his face.

The noise of screaming was suddenly overwhelming because the dogs were upon them.

The first one slammed into Kendrick's back like slingshot fired at close quarters, forty kilograms of bone and sinew, knocking him off his feet and keeping its place on his back, its agility terrifying, its jaws snapping and probing for his neck. From his position on the ground at the man's legs Purkiss groped upwards for the rifle but it was out of reach. It was too late anyway because he felt movement behind him and he kicked out blindly, felt his foot connect with softness underlaid with bone and heard an outraged yelp.

He didn't wait to look back but lunged on his knees for the sharpened branch Kendrick had dropped. He pivoted and jabbed and got the dog in mid-leap, an awkward blow to the chest which struck the ribcage, and although it broke the dog's momentum it only inflamed it further. The beast darted its head in around the stick and got its paws on Purkiss's chest. He lost his balance and it was on him and over him, drool spattering his face like hot rancid hail, the whites of its eyes flaring in derangement.

On the ground a few feet away Kendrick was roaring. The other two dogs had caught up and they lunged for Purkiss's feet. He thrashed and jerked, not just to try and hit the snapping snouts but also to keep his legs moving as targets. He got the stick in both hands and used it as a bar against the throat of the dog above him, forcing its head up and away from his face. Dimly he heard a series of wet thuds and a prolonged and diminishing screech from out of his line of sight. It gave him a new impetus. Instead of trying to push the dog backwards and away from him, he rolled back on to his shoulders, carrying the animal over him and pushing hard with the stick when the dog had passed the point of no return, so that it toppled off him. Before he could rise, one of the others sprang to take its place. This time he was ready with the stick. He rammed it straight into the dog's snarl, the animal's momentum driving it on to the pointed end so that the back of its throat was impaled. It thrashed away, wrenching the stick from Purkiss's grasp, and stumbled, choking, pawing at the fragment jutting from its maw.

The blast was shocking, jolting Purkiss almost to his knees again. It set off a high tinnital whine in his ears which was flooded out by a second explosion, a third. He peered about, disorientated, saw the fanned-out group of men yelling and charging across the field, the huddled and ungainly piles of dog pockmarking the ground around him.

In his ear Kendrick's shout sounded distant in the aftermath of the shots. 'Let's *go*.'

Purkiss blinked, looked round. Kendrick's left leg was black with blood below the knee, the trouser cuff shredded. The sleeves of his bomber jacket too were ripped, though his arms looked relatively unscathed. The collar of the jacket appeared to have protected his neck. The gun was an assault rifle, Purkiss saw, a Russian AK-74. Near Kendrick's feet was the bloodied club he'd used to despatch the dog, which itself lay several feet away, its head almost flattened.

They sprinted back into the copse, Kendrick lurching, his injured leg dragging him back. When Purkiss showed signs of slowing Kendrick yelled, 'Run, you idiot.' Through the trees loomed the shape of the other man with the rifle, approaching from the opposite side, weapon raised. The clattering began an instant after Purkiss saw him, the man's rifle switched to fully automatic fire rather than single-shot mode, and around them gouges and chocks were blasted out of the trunks and a shower of splinters erupted. Kendrick paused behind a tree, stepped out and quickly raised the rifle. He loosed off a burst of three shots. The man bellowed and dropped.

Purkiss reached the wall and his hands slapped against its hard smooth surface at the very moment the approaching group of men opened fire from the other side of the trees. The rain of gunfire smashed and chopped through the trees, making the whole copse shake and hiss like a single animate being. Ricochets whined off into the night like tiny fireworks. Purkiss jerked his head away as a stray shot sizzled past his face and chinked off the wall, sending slivers of stone across his cheek. He looked back and Kendrick crouched, waiting, the rifle in his hands. When two men appeared round the side of the copse he opened fire, fully automatic now, the impact flinging the men backwards and into one another. Another man had appeared round the other side and the man got a burst off which came close, *so close*, causing Purkiss to drop flat to the piney carpet at the foot of the wall. Kendrick threw himself flat on to his belly and fired from the ground. The man danced away in a grotesque pirouette and fell.

With a short run Purkiss leaped up and gripped the top of the wall and hauled his torso over the edge. He folded himself belly-down so that his legs were hanging over the outside and reached down to grab Kendrick's hand. Kendrick passed up the AK-74 and Purkiss took it. With one hand he pulled on Kendrick's, while with the other he pointed the rifle, all eight-plus pounds of it. Just as Kendrick was at the top of the wall and able to support himself another two men appeared round the trees, firing in mid-run. Purkiss squeezed the trigger, the recoil almost too much for him to control in a single-hand grip. The bursts went wild, over the men's heads and into the trees, but it was enough to make them drop back. Purkiss flung the gun down to Kendrick who was already on the other side. He dropped down himself.

They ran, plunging into the mouth of the forest, lashed by branches and grabbed at by roots and cannoning here and there off trunks but not caring. They ignored the pain, oblivious to everything but the need to get away from the noises behind them, the shouts of the remaining men as they mounted the wall and gathered in pursuit.

*

Venedikt dragged a sleeve across his forehead, the sweat stinging in his eyes. From his right a man sobbed, one of the few hit who was alive. Another, more terrible sound, a low primeval howling, rose from further away, breaking off sharply as a shot came. One of the dogs, hanging on despite everything.

The air was hazed with the stench of blood and ordure and the muzzle gases from the weapons. In front of Venedikt the last two men clambered up the wall. Six of them. In a straight firefight it would have been enough. Now, in pursuit of two men through terrain in which agility and the ability to hide were important, they no longer had the upper hand.

He forced down the rage and thought quickly. Dobrynin was heading towards him at a lope, pushing his own gun into his belt with his undamaged hand.

'We have lost four, Venedikt Vasilyevich.'

Venedikt listened to the dwindling clamour in the forest.

Dobrynin said, 'I await your instructions.'

Venedikt drew a deep breath. 'Start the move.'

*

Kendrick staggered against a trunk and slid down, his face waxen. Without speaking he waved Purkiss onwards. Purkiss strained to see back through the trees. There had been no human sound other than their own for – how long? Ten minutes? – and it might be safe to stop. In the sudden relative quiet now that their boots were no longer churning the forest floor he had the impression of another sound, ahead of them. He took a few steps more and saw it, below them and a hundred yards ahead. A road, with a solitary car sweeping by.

'No.' He grabbed Kendrick beneath the arm, hauling him to his feet. Purkiss had already taken the rifle and strapped it across his own back.

He'd noticed an extra magazine clip in Kendrick's belt, and assumed he'd had the presence of mind to take it off the man along with the rifle. 'A bit further.' He hoisted Kendrick's arm across his shoulders.

More slowly now, their momentum broken, they scrambled across the sloping terrain down towards the road, a narrow single-lane curve of tarmac that disappeared into blackness at each end. The evenness of the road surface was jarring at first and Purkiss almost lost his footing. On the other side they disappeared again into the trees. Purkiss took them another fifty yards till he found a ditch. He said, 'All right.'

Kendrick sank so that he was half-supine. Purkiss sat on a rock, rested his forearms on his knees. Getting to the other side of the road had been of tactical importance. If their pursuers made it this far, they might assume the two of them had followed the road in one or other direction.

Kendrick winced himself into a position where he could inspect his leg. Oozing puncture marks were visible in the calves and shin, and a couple of ragged holes had been torn from the muscle. No arterial damage was apparent, though Purkiss knew they wouldn't have made it this far if there had been.

"King dogs,' Kendrick managed through dry lips. 'I normally like them.'

Purkiss checked his phone. No signal.

'How do you think they got on to us?' said Kendrick. 'Reckon they saw us come over the wall?'

'They might have. But we couldn't see the men patrolling the wall, which suggests they were too far away to have spotted us.' Purkiss stood unsteadily and walked up the slope a few paces. The display showed a single bar: a weak signal. Before he could dial, Abby's number came up as a missed call, fifteen minutes earlier. There was no message.

Again he was about to key in her number when the phone rang. Once more it was Abby's number.

'Abby?'

Silence for a moment, then, 'John.'

A man's voice. Low, muted. Unmistakeable.

'*Fallon?*'

'I have your friend.'

The connection was poor, and occasionally a consonant was lost; but there was no doubting the voice, with its trace of Irish.

'Don't go to the police, John, or the Service, or anyone else. If you do, I'll kill her.'

'Fallon, damn you –'

He was gripping the phone so tightly it almost sprang from his sweaty fingers. There was a band around his throat, choking off not only his words but his breathing as well.

'Remember, John. No outside involvement.'

'Listen –'

'I'll be in touch.'

Purkiss dropped the phone. He clenched his fists and raised his face to the canopy of trees and the night sky beyond. The choking feeling left him.

It was completely unprofessional because the danger of being hunted down was still present, but through clamped teeth he roared, a long deep primal sound that bounced off the depths of the forest and sent small things skittering in fear.

Twenty-Three

It was a setback, nothing more. All thoughts of trying to get some sleep gone, Venedikt stood motionless, watching his men at work. The doors were hauled open and the preparations began for the transfer.

Rather than fury he felt a quiet pride in his foresight. There had always been a possibility that the farm would be discovered, and to fail in the mission at this late hour because of having failed to anticipate this possibility would have been a shame too enormous for him to bear. An hour's swift work, and it would be as if nothing had happened.

He could, Venedikt supposed as he stepped aside to give more room to two of his people who were running at a stoop and laying the charges, have committed more men to the pursuit of Purkiss and his colleague. To his mind that would have been irresponsible, would have left the rest of the farm dangerously underprotected. In any case, a larger group wouldn't necessarily have managed to hunt Purkiss down.

Venedikt's phone rang.

'Yes.'

'I've warned Purkiss off. You don't need to relocate.'

'Warned him.'

'I have his friend. The contact he had here in the city. I've told him she'll die if he alerts the authorities.'

Venedikt watched a truck reverse into position and wheeze to a standstill. Two men came running to drag the rear doors wide. 'It's not enough.'

'He cares for this woman. He won't do anything to jeopardize her safety. I know him.'

'But we're still exposed here. He might come back.'

'If he comes back you'll be ready for him. And the woman dies.'

'It's my decision to make.'

'I know it is. And if you choose the upheaval of relocation, it's more of a problem for you than for me. But it is my problem too, because it increases the risk of something going wrong with the operation, of your being discovered along the way.'

Venedikt sucked hard on his teeth. He hated to change his mind once he'd made it up, especially at the urging of another whom he did not respect. Especially when that person was an English. But the possibility that they were still secure, could proceed as planned without the disruption of changing bases... it was attractive.

He said, 'I'll stay put for the time being.'

'Good.'

'Any change in circumstances, any hint you get that Purkiss is alerting anybody else, you let me know immediately.'

There was no reply. Venedikt thought that showed contempt.

He stepped forward, raised his hand, and gave the orders. One or two of the men glanced at him but they were all finely trained, obeyed without question. He went to look for Dobrynin who was supervising the wiring of the farmhouse. The charges, the detonators, would remain in place, just in case circumstances changed.

*

After an age they were surprised by another road. Again they crossed it, its surface slick with the drizzle that was beginning now that the cloud cover had ceased its drifting. The compass on Purkiss's phone told him they were heading east-south-east, but they were still far from anywhere that looked familiar. Soon they would have to leave the cover of the forest and chance the road.

Beside him Kendrick kept pace, hobbling slightly, his leg bound with strips torn from his shirtsleeves. His mouth moved, bitten-off mutters barely audible over the tramp of their feet.

There had been no telephone signal now for half an hour. Purkiss checked the display periodically. The time was just after eleven p.m. Nine hours until the summit, and he didn't care.

He had let Abby down.

Guilt was a phenomenon – not a feeling, that was too slight, too ephemeral a word – with which he was familiar. In the weeks and the months after Claire's death it had lived with him constantly, on the good days a weight pressing down on his head and driving him into the ground, on the bad an internal parasite clawing and sucking the innards of his chest and his abdomen into a compact ball. Now it was a slash from a scalpel blade, so pure and shocking that it was cold rather than painful.

When he'd told Kendrick, the first thing Kendrick said was, 'Shit. Jesus,' and the second was, 'How?'

Purkiss knew the answer. The memory stick in Seppo's flat, the one he'd conveniently been allowed to find, the one with the password that even Abby couldn't crack – *there it was, you* idiot, *the giveaway* – hadn't been a memory stick at all, but a tracking device. Fallon had been on to Abby and her whereabouts from the moment Purkiss had given her the stick.

They got moving at once after that, Kendrick binding his own wounds with concentrated grimness, Purkiss pacing about helplessly, understanding how caged animals felt. Kendrick didn't say *it's not your fault* or anything like it. It wasn't his style. When they were ready to set off he hefted the rifle – he'd insisted on taking it back from Purkiss – and said, very low and very precisely: 'I tell you what, Purkiss. If you see this Fallon, you better kill him quickly. Because if I get my hands on him first, he's mine.'

They used their goggles in the deeper parts of the forest now that there was no moonlight, and saw a startlingly wide variety of cowering and scampering shapes. As they walked Purkiss cast his mind back to his movements after he'd found the memory stick. Had he inadvertently revealed the location of anyone or anywhere else significant? He didn't think so. Fallon would have tracked him to the nightclub, and perhaps that explained why Lyuba Ilkun had been able to summon her colleagues so quickly after he'd talked to her. They had already known he was there.

It still didn't hang together. The surprise the man at Rodina Security, Dobrynin, had shown at the mention of Fallon's background in the Service, as well as his involvement in the events planned for the following day, suggested Fallon wasn't working with Kuznetsov's group. But presumably Fallon had alerted the group to Purkiss and Kendrick's presence on the farm after he'd grabbed Abby, and had either forced her to tell him where they were – he doubted it, it wasn't the sort of thing Abby would do unless under extreme duress, something he didn't want to think about – or, more likely, had seen the farm displayed on Google Earth on her computer and had put two and two together. Which suggested that he was in some way helping Kuznetsov. And where did the traitor among the three British agents come in? Was he – or, conceiveably, she – working with Fallon, as well as with Kuznetsov?

Damn it, they needed to get back to the city, and they were making maddeningly slow progress. Purkiss began heading up a slope towards the road again. Kendrick said, 'We hitchhiking?'

'If need be.'

'Going to be difficult.'

Purkiss half turned and looked at Kendrick, at his bloodied legs and lank hair and stubble. Most of all at the rifle.

'You reckon?'

*

Hitchhiking wasn't in fact an option – with the gun it would be more like hijacking – but Purkiss wanted to get to the exposed higher ground of the road because he was more likely to get a phone signal there. After a few seconds he was rewarded with one bar's worth. He checked the map facility, got the name of the road they were on and that of another one branching off half a kilometre ahead.

'Klavan.' She answered before the first ring had finished.

'It's me, Purkiss.'

'John –'

'I'm in the middle of nowhere, out in the forest to the east of the city. Things are blowing up a bit. Fallon's been in contact with me.' At his side he sensed Kendrick's warning growl. He held up a hand. 'Where are you?'

'Driving the routes the presidents are going to be taking tomorrow, trying again to work out where an attack might come from. There's not much more we *can* do. For God's sake, John, where did you run off to? What have you discovered?'

'Are you with the others?'

'No. On my own.'

'Pick us up, and I'll tell you everything. No more working behind your back, I promise.'

'Us?'

'I'm with a friend.'

After the briefest pause she said, 'All right.' She sounded fatigued.

He gave her the names of the two roads. 'Stop when you get there if you don't see us immediately. We'll be among the trees. And Elle.'

'Yes.'

'Don't tell the other two.'

Kendrick was snarling as he put the phone away: 'Fallon told you not to involve anybody else.'

'It's not the same as going to the police, or SIS at the embassy. She'll be discreet.'

'She could be the one. The traitor. You said so yourself.'

'She's the least likely. She's our best hope of getting back to the city before dawn.'

'I don't fucking like it.'

'I don't pay you to like things.'

*

Half an hour, it had taken her. As they stepped out beside the car Purkiss had the now familiar feeling of tension between his shoulder blades as he waited for the shot to come from whomever she'd brought with her. It didn't happen. He took the front passenger seat and Kendrick got in the back, hoisting his ragged leg up onto the upholstery.

'Elle Klavan, this is Kendrick.'

Kendrick stared at her. Elle craned round to look at his leg.

'Shot?'

'Just a scratch,' said Purkiss.

In the dull light from the dashboard her face was drawn, a tightness around the eyes that he hadn't seen earlier. She took off, handling the car smoothly on the wet road, navigating the curves down through the forest with an ease that contrasted with her grip on the wheel.

'Where are the others?'

'Chris – oh, you might not know this yet. Rodina Security began shutting down soon after we left it. Literally shutting down, the office dismantled, the plaques removed. Chris has been following the removal vans. Last I heard from him was an hour ago. They're out of town, heading south. He's sticking with them.'

'Red herring.'

'Maybe. Richard's back at the office, doing what he can with the background we've unearthed on Rodina – which isn't much – and phoning the few contacts we have around the city, trying to get a new lead on Fallon.' She looked over. 'So tell me.'

Purkiss took a breath and gave it to her, how he'd got the address from the satnav, his and Kendrick's investigation of the farm, Abby and the call from Fallon. She absorbed it in silence.

When he'd finished she said, 'Lots that doesn't add up.'

'Tell me about it.'

'This barn.'

'Yes. I've been thinking about it.'

'And?'

'It could be a hangar.' He glanced round at Kendrick, who shrugged.

'The thought had crossed my mind, yeah.'

Purkiss stared ahead at the rain that was starting to come harder against the windscreen. 'So they're planning to, what – fly a plane in and bomb the summit at the War Memorial? Crash into it like 9/11?'

'They'd never get close,' said Elle. 'There's a ten-kilometre no-fly zone radiating from the site, including over the sea. The airspace will be jam-packed with security. Any aircraft seriously violating the exclusion zone will be shot out of the sky, no questions asked.'

Silence again for a few moments. Elle said, 'Something else. Not new information, but there's a possible connection.'

Purkiss waited.

'Five months ago there was a heist just outside Tallinn. Two armoured vans carrying currency from one of the big banks were attacked in the forest by what must have been a heavily armed gang. There were no survivors, every one of the guards was shot dead. But the sides of the vans had been blown open with RPG rounds. It was huge news at the time, one of the biggest hauls in Estonia's history. Two hundred and fifty million *krooni*. That's over sixteen million euros.'

'Kuznetsov's crew, you think?'

'Possibly. The police made no progress, at least none they disclosed publicly. A well-trained team, carrying out a military-style ambush with sophisticated weapons... Kuznetsov's definitely up there on the board.'

Through the trees was the glimmer of the horizon's lights.

'Where are we going now?' said Elle.

'To the hotel where our friend was when she got taken. To ask if anyone saw anybody matching Fallon's description, and to search her room.'

'It's what Fallon would expect you to do.'

'Exactly.'

'And he's probably got it under surveillance.'

'I hope so. From now on I'm putting myself in harm's way wherever I can. It's the only way in.'

They crested a hill There was the city in the near distance, its brightness blurred by the rain, the firefly glow of helicopters sparking here and there above it. She skirted the centre, Purkiss assumed to avoid the roadblocks and detours as he had earlier. Still progress was slow once they reached the commercial hub.

Elle's phone rang in its cradle on the dashboard. She glanced at the display, said, 'Rossiter,' and hit the speakerphone button.

A rasp, a wheeze, and a burst of static. Then, harsh but clear, Rossiter's voice.

'Elle. It's… Teague. Chris Teague. *He's the one…*'

'Richard?' Her voice rose.

'He's… I've been stabbed…'

Twenty-Four

He sprawled on the living room carpet with his back propped against a sofa, hands clamped to a wad of bloodied cloth against his chest. The room was a riot of disorder. A coffee table sagged in splintered halves, a heavy armchair lay overturned by what could only have been the impact of a human bulk. Glass from smashed ornaments was splashed across the carpet.

Rossiter's teeth were bared and clenched, the breath hissing through them in rapid jerks, sweat sheening his face and slicking his sparse hair to his brow. The carpet was a Pollock painting of cream fabric and spattered blood, a broader smudge marking his path across the floor to his current position.

Elle had said, 'Where are you,' and he replied, '*At my flat,*' and she said 'We're two minutes away. I'll call an ambulance.' He said, '*No. No ambulance, it's not that serious,*' the sibilants drawn out like air from a tyre. Elle seemed to Purkiss to be debating. Then she hung up and hauled the wheel sideways. The car crossed the corner of a pavement.

249

The flat was a second-floor one. They took the stairs three at a time, Purkiss and Elle in the lead, Elle holding the pistol from the car low at her thigh, Kendrick in the rear with the rifle, doing what he could to conceal it across the short distance between the car and the entrance to the block. The door to the flat itself was shut but unlocked when Purkiss tried it. They piled in.

Close up, Purkiss could see that Rossiter had been wrong, that it was in fact serious. His face had the hue and texture of lard, except at his lips where a veiny blue was apparent. His eyes rolled like those of a horse after a fall. Purkiss took his hands, prised them away from his chest, bringing the soaked wad of cloth with them. Rossiter was in shirtsleeves. The front of the shirt was wallpapered to his chest, apart from low down on the left hand side where a ragged tear started to weep fresh blood as its covering was removed. Shreds of cloth from his shirt were mingled with the torn flesh.

Purkiss used the tail of Rossiter's shirt to sponge the wound, feeling the chest flinch under the pressure. He watched the blood well again. No spurting. He put the back of his hand near the wound, felt no air against his skin. Nor, when he put an ear close, was there any tell-tale sucking sound. Rossiter started coughing and there was foam at his lips, but it was clear, not pink or bloody.

Purkiss watched Rossiter's chest, his throat. His eyelids were fluttering and his breathing was quickening and becoming shallower until it was no more than a rapid sequence of tiny gasps, the breaths barely slipping across the threshold of his blueing lips. Purkiss put three fingers of his hand on his throat, the middle one on the thyroid notch and the ring and index ones on either side. The cartilage was off-centre. He pressed his ear against Rossiter's ribs, first the right side and then the left, trying to avoid the blood. It was a poor substitute for a stethoscope, but even so Purkiss could detect the difference between the two sides.

On the right, the echo of air throught the pulmonary tubes. On the left, ominous silence.

Purkiss turned his head to Elle. 'Give me a pen.'

She stared back. 'What?'

'Give me a bloody pen, will you? A ball-point.'

She fumbled in her pockets, passed one across, a cheap and basic piece of plastic.

'Got a knife?'

This time she was quicker and handed him a pen-knife. Purkiss removed the cap from the pen, pulled out the nib with its inky tail, and picked off the round plastic tab at the other end, leaving a hollow tube. Carefully he broke the other end so that the plastic came to a sharp point. He probed Rossiter's chest just in front of the armpit on the left, feeling for the space between the fourth and fifth ribs. Then he opened the smallest of the blades on the pen-knife and made a shallow slit with the tip. Rossiter gave a tiny cry, as much as he could muster given the minimal quantity of air that was getting into and out of his lungs. With his finger Purkiss enlarged the slit a little before positioning the thin end of the hollow plastic tube against the hole and pressing it in. There was the faintest crackle as the tube slid through the subcutaneous fat and fibres before he felt resistance. He pushed harder and the membrane gave and he was through into the pleural space. The air shot through the tube with a hiss. As it escaped, so did a long, drawn-out groan from Rossiter's mouth. Purkiss felt the thyroid cartilage again. It had shifted back to the midline.

He took a long breath.

'What happened?' Elle's voice was raised in volume a notch but the pitch was calm.

'It's called a tension pneumothorax. Air was getting sucked into the sac around his lung but couldn't escape, and it was compressing the other side. I've relieved it for now, but he needs medical attention urgently.'

Through lips that were pinking up rapidly Rossiter hissed, 'Impressive.'

'You pick up a few things here and there.' Purkiss's hands were roving, probing at Rossiter's abdomen. There was no wincing, no involuntary resistance from the muscles. 'It didn't get you below the diaphragm, luckily for you.' To Elle: 'He needs an ambulance.'

'No.' Rossiter spoke perhaps more loudly than he'd been intending, and grimaced. 'Too many... questions. Slow us down.'

After a moment Purkiss said, 'He's right. The ambulance crew would call in a stabbing. We'd have the police to deal with. They're bound to be on the alert tonight and they might get difficult with us, especially given how messed up Kendrick and I look.'

'But you said he needed a doctor.'

Kendrick came back from the sideboard with masking tape. He tore off a length of Rossiter's sleeve and began binding the stab wound. Purkiss said, 'He does. We take him to the hospital, drop him off and get out of there.'

He used some of the tape Kendrick had brought to secure the shell of the ballpoint pen in place where it protruded from Rossiter's chest. Rossiter gasped against the sting of the dressing, nodded. 'I can... spin them a yarn. It'll give you three a chance to keep working.'

Elle sighed, shook her head. She helped Rossiter to sips of water from a glass from the kitchen, then hoisted one of his arms over her shoulders. Purkiss took Rossiter's right hand and curled it around the protruding plastic tube.

'Keep hold of that.'

Ideally there should be a sealed bag on the end to prevent re-entry of the air, but there wasn't time to look for something suitable. He supported Rossiter from the right and the injured man half stumbled between them towards the door. Kendrick went ahead, checked that the coast was clear on the street below. They moved as quickly as they could to Elle's car, and lowered Rossiter into the back, Kendrick sliding in beside him.

Purkiss turned in his seat. 'What happened?'

Another bout of coughing from Rossiter. His voice was a rasp. 'Went home for some clean clothes, knowing... I'd be at the office all night. Teague was there – surprised him, he was rummaging through drawers and didn't hear me come in – and just went for me. Wasn't... armed, just grabbed a paper-knife when the fight started going against him. Stuck me.' He paused for breath. 'He didn't... didn't hang around after that. Must have thought he'd got me somewhere vital. The heart, perhaps.' He gave a bitter, choked laugh. 'Not the first to have difficulty finding it. My heart.'

Purkiss wondered if the man was starting to rave. He cursed himself inwardly that he hadn't checked for signs of head injury.

Elle watched the rear mirror, her foot down. 'He obviously lied about following the removal vans from the Rodina offices. What was he doing in your flat, do you think?'

'God knows.'

Purkiss watched him in the wing mirror. Again Rossiter appeared to be drifting away. Was there more blood, escaping the makeshift dressings?

Kendrick, who hadn't spoken a word since they had arrived at Rossiter's, said, 'This other bloke, Teague. You said the fight was going against him.'

Rossiter nodded.

'Is he injured?'

'Hurt his arm, I think. Got a few blows in to his face and neck. Probably not enough to affect his – to affect his mobility.' In the mirror Purkiss saw a fresh tide of pain ripple across Rossiter's face.

Blue strobes were suddenly swarming before them. Elle swung into the forecourt of the hospital's casualty department. She and Purkiss were out the doors, helping Rossiter from the seat, his face paling again in the harsh fluorescent light over the entrance.

Among the cries and jostling of the Friday night custom they found the triage desk. Elle shouted something in Estonian to the young nurse who was rising from her chair, and three more nurses ran forward to support Rossiter and turn him on to his back on a stretcher.

As Purkiss and Elle were turning to go Rossiter grabbed Purkiss's forearm and whispered, 'Thanks.'

Purkiss nodded, and they took off.

Twenty-Five

The hotel Abby had been using was on a corner. Elle parked three blocks away across the road within sight of the entrance. They watched the front for a while. There wasn't much traffic in and out of the glass doors, and the street, while doubtless busier than usual for this time of night, had lost the press of shoppers Purkiss had noticed when he'd been there before.

'I'm going in on my own,' he'd said, and she immediately objected. But he prevailed. If Fallon or his people had set up an ambush then at least some of them would be outside to block any escape. It made sense to keep the entrance under watch with Elle at the wheel and Kendrick riding shotgun, rather than corralling one or both of them inside the hotel.

Purkiss stepped out of the car and crossed towards the entrance without looking back, flinching at the squeal of tyres somewhere off in the distance but not breaking his stride. The midnight air was cold and the wind was up, whip points of rain flicking the exposed skin of his face and hands.

257

In the foyer, a post-dinner business party milled boozily and a cleaner pushed a desultory mop across the tiled floor. Purkiss went up to the reception desk and waited for the woman seated there to come off the phone.

He said, trying English and his best smile, 'Good evening. I know it's late but I wonder if you might have a room.'

She glanced at the mark on his neck, at his unshaven cheeks, but only briefly. There was blood on his cuffs from where he'd worked on Rossiter, but he'd rolled them up. In any case she wouldn't be able to see them from where she was sitting. With a tight smile she peered at her computer screen.

'Yes, sir, we do.'

He cut in: 'Something on the first floor?'

Her eyebrows twitched. It was an odd request. Pursing her lips slightly, she considered. 'One three one's available –'

'And overlooking the courtyard, if possible.'

He could see she was fighting the urge to roll her eyes. 'One one seven?'

'Perfect.' It was the one next door to Abby's.

He took the registration card and filled it in below the level of the desk so she couldn't see the blood on his sleeves. He handed it across with his Martin Hughes credit card, and waited while she entered the details, hoping she wouldn't ask about luggage. After she handed across two key cards he thanked her and turned, expecting either the hotel's security or someone worse to be bearing down on him. There was nobody.

Purkiss ignored the lift and walked across to the stairs. He climbed them to the first floor. Stepping into the carpeted gloom of the landing he waited, listening. Voices somewhere, the low murmur of a television set through one of the walls. He walked to a bend in the landing and risked a look round. A defective lighting panel in the ceiling gave an occasional flicker, but otherwise the corridor was empty.

Abby's room was 119. He resisted the temptation to listen at the door and instead approached 117. As softly as he could he slipped in the key card, wincing at the electronic click. He pushed open the door, controlling it as it closed behind him. He took a glass from the bathroom and put its open end against the wall adjoining room 119, pressing his ear to the base. Within a minute he had become acclimatised to the creaks and hollow noises being conducted from far-off parts of the hotel, and was able to distinguish them from the nearer sounds on the other side of the wall: the rustling of cloth, the shift of bedsprings, a footfall.

Purkiss went back into the bathroom. He saw a round shaving mirror affixed to the wall with an extendable arm. He fished a handful of change from his pocket and sorted through it till he found a coin of the right size, then used it to unscrew the arm of the mirror from the wall. Quietly he eased open the sliding door at the far end of the room, the noise muffled by the gathering rain, and stepped out on to the tiny balcony. Below was a courtyard with a scrap of garden. To his right was the identical balcony to room 119. The sliding doors were closed, the heavy curtains drawn.

He pulled the arm of the mirror so that it was maximally extended, and reached across with it as far as he could over the other balcony, tilting it until he had the view he wanted. The curtains were separated a crack at chest height. As he watched the mirror, a man's torso appeared fleetingly inside the room. Purkiss adjusted the angle some more and saw the side of a man's face, his mouth moving as he addressed somebody to the side of and below him.

At least two, then.

Back in the room he squatted down at the minibar. He found a bottle of wine and eight miniature bottles of spirits. Among the coffee things on the dresser were six sachets of sugar. He took everything to the bathroom and poured the wine down the sink, then poured the contents of the miniatures into the wine bottle, half filling it. Using his teeth he ripped the edge of a hand towel and tore it lengthways. He rolled it and pushed it deep into the neck of the bottle, dousing in the mixture, before removing it and emptying the sugar over the soaked cloth. He reinserted one end into the bottle's neck so that it dipped below the surface of the alcohol. It wasn't much, certainly nowhere near as effective as a petrol bomb would have been, but he wasn't looking for something deadly.

He took out his phone. When Elle answered, he said very quietly, 'There are at least two of them in her room. I'm in the one next door. I want you to phone the hotel switchboard and ask to be put through to room one one nine. Speak in Russian. Tell whomever answers that his orders are to withdraw. I'll take your call as my cue.'

'Understood.'

Purkiss used a chair to prop open the door of his room. He stepped along the corridor to the door of room 119 and placed the end of the keycard Abby had given him into the slot, taking care not to push it far enough to unlock the door. He left his door ajar. On his way back to the balcony he picked up the makeshift Molotov cocktail and the complimentary book of matches on the coffee table.

He waited on the balcony, the rain batting gently at his face, the enclosed layout of the courtyard protecting him from the wind. He had counted to twenty-two when the phone began to ring in room 119.

Purkiss lit half the matches at the same time, twisting and tilting the protruding length of towel, smearing the flame over its length. He watched it catch and begin its slow crawl towards the neck of the bottle. Faintly, through the closed glass doors of the room next door, he heard the man's voice. Purkiss drew a breath. As he released it, he hurled the bottle backhanded against the glass doors of the adjacent room.

It smashed in a burst of flame and glass, but he was already running back down the length of his room and out to the corridor. He rammed the keycard home, waited the half second for the click, and pushed the door open. It was as he'd hoped, the phone was on the side of the bed nearer the door as he'd remembered it and the man was still there having just dropped the receiver. The other man had also backed off towards the door, recoiling from the shock of the noise and flame against the balcony doors. Purkiss charged the man at the phone first because he was nearer and caught him with a flying kick square in the chest. It slammed him hard against the wall, and as the man started to slide down Purkiss dropped and grabbed the gun half-grasped in the man's limp hand and spun, keeping low by the side of the bed.

The other man was fast, already taking aim. The noise from the suppressed shot was like a heavy table being tipped over, and the duvet inches from Purkiss's face erupted in a furrow of feathers. At the same time Purkiss fired, his gun fitted with a suppressor too. His shot caught the man in the throat, his head snapped round and back, and he twisted and crashed back against the television set in the corner.

Purkiss hauled the slumped man to a sitting position. He'd hit his head in the impact with the wall and was semiconscious, his eyes fluttering.

Purkiss slapped his cheeks, drove a knuckle into his breastbone. Apart from a moan, the man didn't react.

Purkiss pulled out his phone. 'I have one of them. I need to interrogate him but he'll make too much noise, and somebody might have heard something already anyway. I'm coming down.'

She said, 'Got it.'

He strode over to the balcony doors and flung them open. The fire from the homemade bomb had already burned itself out. Purkiss craned to look up and down the iron steps of the fire escape that ran alongside the balcony. At the bottom was the courtyard, where he would be hemmed in. It would be more straightforward to go out the front door, though he'd have to get the man at least partly mobile first.

He glanced at the man in the corner, the one he'd shot and whose throat had sprayed gore across the television screen. The man was quite dead, but a few inches from his hand was a phone, its display still lit up as if it had been used in the last minute or so. Purkiss had been paying attention to the man's gun, naturally enough, but hadn't noticed what else he had in his hands. Had he had time to make a call before Purkiss had come through the door?

Purkiss's own phone vibrated.

'John.' Elle's voice, low and urgent. 'They're approaching the entrance. Four of them.'

Twenty-Six

Purkiss said, 'Understood,' and rang off.

There would be a back way through the kitchens, but they'd have that covered. Apart from that he knew nothing about the layout of the hotel.

He grabbed the man under the arms and dragged him to a standing position. The man staggered but he kept himself upright. He blinked vacantly. Purkiss hissed in his ear, 'English?'

The man stared at him.

'Russian?'

The man didn't nod his head but Purkiss could see he'd understood. He said, 'Come on,' and, an arm across the man's shoulders, he led him to the door, stowing the gun in the waistband of his trousers and covering it with his jacket.

The corridor was empty. There was no approaching commotion to suggest anyone had been alarmed by the banging. Purkiss hurried the man, not allowing him to stumble, towards the stairs. Instead of descending he urged the man up to the second floor.

At the top of the steps he pushed him along the corridor and round a corner. To their left the lift was coming, the numbers above the door counting the floors as it rose. It wouldn't be the four others; they were unlikely to take the lift. With his free hand Purkiss gripped the man's throat on either side of the tracheal cartilage and massaged the carotid arteries with thumb and fingertips. It stimulated the vagal nerves which in turn slowed the heartbeat, a trick Purkiss had learned from a doctor in Morocco. The man's eyes rolled up and he sank. Purkiss held him under the arms and lowered his dead weight to the carpet in front of the lift. Then he slipped back round the corner.

The lift door opened to the murmur of voices, which changed to sharp cries. Purkiss stepped round the corner and saw a middle-aged couple crowding round the body on the floor. They looked like tourists. He strode forward.

'Move aside, please. I'm a doctor,' he said in English, with a Russian accent.

They looked up in bewilderment. He put a little impatience into the voice.

'Move *out* of the *way*.'

The man on the floor looked awful, his face like the sweating underbelly of a fish. His breathing came in laboured rasps. Purkiss crouched beside him and lifted his eyelids with his thumbs to reveal a rind of white on each side. He felt his pulse – thirty-eight beats per minute but at least full – and peered in his mouth at his tongue.

He looked up at the couple. 'You speak English?'

'Yes.' The man was American.

'You know this man?'

'Never seen him before. We came out of the elevator and he was just there.'

'He needs urgent attention. I need to get him on a bed, quickly. Where's your room?'

The woman said, 'Well, I don't know if –'

'Where's your *room*.'

The man said, 'Opposite. Two oh three.'

He walked quickly to the door a few paces down the corridor and unlocked it. He came back and took the supine man's feet while Purkiss got a grip beneath his arms. They hauled him into the room and laid him on the double bed. Purkiss bent over him, busying himself, loosening the man's collar, turning him on his side so that he wouldn't aspirate if he vomited. He addressed the couple without looking at them.

'Sir, I need you to go down to the front desk and tell them to call an ambulance. Don't try calling from the room because they may not understand you. Their English is not so good here. Ma'am, I want you please to go upstairs to room 507 – that's the fifth floor – and get my medical bag. It's beside the bed.'

He groped in his pocket and took out the keycard to room 121. She seemed about to protest again, but her husband took her arm and they left. It was a tissue-thin story and it wouldn't be long before they saw through it, but at the moment Purkiss was on a floor and in a room where his opponents were not expecting him to be. That gave him an edge, however slight.

The Americans had left their room keycards on the bedside table. Purkiss opened the mini-bar and took out a cold bottle of soda water and pushed it down the back of the man's collar. He moaned and flailed his arms. Purkiss felt his neck. The pulse was up to fifty.

He was recovering, but not quickly enough. Purkiss put the bottle in his pocket and went into the bathroom. The tiny window opened on to the side of the building. Through it, he could see the black iron railing of the fire escape.

Back in the bedroom the man was stirring again. Purkiss got him in a fireman's lift and carried him into the bathroom, locking the door behind him.

Below the window that opened was another immovable one, an opaque sheet of glass. Purkiss took off his jacket and wrapped it around his fist and broke the glass with a sharp jab. Behind him he could hear the rattle of somebody trying the door to the bedroom, then a woman's voice calling out, the American's. She would have gone up to room 507, found that the key Purkiss had given them didn't work, and come straight back down. Her husband would probably still be on the ground floor, alerting the staff.

*

Like many continental hotel bathrooms this one had a bidet, positioned under the window. Purkiss stood on it and leaned out the gap left by the breaking of the window. The cast-iron fire escape plunged three floors to an alley along the side of the hotel, and stretched up beyond the fourth, fifth and sixth floors to the roof. He put his head back inside and propped the man upright on the bidet, jamming him so that he didn't slide sideways. It wasn't going to do much good for the blood flow to his brain, but Purkiss had more pressing concerns.

He squeezed through the window space and hauled himself on to the steps, teetering for a horrible instant in the grip of that inbuilt insanity that whispers to human beings to jump when they're on the lip of a long drop. Then he sat and braced his feet against the banister and the window frame. Gripping the man beneath his arms, he leaned backwards.

The man was about Purkiss's size but he was dead weight. Purkiss strained, the muscles of his arms and shoulders burning. Distantly he could hear pounding on the door, shouting. With luck, whoever came upstairs with the husband would not have keys to the room on them and would have to go back downstairs again. The man flopped over the rim of the window. Purkiss heaved him the rest of the way by grabbing his arms. For a second he felt him start slipping down the slick metal of the steps and Purkiss fought to regain control. Then he stooped awkwardly and lifted him fireman-style again.

Gasping under the effort, he began to climb. The night air was cold, and flickers of rain whipped about as if a deluge was toying with the idea of making an appearance. The alley below didn't go anywhere. Chances were fair that there would be nobody down there to look up and see them. Far greater was the likelihood that somebody would get into the room and stick his head out the window. If Purkiss could make it to the roof before this happened, he might have a few minutes to spare, because the natural assumption would be that he had climbed down rather than up.

He reached the top where there was an unlocked metal door, pushed the man through, and shut it behind them as softly as he could. Voices suddenly broke into the empty air below. The door was in a low wall that ran around the edge of the roof. In the centre of the open rectangle were two blocks with doors in their walls that he assumed led to the inner staircases. He didn't have a great deal of time because the hotel would be crawling with police in a few minutes, and they would certainly check the roof.

Purkiss sat the man against one of the walls. He tore off the gag, pulled the bottle of soda from his pocket. The shaken carbonated water sizzled over his hands. Purkiss shook it over the man's waxy face. The man sighed and mumbled, opening his eyes a crack and squinting against the glare of a spotlight from a nearby building. Purkiss took out the pistol – a SIG Sauer P226, he noticed – and laid it on the ground.

'What's your name?'

His lips moved silently. Purkiss slapped him.

'What's your name?'

'Braginsky.' His eyes were open and focused on Purkiss's. He was on the right side of the twilight that separated consciousness from its counterpart.

'Okay.' Purkiss squatted back on his haunches. 'You know how this sort of thing usually works, Braginsky. You give me the runaround a bit, I cut up rough, you start feeding me scraps, I go easy, you clam up again, I escalate the violence, et cetera, et cetera. Except I haven't got much time. And when I'm pushed for time, I skip the niceties.'

One of the mistakes that Purkiss had come to learn was frequently made about interrogation science was that the more immediately the urge to be free from the distressing stimulus, the more likely the person being interrogated was to say anything, even if it were untrue. So, a man in extreme pain will reflexively tell his tormentor what he believes he wants to hear. A man facing the less immediate threat of impending death or disfigurement, and who has time to contemplate the consequences of his non-cooperation, may still lie, but is less likely to do so, as the demons generated by his own imagination do their work.

Purkiss picked up the SIG Sauer, pushed the tip of the silencer against the man's forehead, and motioned for him to stand. He did so, shakily. Purkiss grabbed his collar and turned him and shoved him towards the adjacent wall which was lower, hip height. He kept pushing so that the man was bent over the wall at the waist. Laying the gun down on the wall, Purkiss squatted and gripped the man's ankles. He pushed up so that he tipped past his centre of gravity with a cry.

Braginsky hung suspended over the drop, his arms flailing.

'Where's my friend? The woman.'

The man yelled some more. Purkiss let go and immediately gripped the ankles again.

'Whoops.' He peered over at Braginsky's face, which arched back at him, eyes rolling in terror. 'You'll notice it's not a clean drop. You'll hit a balcony or two on the way down. It'll be messy.'

'I don't know –'

'You're getting awfully heavy, Braginsky.' He let the ankles slip a few inches more.

'For the love of God, I swear I don't know. The Englishman took her.'

'Fallon.'

'I don't know his name. It was never told to us by the boss.'

'The boss. You mean Kuznetsov.'

'Yes.' He shouted it unhesitatingly. It made Purkiss think he was telling the truth about the rest.

'Where's Fallon?'

'I don't know.'

'Back at the farm?'

'No. It's –' He broke off, and Purkiss gave him an encouraging jolt. 'Ah, *God*, don't – The farm's being closed down.'

From far away, somewhere below in the streets, came the noise of sirens.

'What's planned for tomorrow?' He combined the question with a shake of the man's legs. He could feel his grip genuinely starting to slacken.

'An attack on the President.'

That was interesting. He hadn't said *on the summit*.

'Which one?'

'Russian.'

Purkiss took this in, the implications not immediately clear. But it became a secondary concern. Behind him a door crashed open in one of the stairwell blocks and men began to stream out, too early to be the police, and looking too murderous.

Twenty-Seven

They were four, just as Elle had said, hard and ugly men who fanned out across the rooftop. Each was armed with a pistol, apart from one who gripped one-handed a single-barrelled shotgun, the end sawn short.

Purkiss dragged Braginsky back over the edge and let him fall gasping near his feet. He grabbed the SIG Sauer. The block the men emerged from was the farther of the two from Purkiss. The men were perhaps fifty feet away, advancing. Purkiss hauled Braginsky to his feet, pressed the gun against his head. One of the men took aim at Braginsky himself. No good: they'd riddle their own man if they had to. Purkiss placed the gun on the ground and raised his hands. Braginsky's legs buckled and he slid to the ground, his face a gargoyle mask of fear.

Purkiss scanned the environment. There was nothing he could do, *nothing*. The door to the fire escape was too far away to be of any use, and the men were between him and the doors to the inner stairs. If they didn't take his phone away from him immediately he might be able to get a message to Elle and Kendrick. The likelihood of that was almost non-existent.

One of the men coughed, and frowned at the rope of blood his mouth flung out on to the concrete. An instant later the crash of a shot rang off the walls around the roof. The man hit the ground face-down as the other three spun and crouched, one of them knocked off his feet immediately by a second shot. The man with the shotgun pulled the triggers of his weapon. The boom of the firing mechanism was followed by the stinging spatter of lead shot against the wall of one of the blocks. His body jerked twice and he twisted towards Purkiss as he fell. The fourth man got to his feet, swung his gun arm over to point it at Purkiss. Purkiss dived and rolled on his shoulder and the shots sang off the wall. Braginsky screamed and spun face-down, hit by a ricochet, Purkiss assumed. The man was taking aim again when the rifle hammered. He was hit three times before he could fire. He sprawled awkwardly, the gun spinning and skittering away from him across the surface of the roof.

The aftershock of the gunfire had left a high peal in Purkiss's ears. Below, the sirens were becoming more insistent, the notes from assorted vehicles overlapping. Purkiss crouched, holding the SIG Sauer lowered in a two-handed grip. From the doorway of one of the stairwell blocks Elle and Kendrick had broken into a run towards him, Kendrick with the rifle at the ready and Elle holding her pistol at her side. As they got near

Purkiss saw her eyes were dazed. It was the first time she'd killed, he thought.

'There may be more coming up behind,' she said, her voice steady. 'And the police are on the way.'

Purkiss said, 'The fire escape.' He pulled open the door and looked down. Nobody in the alley yet. They began to descend, Purkiss in the lead and Kendrick at the back, their soles squealing on the metal steps. As they approached the window Purkiss had climbed out of, voices from the room beyond became louder. He ignored them and slipped past, hearing them turn to shouts.

Two floors from the bottom Kendrick said, 'Ah, *bollocks*,' as a police car pulled across the mouth of the alley.

There was nothing to do but keep going. One floor down Purkiss said, 'Jump', and swung himself over the banister. His shirt caught on a spur of metal and tore all the way down. The doors of the car were opening, uniformed men emerging and yelling. Purkiss hung in space for a second, then hit the floor, rolling. Something spanged and chipped off the tarmac beside him. The low crack of the shot trailed after it.

Why are they shooting at us, he thought, before realising the shot had come from far away and another direction. He rolled over and over, deeper into the alley, sounds coming disorientatingly from all around, shouting and sirens and two more cracks (from above, he now understood; reinforcements had arrived on the roof). Then he was up and running at a low crouch, glancing behind him, seeing Elle and Kendrick close at his back.

Behind them a couple of the policemen were shouting something. One of them tried to come forward, but he cringed back as a rain of shots spackled off the steps. The police seemed torn between returning the fire from above and covering Purkiss and his colleagues, especially as the firing from the roof didn't appear to be aimed at them. Kendrick crouched behind some steel bins and started to lay down covering fire, aiming diagonally upwards at the fire escape door. Purkiss hoped to God he didn't start shooting at the police.

The alley didn't, as Purkiss had thought before, end blindly. There was a narrow gap, wide enough to fit a single person, leading through to a street at the back of the hotel. Elle pointed at the gap and nodded. Purkiss waved her ahead of him and yelled at Kendrick, 'Come on.'

The shooting from above had stopped. That was a bad sign, because the police would now be free to come after them or, worse, start firing. Purkiss grabbed two dustbin lids and held them up as makeshift shields. He winced as a bullet smashed into the wall of the alley. Another sang off one of the lids, the impact almost knocking it from his hand. He waited till Kendrick disappeared through the gap, then crammed himself through. Ahead Elle was sprinting, not waiting for them. He understood that she needed to get to the car and start it up.

They weaved and cannoned through the maze of streets, bouncing off the rain-slicked walls. Purkiss was aware of a terrifying claustrophobia. He felt hemmed in on all sides by the clusters of people, the coloured lights, the vehicles. He had no idea where he was running, kept his gaze on Elle several yards ahead, who was a faster runner than he'd realised. He saw a screaming couple recoil from them. As if for the first time he noticed the rifle in Kendrick's grip. He yelled, 'Get rid of that.' Kendrick snarled something bestial in reply and kept hold of the gun.

And they were at the car, its exhaust already alive and growling. They piled inside. Elle looked in the mirrors, pulled away gently and kept the speed slow, maddeningly so. Much as Purkiss wanted to shout at her to put her foot down, he understood the need to be unobtrusive. He turned in his seat and stared back through the rear window. High on the roof of the hotel he saw helmeted figures swarming under the spotlights, the occasional prick of light from a gunshot. On the streets below people were massing in fear and wonder, craning their gazes upwards, like peasant villagers staring up at a Gothic castle where terrible deeds were being perpetrated.

*

Never in front of his men would Venedikt lose control. To do so would be humiliating, unmanly. It would also be tactically unwise, because every display of fear and doubt in the leader would kindle such feelings in his followers, where they would be magnified a thousandfold.

'We believe all eight are dead, sir.'

It was *sir* now, not *Venedikt Vasilyevich*. Dobrynin had been making and taking phone calls. Now he stood before Venedikt, his mutilated hand grasped in the other, the only sign of his nerves.

'Eight.'.

'Yes. Braginsky and Ivanov from the room, the remaining six on the roof.'

'All dead.'

'None in custody, as far as we know. The police have not been seen to take anybody away yet. The only ambulance has been to attend to an injured policeman on the ground.'

'And no Purkiss.'

'No, sir. He and the other two have escaped.'

Venedikt felt the urge to probe his temples with his fingertips but resisted. *Control.*

'And we don't know if Purkiss learned anything from any of the men.'

'No, sir.'

The office was spartan, unused before now. He would have preferred that they hadn't had to use it. Now, perhaps, they would have to move again. But where to? He watched Dobrynin's face, the grave, calm expression. On the periphery of Venedikt's vision the wall clock said ten past one.

Seven hours.

'It's a setback.'

Dobrynin stood poised, waiting for the next.

'A setback. But no more.'

'Yes, sir.' Dobrynin exhaled, audibly, grasping the meaning. *We stay put. We proceed as planned.*

Venedikt waved him into a seat. With pen and paper they made rapid calculations. Eight men down. A third of their number. It was a setback, indeed, a serious though not a fatal one.

After Dobrynin had left Venedikt walked outside and stood in the sharp cold, relishing the tingle of the fine rain on his upturned face. The row of disused hangars in the distance resembled the tailbones of some gigantic fossilised prehistoric beast. Only one, the nearest, was illuminated, the men moving about moth-like under the arc lights. They had worked swiftly, transporting everything to the new location within ninety minutes.

No. The energy and manpower that would have to be spent in moving everything again would be better directed towards another goal. Finding Purkiss, and neutralising him.

First, Venedikt needed to speak to his English 'friend'. The word was increasingly bitter in his mind. The 'friend' was playing games with him. It was time for a reminder of who was in charge.

He stepped back into his office and took out his phone.

*

'Nothing.' Purkiss wanted to thump the dashboard in frustration. 'Absolutely nothing.'

Beside him Elle said, 'We took down several of them. And the police may have taken some of them alive. Might find out something useful.'

'That doesn't help us. Or Abby.'

The cacophony of the hotel was fifteen minutes behind them, an occasional emergency vehicle still blasting past. Purkiss had rattled off the little he'd learned. The farmhouse base was being shut down – no doubt his and Kendrick's appearance there and subsequent escape had triggered this – and the target the next day was going to be the Russian president.

'An ethnic Russian group planning to kill the leader of what presumably they regard as their home nation,' said Elle. 'Two possibilities. Either they see him as too conciliatory, too liberal, or it's meant as a provocation, intended to harden Russian attitudes towards the Estonian government and people.'

'I'd go for the second,' said Purkiss.

In the back Kendrick was agitated, shifting about in his seat as if it were heated, hands playing over the AK-74. He said, 'What's on the agenda?'

Elle answered. 'We hole up, take stock. I've a safe house a couple of miles away.'

Purkiss knew it was standard procedure. Every agent in the field arranged his or her own safe house, the whereabouts of which was unknown to anybody else, even trusted colleagues. They couldn't return to her usual flat in case Teague showed up.

'So he hates the Russian president too,' said Purkiss. 'Teague.'

She shook her head, her eyes weary. 'Not that he ever mentioned. But I don't know. God. Nothing's certain any more.'

The safe house was a second-floor flat in a nondescript suburban area. Purkiss had a notion they were west of the Old Town. He trooped upstairs with the others two, fatigue pulling at his limbs.

The living room was barely furnished and cold as only a room left unheated for months can be. Elle flicked the boiler into life, went into the kitchenette. Purkiss sank onto a reconditioned sofa and Kendrick seated himself at the tiny dining table. He placed the rifle across it and began to strip it.

'Thing about these old Soviet weapons,' he said, 'you can treat them like shit. Leave them out in the rain, drag them through swamps, bury them under an avalanche. They go on working like loyal old mutts.'

The aroma of coffee began to replace the mustiness. Purkiss put his hands round the mug Elle handed him and drank gratefully. She'd provided sandwiches as well, huge doorsteps of granary and ham and cheese.

Purkiss's phone vibrated. He snatched it from his pocket.

Caller's number blocked.

'John. It's me.'

'Fallon.'

He felt Elle stiffen beside him on the sofa, saw Kendrick sit up in the chair.

'Here's something to establish good faith.' The voice was low and grating.

An instant later another voice, so close to the mouthpiece it was distorted, whispered:

'Mr Purkiss. He's –'

'*Abby*. Are you hurt –'

Fallon's voice came back, Abby's having ended so abruptly it must have been clamped off by a hand or a gag of some sort.

'She's fine, at the moment. This is the deal. Listening?'

'Yes.'

'You for her. You come in, and she walks.' A pause. 'What time do you have?'

'One thirty.'

'Four a.m., Kiek in de Kök.'

He was gone.

Twenty-Eight

The rain was becoming more determined, as if claiming the streets now that so few people were about any longer. The Jacobin worked as quickly as he could, making sure the boot was locked, and doing a routine sweep for bugs under the bonnet and the chassis even though the likelihood was remote.

He hadn't expected Purkiss to return to the hotel. He'd told Kuznetsov about the hotel to get the man off his back. The Russian had of course wanted to use the woman immediately as bait to draw Purkiss in, but the Jacobin had held off, still clinging to the hope that Purkiss might lead him to Fallon. He'd known Kuznetsov would stake the hotel room out, but assumed he'd post a couple of men at most, not mount an eight-man surveillance operation.

As it turned out, Kuznetsov had been right. Purkiss *had* gone back, and now Kuznetsov had lost a third of his personnel, and the police were involved. All in all, a chaotic couple of hours.

Now the Jacobin was forced to agree with Kuznetsov. It was time to bring Purkiss in, and his friend, Abby, was the lure. He'd agreed the venue with Kuznetsov, Kiek in de Kök, as well as the time. Two and a half hours from now, which would give Kuznetsov's depleted crew time to finish the transfer to the new site and the securing of the base, and to set up position at the venue. The delay wouldn't give Purkiss a significant advantage because he didn't have vast reserves on which to draw. Just that sidekick of his, and Elle.

Elle. As the Jacobin went back indoors for his coat, he reflected that it was a pity she was probably going to die. He had cared for her, of course. Had he loved her, even, once? He supposed the flicker of loosening that her voice, her presence, had stirred in his chest could be interpreted as love, or as close as he had ever come to experiencing it. But that had been some time ago, and when he'd feared the feelings might get in the way of what he needed to do, he'd rooted them out. Now he felt nothing.

Less even, perhaps, than the body face down in the empty bath, invisible from where he stood at the front door of the flat.

He dragged on his coat and killed the lights and went out to the car.

*

'Kiek in de Kök.' Kendrick had stripped and cleaned and reassembled the gun and he sat at the table, practising his aim. 'It sounds like –'

'Yes, I know what it sounds like.' Purkiss mopped sandwich crumbs from the table with his finger, caught Elle watching him.

Kendrick said: 'Craziest idea I've ever heard.'

'No. I've come up with crazier.'

There really weren't any other options. If they simply didn't turn up at the venue, Abby would be killed. If they turned up but Purkiss didn't hand himself over, she'd be killed. If he gave himself up as Fallon was asking, he'd probably be killed. But if he wasn't, if they kept him alive even an hour, then Abby, back in action again, might be able to work her magic.

Purkiss asked Elle, 'Do you have anything to wrap it in? Cling film, a small zippable sandwich bag?'

She emerged from the kitchen with a roll of plastic wrap. He tore off a small rectangle and put it in his pocket.

He'd explained his plan to them. 'Abby was tracking my phone via a website which she had password-protected access to, so you two wouldn't be able to use it. If they swap her for me, she'll be able to track me and find out where they've taken me, assuming they don't kill me immediately.'

'But they'll anticipate that and get rid of your phone as soon as they've got you,' said Elle.

'The tracking's done through the phone's SIM card,' he said. 'If I take that with me and manage to install it in another phone, she'll be able to track that phone.'

'So how will you get the card in a new handset?'

'Smuggling the card in with me is the easy bit.' He pointed at his open mouth. 'Getting it into a handset's going to be tricky.'

He had no idea if a SIM card would be damaged by stomach acids, but assumed it might be, so he asked for the plastic wrap. He'd have to remove it from his phone and swallow it at the last minute, since he needed to keep his phone on standby in case Fallon rang again.

Two a.m. The safe house was in the Old Town. The rendezvous point, Kiek in de Kök, was ten minutes' drive away. Even though they planned to get there early, there was still an agony of time to kill.

Kendrick did a rapid strip and reassembly of the rifle again. He said, 'Can't stand this. I'm going for a walk.' He stood and pulled on his jacket.

Elle raised her eyebrows, looked at Purkiss. Purkiss said, 'He's always like this before a job. Best we let him walk off some steam or he'll be unbearable to be around.' To Kendrick he said, 'Go easy.' His eyes flashed a warning. Kendrick nodded distractedly and banged out of the flat.

'A bit worked up,' said Elle.

'He'll be fine.'

Purkiss hoped he would be, that he didn't overdo it. Since leaving the Army Kendrick had developed a tendency to enhance his natural edginess with amphetamines at times when added alertness was needed. When he'd first discovered this, Purkiss had been alarmed, but Kendrick wasn't to be told, and the extra stamina he derived from the stimulants did, Purkiss had to admit, seem to give him an advantage.

Purkiss and Elle sat in silence for several minutes, listening to the distant nighttime sounds, the flat's creaks and echoes.

'She's a close friend.' Her glance was questioning even though the words came out as a statement.

'Abby. Yes. Salt of the earth.'

He'd known Abby three years, encountering her first on a web forum where he was seeking technical advice, back in the early days of his work with Vale when he was still doing his own searches and becoming frustratingly aware that his skills as a computer geek weren't up to par. After she proved helpful with more than one of his enquiries, he suggested they meet to discuss possible employment options. He discovered that she worked freelance for the Metropolitan Police, among other organisations. Eventually she came to take on jobs exclusively for him. The rates he paid made this worthwhile. Despite their close association he knew very little about her. She'd mentioned parents back in Lancashire, but that was about all.

'And Kendrick. There's a rapport there. The kind we develop with other Service colleagues, if we're lucky.'

'Yes.' She'd sounded wistful. He was about to say that Abby and Kendrick were the closest thing he had to friends, but the suddenness of the realisation brought him up short.

To change the subject he said, 'Teague being the traitor. That's got to be difficult for you.'

She shrugged. 'To be honest, I wasn't convinced he wasn't, even when I told you otherwise. What bothers me more is Rossiter. Seeing him there, stabbed, bleeding… he can be a difficult sod to work for, but my God, he didn't deserve that.'

'He'll be all right. They'll put a drain in his chest for a couple of days.'

She shifted closer, her legs tucked under her on the sofa, and put a shy hand on his arm. 'He thanked you, but I haven't yet. So, thanks.'

Purkiss looked at her eyes, dark in the pale, drawn face. At her mouth, her throat. Through the layers of fatigue he felt a stirring.

Somehow she was closer still. He leant his face in and kissed her forehead, then her mouth. Her lips yielded at first, then responded, pressing back. His hands slid round across her back and up to her hair, drawing her head towards him. Her own arms came up and her hands grabbed at his back, his shoulders, and he broke the kiss to pull at her sweater and drag it off in a cascade of hair which she shook out of her face. Then his hands were on her breasts through her thin blouse and hers clasped his face. She said, 'Wait,' rose and tugged on his arm.

He half followed, half propelled her towards the door of the solitary bedroom. Once inside he kicked the door shut and they were clawing at each other's clothes, tumbling and rolling on the cold bedspread, enveloped in each other's heat in a raging joy that was so complete it made time cease for hours.

*

She lay naked against his side, her breast pressed against his chest, her hair pushing up under his chin every time he breathed in. Purkiss watched the ceiling, letting the night vision work its way into his retinas.

He hadn't been expecting it, wondered if she had. The nearness of death no doubt had something to do with it, the need to respond by engaging in the most life-affirming act of all. There had been other women, since Claire, including one with whom he'd become very close until she'd come up against the impenetrable bedrock of his grief. Usually the women ended it, saddened by his distance.

The evenness of her breathing made him wonder if she'd fallen asleep. He said, 'We should get ready.'

'No. Not… all that, out there, yet. Not for a few minutes. Let's be normal for a while.' She shifted against him, easing herself. 'Ask me something normal.'

'All right.' He thought for a moment. 'Elle. Not the commonest name nowadays.'

'A long story. Well, not long so much as dull.'

'Try me.'

'First week at university. I was registering for a class. I was asked for my name, and for some reason instead of Louise Klavan – Louise, that's my name – I said "L. Klavan". The woman wrote down "Elle". It sort of stuck.'

'I prefer Louise.'

'That's too bad.' She pinched his arm. 'Your middle name. Rutherford. I noticed it when I did the background search on you. What's that all about? It wasn't your mother's maiden name.'

'My father was an amateur scientist. He wanted me to pursue a career in physics. Like Ernest Rutherford.'

'You must have been a great disappointment to him.' He felt her smile against his shoulder.

'You don't know the half of it.'

After a pause she said, 'Now comes the part where I ask you how, or why, you came to join the Service.'

'And where I give you the usual reasons. A young man's restlessness and desire for adventure. A bookish intellectual's wish to serve abstract ideals of freedom and justice. Or the self-indulgence of an immature existentialist who lacks the imagination to seek out normal ways to live a worthwhile life, and chooses a life of danger as a tragic gesture against the void.'

She sat up and drew the covers around herself and stared at him, still smiling, genuine interest in her eyes. 'I don't believe any of those apply to you. But clearly you've considered them.'

'Everyone in this job asks themselves sooner or later why the hell they chose it, as you well know.' He shrugged, feeling suddenly self-conscious. 'You know what I read at university.'

'Philosophy, English literature and history, in which you achieved a first,' she recited. 'So... I'm guessing it was the history that motivated you? You saw yourself as an agent of history, destined to carry it forward. I'm not being facetious, by the way.'

'Don't worry, I didn't think you were. But you're exactly wrong, one hundred and eighty degrees out. There are no grand sweeping narratives in history, other than the ones we construct. Something happens and then another something happens, and then another, and in retrospect we impose a contrived causal link between them, so it seems like one progressed inevitably from the last.'

She said nothing, absorbing it. Purkiss sat up, warming to his theme.

'Take tomorrow, or later today, rather. The presidents are meeting, and if all goes according to plan, they'll seal an agreement which will make it less likely that their two countries, Russia and Estonia, and by extension Russia and the NATO powers, will go to war. But there are thousands of other potential triggers, manmade and otherwise, that could lead to such a war. Yet in a year's time, ten years' time, if we haven't gone to war then the historians will attribute this achievement directly to today's meeting. Baselessly so.'

'But if the meeting is sabotaged, if the Russian president is assassinated... the chance of war is dramatically increased.'

'Exactly. Chances, probabilities – that's all we can deal in. Not certainties. It's what Hume taught me. That's why I chose the Service.' He sat back against the pillows again. 'You can't make the world a better place. But you can help reduce the probability of awful things happening, not awful things in principle but individual things. And if that's the most you do with your life then I think you can say you've had a life worth living.'

Her eyes were soft and he thought he saw a sadness in her smile.

'And where does *this* fit in? What we're doing?'

She waved vaguely at them, at the bed. Before he could be lost for words, she let the cover drop away from her body, leaned in towards him, and he reached for her once more.

Twenty-Nine

Purkiss was dressed by the time Kendrick let himself in. Kendrick's face was taut, the cheeks stretched hollow, his limbs tense as claspknives. He barely nodded at Purkiss as he strode over to the table, where he picked up the gun and hefted it as if it were a prosthetic arm he'd temporarily misplaced.

Elle emerged from the bedroom in a dressing gown. Purkiss handed her the mug of coffee he'd made. She waved at Kendrick's stare and disappeared again into the bedroom.

'Have a good walk?' Purkiss asked. Kendrick had none of the jitteriness of the true speed freak, so probably hadn't overdone it.

Kendrick sat himself in Purkiss's line of sight and leered. 'Filthy bastard.'

Purkiss looked at the smirking face, managed to stop his mouth from twitching in a smile. 'There's coffee in the pot. Help yourself. If you need any caffeine on top, that is.'

'I won't tell Abby.' Kendrick laid a forefinger alongside his nose.

Purkiss sighed, exasperated. Perhaps Kendrick had overindulged after all. 'Why would she care?'

The silence went on longer than was comfortable. Purkiss noticed that Kendrick's gaze had changed, turned from mocking to wondering.

'My God. You genuinely don't know, do you?'

'What?'

Kendrick let out his breath in a great hiss between his teeth, propping his boots up on a chair. 'Purkiss... for someone who's only slightly less educated than God, you can be a right stupid bugger at times.'

'*What?*' Purkiss spread his palms.

'She's crazy about you. Batshit insane. Like a teenager with a pop star.'

'Abby?'

'Yes. Abby.' Kendrick shook his head. 'And you haven't seen it. All that wisecracking, all those chirpy *Mister Purkiss* remarks... it's all a front. She's besotted. Christ knows why, she could do better.'

Purkiss said nothing, his thoughts churning. Was it possible? He'd had a vague notion Abby admired what he did, that her loyalty wasn't just due to the money he paid her, but... *that*? Comments, snatches of conversation, nonverbal signs began to play themselves again in his head.

Elle emerged again, dressed and glancing from one man to the other, aware that something had passed between them. Kendrick chuckled softly, and the moment was gone.

*

They did an inventory. Elle's Glock 19, a lighter version of the Glock 17 with which Purkiss was more familiar. The SIG Sauer he'd taken off the man Braginsky in the hotel. Kendrick's AK-74. Elle had six rounds left as well as a spare 15-round magazine, while the SIG Sauer still had all ten of its rounds but no spare clip. The assault rifle had one spare magazine holding 30 rounds. And that was it.

The priority, Purkiss had made them agree, was to see Abby to safety before revealing themselves. Any appearance by the two of them before Abby was home and dry, and they would likely all be cut down. Kendrick in particular had to stay hidden. As the one whose weapon gave him sniping capacity, he was their wild card, the guardian in the shadows. Purkiss had no idea how many people they would be facing, but had to assume they would be vastly outnumbered. Priority one was to get Abby out. Lesser priorities were to retrieve Purkiss himself at the same time, which was unlikely to be possible, and to take one or more of the opposition alive.

Twenty past three. It was time to go.

*

Kiek in de Kök was, Elle explained, a fifteenth century artillery tower on a hill to the west of the Old Town's centre. The tower was home to a museum showcasing mediaeval weapons. The name was Low German for 'peep in the kitchen' and referred to the ability of soldiers manning it to peer into the houses in the Old Town below. Fallon hadn't said where they were to meet. Purkiss assumed it was to be at the base of the tower, that the location had been chosen because of its position on a hill with the advantages this conferred on whomever got there first.

Although the tower was within walking distance of the safe house, they decided to take Elle's car in case a quick getaway was needed. By now the streets were mostly silent, the cobbles slick, street lights often absent so that the turrets rose blackly against the rain.

Elle parked up on the kerb of a narrow street that was part of a tightly woven warren of cobbled passageways, which together with the tiny top-heavy cottages and quaintly lettered shop signs that lined them gave the impression of a village for some kind of mythical folk. She led them round a bend through an arch, and pointed upwards where a steep flight of steps twisted in a gap between two houses. Beyond rose a hill at the top of which Purkiss could see in silhouette a cylindrical tower with a coned roof.

Twenty to four.

'You and I go first,' said Purkiss. 'Tony, you keep back. At the top of the steps you move away, approach the tower by a separate route.'

'Got it.' Kendrick fitted the night-vision goggles in place.

They began to climb the steps.

*

Kuznetsov stepped forward and popped the catch on the boot – it was the Jacobin's car but Kuznetsov always had to be the man doing things, the one in control, and the Jacobin let him. They stood gazing down.

The woman was tiny, made even more so by the bindings that narrowed her arms against her sides and her legs together. Above the gag her face was yellow in the light from the streetlamp, her eyes huge. The Jacobin couldn't read them because of the light, and so couldn't see if they held fear or defiance or even contempt. He hoped it wasn't the last. It wouldn't bother him, but Kuznetsov's ego wouldn't take kindly to it and he might snap and get rough.

Two of Kuznetsov's men, one of them Dobrynin, his second in command with the damaged hand, took hold of the girl under her arms, hauled her out, and deposited her on the pavement of the car park. She lay trussed, not struggling or whimpering. In the dim light the Jacobin could see a thread of blood from the corner of her mouth where the gag had cut into the skin.

'Untie her legs,' said Kuznetsov. The men cut the cords at her knees and ankles and dragged her to her feet, dwarfing her between them.

One of them reached for the gag. The Jacobin said, 'No. Leave that.'

The man glanced at Kuznetsov, looking almost astonished that the Englishman had given him an instruction. The Jacobin said: 'She won't run, but she will call out, try to warn him.'

Kuznetsov nodded at his man and turned away. They pulled the girl along after him. Beyond him four more of his people waited, all wearing overcoats to conceal their weapons more than to protect them from the rain. They too began to move up the slope towards the tower.

Kuznetsov stopped, half-turned as if surprised to see the Jacobin keeping pace with him. 'You'll want to keep out of the way.'

'Just the opposite. I want to be right there when he appears.' *And to see that you don't balls it up.*

Kuznetsov raised his eyebrows in a shrug. He continued after his men and the stumbling girl.

*

The tower was in darkness, sodium lamps throwing a fringe of brightness across the small lawns and paved pathways around its base. Purkiss and Elle stopped at the edge of one of the lawns between a small clump of trees, watching and listening. No movement in the shadows. From somewhere, low voices murmured, but it was impossible to tell how distant they were. The rain was steady, soft, its drumming setting up low-grade interference both visually and aurally.

Purkiss glanced behind him. Kendrick was already gone, invisible somewhere in the shadows.

They moved forwards, closer to the tower. Purkiss had one hand in his pocket, his fingertips touching his phone.

'There,' breathed Elle. He crouched as she did, arm coming up with the SIG Sauer extended. It was a man's shape, emerging from the shadows and standing at the foot of the tower, perhaps sixty feet away.

'Purkiss.'

The voice was quiet but carried against the rain. He recognised it: Dobrynin, the man they'd met at the offices of Rodina Security.

'Where is she?'

'Your friend's here. Is it just the two of you?'

'Of course not.'

Because of the rain it was difficult to tell if the man laughed. 'Point taken. I have back up myself.'

'Where's Fallon?'

'You're here to trade yourself for the woman. It doesn't matter where Fallon is.'

'Bring her out, then.'

Dobrynin looked to one side, over to the trees. Two men stepped out, sandwiching a smaller figure as though in a rugby scrum.

'Her?' Elle murmured. He nodded.

The men gave Abby a push. She staggered but kept her footing. One of the men said something harsh. Over to the right Dobrynin made motions with his good hand: *go on, walk.* Behind her, the men had handguns drawn.

Purkiss looked up and off to the left and the right, making a show of it, as if he had an army hidden in the darkness waiting for their orders. He had no idea where Kendrick had positioned himself. With his hand still in his pocket Purkiss used his fingernails to prise the SIM card from his phone and wrap the plastic around it. He brought it up to his mouth and swallowed, wincing at the hardness, feeling it scrape as it went down.

Abby began to take slow steps in his direction. He realised her wrists were bound together behind her back and she had some sort of gag in her mouth. She was too far away for him to be sure, but she didn't look marked.

Dobrynin called out, in English, 'Stop.' She did. Her eyes were on Purkiss.

Dobrynin said, 'Now Purkiss. Gun on the ground, hands raised, and approach those two men.'

He kept his gaze on the two men. Abby was in his line of sight, nearer, out of focus. He knelt, laid the gun on the ground, folded his hands on top of his head, and began to walk.

The two men raised their guns to shoulder height, both adopting the Weaver stance, free hands cupping the ones that held their pistols. Purkiss watched them over the tousle of Abby's hair.

As if obeying some unseen choreographer, Purkiss and Abby timed their progress so that they reached one another at what appeared to be the midpoint between the two men and Elle. For a moment Purkiss took his gaze off the two men with the guns and looked down at Abby's face. He realised she'd been trying to get his attention. Her eyes were flashing frantically above the gag, and he could see the dirty material billowing and sucking as she tried to articulate words. Low sounds came from her throat.

Just as he passed her he lowered his head to catch what she was saying, but it was no good, the gag was too secure. He whispered, 'Tell Kendrick.'

Then she was out of sight behind him.

*

Later he had time, plenty of it, to reflect on what happened, on whether he could have averted it in some way with a shouted instruction, a warning of some sort. Whether, indeed, he was responsible for it by omission. But as the men shifted their stance and tightened their grips on their weapons and he drew close enough to see the dilation of their pupils in the darkness, all Purkiss was thinking of were the chances of not only taking down two armed men who were fully expecting him to make such a move, but also surviving the assault from whatever backup they had waiting in the shadows.

Signals were useful things when preparing for a combat situation. The fall of the drop of sweat that had been gathering in the armpit, the next cry of the owl off in the trees, the final chime of a clock striking the hour: all could provide a focus point for the launching of an attack. This time he was waiting for Elle's shout, the sign that Abby had reached the point of safety.

And Elle's voice came, high and clear against the thrumming of the rain, though it wasn't the word they'd agreed – *now* – but rather one that while sounding similar carried an altogether more terrible significance.

'No.'

Thirty

Purkiss had once read about the intriguing hypothesis that time was an entirely human construct, and did not, in any valid sense, exist. Instead, what people regarded as units of time – minutes, seconds, moments or instants – were really quantum states that happened to be stacked up alongside one another in space (which *did* exist, provably), like the infinitesimally altered series of pictures that when run together tricked the human eye and became a cartoon.

He'd found the concept a tricky one to get to grips with. He came close to grasping it during the events that followed Elle's cry. The free flow of time became a series of snapshot images that engrained themselves on his memory.

In the first picture, the two men immediately in front of him were bracing their bent legs and sighting horizontally down their arms, their eyes widened slightly, ready to fire imminently; but one of the men had his gaze fixed not on Purkiss's face but on a point past his left shoulder.

In the next picture Purkiss, whose head was now turned slightly to the left, was looking at a human figure in the sparse trees over to his left, a black-clad man with a rifle gripped in his hands, not Kendrick. In the corner of his vision was Abby's small figure.

In the third picture the man among the trees had lifted the rifle and was taking aim at a point off to Purkiss's left, while a second man beside him held a pistol in a two-handed grip and aimed in the same direction. Still on the periphery of Purkiss's visual field, Abby's leg was extended behind her in the first thrust of a running movement.

Picture number four: Purkiss was in the middle of a lunge towards the trees and the men among the trees were larger and one, the man with the handgun, was facing Purkiss, his mouth an O of surprise and anger, his gun arm lagging and still pointed away. In the left corner of the visual field Abby was several yards further with her run. On the right, one of the two gunmen towards whom Purkiss had been walking was airborne, diving towards him at an angle to head him off.

In the fifth picture, Purkiss was half-turned towards the man diving from his right, his fist inches past the man's jaw. The man's head was snapped sideways, while among the trees the men were looking back in Abby's direction.

In the sixth picture Purkiss was almost at the trees. The man with the rifle was ducking and looking askance at the other man, the one with the handgun in the two-handed grip, whose head was shearing in a fan of blood and bone.

In the seventh picture Purkiss was on the ground, felled, and looking with his head to one side along the expanse of lawn and path away from the tower. Far on the edge of the pool of light was Kendrick, tiny and beetly at this distance, his mouth stretched wide, the flash from his gun's muzzle a bright star above his hands.

In the eighth picture Purkiss, still on the ground, saw beyond the towering forest of lawn grass Abby's shape suspended in the air, legs buckled and hands still trussed behind her.

In the ninth and final picture: the same landscape of grass blades made huge by nearness, but no people.

No Abby.

*

The Jacobin wanted to seize him by the lapels.

'What are you doing?'

Kuznetsov ignored him, shouted an order. Two of the men, running at a crouch, moved in, the others provising covering fire.

'Shoot him there.'

Again Kuznetsov ignored him. The Jacobin backed away several steps around the curve of the tower, away from the crashing of the guns, the screaming. He kept his eyes on the tableau. Elle was out of sight, having retreated over the crest of the hill, driven back by the barrage of gunfire. The man, Purkiss's other friend, was somewhere over to the right, lost in the trees. The Jacobin had seen the man's shot take down Kuznetsov's man, had watched the concentrated fire sent in return.

The girl, Abby, had been lifted impossibly high into the air by the burst from Kuznetsov's man's rifle, so high that a ripple of awe, of disbelief, had spread among even these battle-hardened men. The sound of her body hitting the ground had been audible even through the gunfire and the rain. She hadn't moved after that.

The rifleman had shown himself too soon. Yes, the girl had had to die, they'd agreed on that. She couldn't be allowed to reveal what she knew, had seemed to be trying to pass the information on to Purkiss himself when she passed him during the exchange. But if they'd waited until they had Purkiss, they could have taken her out with ease, then dealt with Elle and Purkiss's other sidekick at their leisure. Instead, Elle had shouted a warning, having seen the rifle emerge from the trees. Purkiss had tried heroics, had managed to knock down one of the gunmen.

They should have shot him where he lay. What was to be gained by taking him prisoner? The Jacobin stared at Kuznetsov's back, thinking of Churchill's description of Russia: *a riddle wrapped inside an enigma*.

*

The roaring in his ears continued, even when he closed his mouth. He realised it wasn't him but the aftershock of the gunfire. He tried to move his arms, but they were pinioned behind him, something slicing into his flesh. He couldn't move his legs because he was kneeling with his torso forced down over his lap and a gun muzzle at the back of his neck. His back hurt from the blow that had dropped him.

He raised his head just enough to see the dark shape on the grass.

Abby, gone. Failed. But, worse than that, *gone*.

From above and behind him he heard a voice, one steeled with authority: 'Forget them. Let's go.'

Men swarmed back across the lawns and the paths, one or two walking backwards with their guns trained into the distance. The ones who reached Abby's body stepped around it, ignoring it.

They were going to leave her there for the dogs and the rats.

Hands jerked him to his feet. He registered a face in front of him, dimly familiar as the bull-necked man who'd stalked him on the streets and in the night club. The man was laughing, his mouth a grotesque gargoyle's rictus in the harsh rainy lamplight.

From a place deep within him that he'd never be able to find if he looked for it, Purkiss summoned something terrible and brought his forehead hammering into the laughing maw.

The blows came, then, to face and belly and the backs of his legs. On his knees once more he continued fighting, shaking his head like a dog resisting a collar so that one man had to brace a knee in the small of his back while another two gripped his head to keep it still. Yet another man pulled the canvas hood over it.

Darkness. A last shattering blow full into his face made the roaring stop as well.

Thirty-One

Venedikt sat in the front passenger seat, Leok driving. He watched the sparse night traffic dwindling as the city receded and they wove through the slumbering fields and flatlands to the west. Full sunrise was nearly four hours away. Even the first flames of light would not light the horizon for another three. Behind his car was another with Dobrynin and two of his men. In front, the nondescript van with the windowless rear compartment, containing four armed men and their prize. Venedikt's prize.

It was a risk. A calculated one, but a risk nevertheless. The Englishman had stood back, watching silently, saying nothing after his initial protests. Venedikt did not need to explain himself to anyone, least of all a turncoat *Angli*. But he understood the Englishman's puzzlement and frustration. Perhaps it would have been better to have offered a reason for keeping Purkiss alive. Venedikt assumed the reason would be guessed: Purkiss had killed or left dead in his wake six of Venedikt's men, and would be made to pay the price for this before he himself was dispatched.

The risk was that the Englishman would work out Venedikt's true intentions. Venedikt thought this unlikely. Even if by some leap of the imagination the Englishman did make the connection, what would he do with the knowledge? Inform the police? Venedikt despised the Englishman – knew his feelings were reciprocated – but had always had a good nose for commitment in another person, and had noticed this quality in the Englishman in abundance. Also, if Kuznetsov went down, the Englishman knew he would go down with him.

The car's heater needed to be on because of the cold, but the air was stuffy. Venedikt pressed the button to lower the window on his side, breathed deeply through his nose, savouring the bright aromas of wet fields and woodsmoke. A year of planning, then the frustration of major complications in the last two days. But here he was, six hours from his goal, the path ahead cleared.

He was going to pull it off.

*

The Jacobin let himself into the flat, pulled up one of the chairs around the dining table. He preferred it over the armchairs: they were too low and rising from them would be difficult before long. He needed rest, badly, and sleep, but could afford neither. The usual stroll through the night-time streets was of course out of the question now.

He made the necessary phone call, then folded the handset away, surprised at how difficult he had found the exchange. It must be the tiredness. Sentimentality, emotional weakness in general, always showed through like a garish undercoat when the outer layers got rubbed thin by fatigue. It wasn't a matter to dwell on because he needed to think about what to do about the Russian.

Up until the Jacobin had impersonated Fallon's voice on the phone to Purkiss, he'd considered the far-fetched notion that Purkiss was somehow in league with Fallon, that his stated pursuit of the man was a smokescreen of some kind. But Purkiss's reaction to hearing "Fallon"'s voice – immediate, unquestioning hatred – convinced the Jacobin. Purkiss was hunting the man, wanted him as badly as he said. This validated the Jacobin's earlier plan, told him he'd been right to play Purkiss along in the hope that he'd find Fallon. But he'd failed, and now he, Purkiss, was in Kuznetsov's hands.

Had Kuznetsov killed Fallon? Tortured him, gone too far and lost him, and now taken Purkiss as a replacement? But why torture either man, unless out of wanton cruelty, something the Jacobin thought unlikely? Perhaps Kuznetsov entertained delusions about being a spymaster, and had decided to kick off his career by beating as much information as he could about the British SIS out of two of its former agents. Again, possible, but implausible.

The problem was, the Jacobin had no idea where Kuznetsov had taken Purkiss, where the new base was. Kuznetsov had mentioned earlier during the planning stages of the operation that there was a second base, as an alternative should the farm be compromised, but he'd kept quiet about its location and the Jacobin hadn't pressed him, assuming the farm would remain secure. With hindsight it had been a mistake. He had tried phoning Kuznetsov earlier, just before reaching the flat. The number was no longer in service. Kuznetsov was cutting all ties, getting rid of his phone so that he couldn't be tracked.

The Jacobin rose uncomfortably from the chair and went into the bathroom and splashed water on his face, then filled a tooth glass and drank. In the bath the body looked cramped, its face turned downward so that only a quarter was visible. There would be plenty of time to move it later on, after eight o'clock had come and gone.

He stood at the sink, finishing the water, gazing at the huddled mass, and was reminded of the much smaller crumpled figure of the girl on the lawn. In mid-swallow the thought struck him.

Purkiss had gone into the exchange knowing there was no escape for him, that if he wasn't killed immediately he'd be taken captive. In which case, what precautions had he taken to allow his colleagues to track his whereabouts after his capture?

314

The Jacobin put down the glass, took out his phone.

*

Down the steps he was shoved, vertigo and the lack of visual cues making them seem steeper than they really were. His shoulders bashed off the walls. At the bottom he finally lost his balance and tipped forwards, unable to use his trussed hands to break his fall, colliding face-first with something wooden – a door, he guessed – that was like yet another punch to his swollen nose and lips, sending a surge of pain all the way through his head to the back of his neck.

Hands steadied Purkiss and he heard the faint whine of hinges and another shove propelled him into a wider space, judging by the slight echo. He regained his footing and stood and a heavy scrape behind him was followed by the jarring of some hefty object against the backs of his knees and now the hands were on his shoulders pressing him down on to the chair and he felt something like plastic cord being lashed around his torso and binding him to the back of the seat. He drew a deep breath, held it as long as he could, inflating his chest so the cords would be looser when he exhaled, trying to ignore the screaming of his bruised and cracked ribs.

The hood was pulled off abruptly, the scab gumming the wet stiff khaki to his nose torn away. The sudden return of vision after an hour or more of varying shades of darkness was shocking as a car crash. To turn his head hurt too much, but he was aware of three men surrounding him. One of them squatted before him and brought hot sour breath close to his face. It was the bull-necked man he'd headbutted earlier, his rotten teeth bent and bloodied in his mouth. The man stared into his eyes for a long minute, then hawked and spat blackly into one of them before Purkiss could blink.

The man stood and looked down at him and Purkiss prepared himself for the beating to start again, but the man muttered something Purkiss didn't catch and he and the other two went through the door to Purkiss's left and closed it. He heard a key being turned in a lock and their footsteps echoing rapidly up the steps. He squeezed his eye, trying to force out as much of the phlegm and blood as he could, blinked several times and peered around.

It was a basement, almost exactly square, the grey walls plastered but unpainted Two strips of blue-yellow fluorescent lighting in the ceiling provided illumination. The only exit was the door he'd been pushed through. There were no windows or skylights. Purkiss was secured to a chair with plastic flex around his torso from chest to hips. His hands remained fastened separately behind his back. The chair was a solid steel one of the sort used in prisons and secure psychiatric units, too heavy to be picked up and used as a projectile.

The three men had left, but he wasn't alone.

Sitting opposite him, ten feet away on a similar chair, was a man, shorter and slighter than Purkiss, his head lowered but his eyes watching him.

The pain in Purkiss's face, the stabs of his ribs with each respiration, the ache throbbing at his kidneys, all faded like a radio signal being tuned out. All sensations, not just sight and sound but those of smell and touch and even taste, seemed focused of their own accord on the man in the chair.

Purkiss had taken a kick to his throat but the word emerged clearly enough, the harshness due to reasons other than injury.

'Fallon.'

Thirty-Two

The laptop was where he'd left it, in the back of the car, and the Jacobin took his time ascending the stairs back up to the flat. He opened the computer on the dining table and typed in the wi-fi key. In a few seconds the internet connection was established.

The girl, Abby, hadn't had time to shut down the sites she'd been connected to when he'd surprised her in the hotel room. They sprang up in a series of windows: Google Earth, which he closed, and another, a GPS tracking site which informed him that the session had expired and inviting him to log in again. He chose this option and was immediately prompted for a user name and password. The user name was already filled in: Abbyholt53.

He sat, elbows on the table and hands folded at his lips, chin propped on his thumbs. He knew nothing about the dead girl, hadn't the faintest idea what she might use as a password.

Before taking her from the hotel room – he'd marched her straight past the reception desk and she'd been calm about it, possibly because of the knife at her back – the Jacobin had grabbed her rucksack as well as the laptop. Now he emptied the rucksack on to the table. Computer disks, an MP3 player with headphones, toiletries which she hadn't got around to unpacking, a wallet.

He gutted the wallet swiftly. Banknotes and loose change, British and Estonian. Credit and debit cards, one each. A clutch of photographs in plastic windows: two people he took to be her parents.

And one of Purkiss, a clear shot of his face even though he wasn't looking at the camera, didn't even seem aware he was being photographed.

The Jacobin frowned at it, then put the wallet aside and pulled the laptop back in front of him and in the space marked *password* he typed *purkiss* and hit enter.

Password incorrect.

He typed *johnpurkiss*.

For a moment the screen went blank. Then a telephone number appeared, and beside it the words: *signal lost*.

He sat back. So, he had access, but no signal, which meant that either Purkiss hadn't taken along his phone, or Kuznetsov had taken it from him and destroyed it.

The Jacobin kept the laptop open on the off chance that the situation changed.

*

Fallon remained motionless, continuing to watch Purkiss from beneath a lowered brow.

Purkiss had wondered what his reaction would be, seeing him for the first time. Would he feel overwhelming fury, be swamped by grief? But all he found himself thinking was, *it wasn't him on the phone.*

There was nothing to say as an opening gambit that wouldn't sound hopelessly melodramatic, so Purkiss said nothing. The silence was boken only by his breathing, harsh and loud through his swollen throat, by intermittent far-off bangs and echoes, and the faint buzzing of the fluorescent strips.

In the end it was Fallon who spoke first. 'What time is it?'

The voice... Last heard in the courtroom, where he'd barely spoken, it now caused time to telescope so that to Purkiss days rather than years had passed since they'd last encountered each other.

All he was able to reply was, 'I don't know.'

'No, of course not. I mean, what time was it when you last looked, and how long ago was that, do you think?'

There was something off about the voice now that he'd spoken for longer, a mushiness in the sibilants, and in a moment Purkiss got it. Several of the man's teeth were missing. Without stopping to wonder why he was answering in so conversational a way, Purkiss said, 'Four o'clock, and it was about an hour ago, I'd say.'

'Four o'clock in the afternoon?'

'The morning.'

'Jesus.'

When they'd been friends, Fallon and Claire and Purkiss, Fallon had used to pronounce the word with a deliberately exaggerated Irishness – *Jaysis* – for comical effect, but he didn't now. It came out quiet, heartfelt.

'How long have you been here?'

'I've no idea.'

Fallon was lashed to the chair just as Purkiss was to his, if anything more securely so, his legs bound one to each chair leg. He wore an open-necked shirt filthy with old dried blood. The whites of his eyes were webbed red and a cut beneath one eye gaped stickily. His nose appeared intact, but his lower lip was a swollen wedge of meat.

Purkiss understood, then, what Fallon's stare had meant in the long minutes after they were left alone. The man had been utterly astonished to see him.

*

It was like a bizarre type of motionless, silent sparring. Purkiss did not know what to say, where to begin. Fallon clearly had lots he wanted to say, urgently, but his words were kept at bay by the huge, the all-encompassing fact that both separated and joined them. *Spliced*, thought

Purkiss absently: that was a good double-edged word to describe the dynamic.

*

An hour passed, or possibly ten minutes. Neither man dropped his gaze.

Fallon ended the silence again, his mouth moving with the sticky sound of somebody deficient in saliva.

'We have two things to talk about. One is more urgent. Why don't we address that first.'

Purkiss said nothing.

'Why are you here?'

Purkiss watched the face but the question seemed genuine.

'I came here to find you.'

'How did you know –'

'Somebody sent me a photo of you in Tallinn.'

Fallon blinked slowly, as if considering this.

'What are *you* doing here?' said Purkiss.

'Trying to stop an attack on the summit.' He coughed, broke off wincing. 'Today, is it? It's the morning of the thirteenth?'

'Yes. There's about three hours to go.' Purkiss would have leaned forward if he could, the urgency beginning to take hold. 'Keep talking.'

'I'm on a Service operation. It's why they got me out of Belmarsh. A rogue Service agent here in Tallinn is helping Kuznetsov, the man who's holding us here.'

'Do you know which one? Which of the three agents?'

Fallon stared. 'You know them?'

'Yes.'

'No, I never discovered which one.'

'Teague.'

'You stopped him?' said Fallon.

'No.'

'He's still at large?'

'Yes.'

Fallon closed his eyes, nodded, then looked at Purkiss again. 'Briefly, I got close to one of Kuznetsov's crew. A woman.'

'Lyuba Ilkun.'

'You know that, too. I was hoping to get on board the operation. I'd convinced her, I think. Kuznetsov on the other hand was suspicious. They grabbed me several days ago, might have been a week – you lose track.'

'You've been down here all the time?'

'No. They were keeping me in some kind of cellar until a few hours ago. Hooded me, brought me here.'

A cellar. It would have been the farmhouse.

Purkiss said: 'You've been roughed up. What did they ask you?'

'The usual. Who I was working for, who I was working with. It was pretty bad in the beginning – they're amateurs at this but what they lack in finesse they make up for in brute force – but they eased up after a while. As though Kuznetsov realised he wasn't going to get me to talk, and wanted to keep me intact until he could find out who I was by other means. They've left me entirely alone for the last day or so, apart from feeding me. And moving me here.'

Purkiss was thinking rapidly, sifting through conversations in his memory. 'They don't know that you're Service?'

'They might suspect it. I certainly didn't tell them.'

It fell into place with what Purkiss thought must be an audible click. 'They do now.'

'How so?'

'Teague doesn't know Kuznetsov has you. Or at least he didn't when I first met him. As soon as I told him and the other two agents I was looking for you, he would have got on to Kuznetsov and asked him if he'd heard of you, without telling him who you were.'

Fallon's frown deepened.

Purkiss went on: 'Kuznetsov didn't tell Teague he had you, but I think Teague suspected that he did. It's why Teague let me carry on, why he didn't just hand me over to Kuznetsov from the word go. Teague wanted me to find you because he wanted to find you himself. He knew you were here to stop the operation, so he needed to be assured that you'd been neutralised. Later, I met Kuznetsov's second in command, Dobrynin –'

'The one with the mutilated hand. He was one of my interrogators.'

'Right. I told him I was looking for you and that you were a former SIS agent. I did it to gauge his reaction. He looked delighted.'

'So why would Kuznetsov hang on to me after he'd learned who I was, and why has he kept it a secret from Teague?'

'Maybe –' Purkiss stopped. There was no *maybe*. He didn't know.

They fell silent, Purkiss listening for footsteps, Kuznetsov's men returning to tell them to stop talking. None came.

'Do you know what's planned for the summit?' said Fallon.

'The assassination of the Russian president.'

'How?'

'I don't know. Do you?'

Again Fallon shook his head. 'The closest I got to finding anything out was when Lyuba used to talk about the "event". All very abstract.'

Purkiss felt the unspoken thing rising between them again. It wasn't time, yet, and he said: 'All right. A full debrief.'

'Agreed.'

'You first.'

*

On the screen a reporter, one of the network's heavyweights and looking unfeasibly bright and awake given the hour, yammered away against the backdrop of the Memorial. Police bearing very visible light arms hove into view from time to time, not accidentally. At the bottom of the screen a ticker tape relayed information about little else. Every now and again the picture cut away to the hotel where the president was staying overnight, an aerial shot making the early morning helicopters look like circling moths.

Venedikt drank tea, replenishing his glass as quickly as he emptied it. On the screen a related human-interest piece showed a group of young people in Moscow raising a raucous toast to their new friends in Estonia. This was followed by the now-familiar footage of the president arriving at the reception banquet the night before. As the camera closed on his face, Venedikt raised his own glass.

The supreme sacrifice, *tovarisch*. Just as his grandfather had made.

And a brilliant plan, meticulously conceived, was now going to be made perfect. All along, Kuznetsov had striven not to leave any fingerprints. In a few hours from now, when the world was picking over the pieces, fingerprints would indeed be found.

The fingerprints of the British Secret Service.

Thirty-Three

Ventilation in the basement was poor, and the sweat was moulding Purkiss's clothes to his body, adding to the sense of restriction imposed by the bonds. He blinked, tried to flick the stinging droplets from the corners of his eyes.

'So, you see,' he said, 'things don't add up.'

Fallon's story had been a masterclass in the art of the debriefing: rapid, clipped, not a word wasted. Released early from Belmarsh with an unconditional pardon, sent to Tallinn because of preliminary intelligence suggesting activity potentially detrimental to the forthcoming summit visit, he'd picked up the Kuznetsov link through old-fashioned legwork, haunting bars and clubs frequented by ex-military types. At the same time he had learned of the unofficial cell of SIS agents, the trio working without Embassy cover. Pillow talk from Lyuba had confirmed that Kuznetsov's operation, whatever it was, was being assisted by a British intelligence agent, and that this person wasn't connected with the Embassy. Fallon didn't think Lyuba knew herself who the agent was.

And he'd been sharing a flat with an SIS agent-in-place called Jaak Seppo. It was the part that didn't make sense.

Purkiss listened without comment, then relayed his own story, less succinctly, leaving out any mention of Vale, saying only that "a contact" in London had passed on to him the picture of Fallon that Seppo had sent him.

Now he said, 'Why would Seppo shop you to my contact, knowing he'd get in touch with me?'

'I don't know.'

Had there been the slightest hesitation there?

'You're not telling me everything, Fallon.'

This time the pause was definite.

'No, I'm not.'

Purkiss waited. When Fallon stayed silent he said, 'A full debrief. We agreed.'

'There's something I can't tell you now.'

'Damn it, Fallon.'

'I can't explain why. It doesn't affect the position we're in.'

'For the love of God –'

'I will explain. I promise. Once we're out of here, once we've stopped Kuznetsov.'

And so it had come to be, without being made explicit by either of them before. They were allies, working together towards a common goal. Old buddies again.

Purkiss hadn't breathed in but he felt his chest swelling, the agony in his ribs so intense it became almost pleasurable. He stared at this man, battered, bloodied, teeth smashed. Pitiable.

'You killed Claire.'

Fallon's head had been hanging forward, his gaze downcast. Now he lifted his eyes.

'Yes,' he said.

*

Understanding came fully formed, not in stealthy increments. The Jacobin sat down under the enormity of it.

He was in the kitchen, forcing himself to take food despite having no appetite. Beyond the window the city napped through the darkest hours, as reluctant to rest as he was.

Kuznetsov had had Fallon, all along. Had taken him captive while he was courting the Ilkun woman, and had found out somehow that he was SIS. Now he had Purkiss, another former SIS operative. Two British agents.

He was going to use them to implicate the Service in the attack.

Fury at oneself was never productive, never ever, and the Jacobin struggled to suppress it. *If you'd worked it out earlier, you'd have taken care of Purkiss yourself rather than deliver him to the Russian.* Kuznetsov might still have used Fallon, but a single agent could have been attributed to coincidence. With two, the hand of SIS would be unmistakeable.

My Service. Destroyed, utterly. Because that would be the result. Conflict on a global scale, and attributable squarely to the British intelligence service. Whatever the eventual outcome, SIS would cease to exist, both in fact and in legend. All the good it had done, all the noble achievements of the previous hundred years, would be dissolved in the acid of its treachery. A treachery not only towards Britain, but towards humanity as a whole.

It was the outcome exactly, *diametrically* opposed to the one the Jacobin had set out to achieve.

He sat staring at the wet city on the other side of the glass, and wondered if it was time to pull the plug.

*

'There are things we need to talk about.'

'We've nothing to talk about. There's nothing I want to say to you, or to hear from you.'

It was true. During Fallon's trial Purkiss had rehearsed in obsessive detail the possible ways a conversation would go between the two of them. He'd never been permitted to communicate with Fallon, and afterwards, after the conviction and sentencing, he'd avoided visiting him in prison. Now he knew why. Words seemed utterly trivial, a form of non-communication between them.

Fallon's eyes were almost closed. 'It's difficult to explain. There are things you don't know about what went on.'

'Excuses? Is that what you're talking about? And you think it would do me good to hear them, would help me to achieve *closure* by understanding your point of view and defusing some of the hate?' Despite himself Purkiss laughed, a guttural sound. 'Thanks for the concern, but if I go to my grave hating you that'll suit me fine.'

'No. Not excuses.'

'Oh, I'm sorry. Is that too value-laden a word?' He fought to stop his voice rising. '*Justifications*, then. Justifications for murder.'

'I didn't murder her.'

'You just said you did.'

'I said I killed her.'

'That's –' Purkiss drew a deep breath, all the way in, ignoring the pain flaring in protest. 'Don't split hairs with me now, Fallon. Don't you dare do that.'

'Or what?' It was Fallon's turn to laugh, without mirth. 'You'll hit me? Kill me? Go ahead, give it a try.'

Purkiss's pulse was up. It wasn't good. The adrenaline would be wasted.

More quietly Fallon said, 'I'm not goading you. It's a serious point. We're trapped here. If we cooperate, you'll be able to kill me. If we don't, we'll both die. As will countless others.'

For the first time Purkiss shut his eyes, not wanting to see the man's face, wishing he could shut his ears as well.

Fallon went on: 'I'm being cryptic because if I tell you everything I need to tell you, we won't be able to cooperate –'

'Nothing more you could say would make me less willing to cooperate with you –'

'Trust me. When I tell you eventually, you'll understand. But I promise you, John. Full disclosure. Nothing held back. After we get out of this.'

Purkiss opened his eyes and stared at the man, taking in every detail of his face, inoculating himself against his presence.

'And then I'm going to kill you.'

'Fair enough.'

'I'm not joking, Fallon.'

'I know you're not.' A beat. 'We need to come up with a plan.'

'I've got one already.'

*

Thumb poised over the green "call" key, the Jacobin stared at the number on the display. It was one he'd never used before, that of the *Kaitsepolitsei*, the Security Police.

He'd be assumed to be a crank, so confident would the KaPo be about its security arrangements, until he revealed how the assassination was going to be carried out; then he'd be taken seriously, and although he wouldn't stay on the phone long enough to be traced, there was no question the summit would be aborted. Then what? It would be a victory of sorts, a major summit derailed by a terrorist threat, but a Pyrrhic one, as the intelligence services of both Estonia and Russia would spin it as a successful example of international cooperation. The summit would simply be rescheduled. And, there was a real risk of Kuznetsov's being tracked down and captured, in which case he, the Jacobin, would be named, and SIS would be implicated after all.

After a long moment the Jacobin hit "cancel" and put the phone away.

*

Purkiss paused, the muscles burning in his thighs and his belly, sweat slicking his hair to his forehead.

Six inches, he estimated. Half a foot of progress after five minutes of struggle.

If his arms had been fastened behind the back of the chair it would have been easier. He could have used them to give him forward momentum. Instead, his wrists were pressed between the small of his back and the back of the chair, secured to each other with plastic ties, the toughest bonds of all. He was able to achieve forward motion only by bracing the balls of his feet on the concrete floor of the basement, and thrusting his pelvis forwards using all the strength in his abdominal and anterior thigh muscles and those of his hamstrings. Each such thrust caused the feet of the chair to scrape a fraction of an inch forward, an almost comically poor return on his efforts.

Facing him, Fallon urged him on, silently. They would have reached each other more quickly if Fallon had been inching forward similarly, but Fallon's ankles were tied to the legs of the chair and no amount of rocking would budge him.

In between surges of exertion, Purkiss felt the blood hammering in his ears. He tried not to listen out for footsteps coming down the stairs, because if he heard them there'd be nothing he could do about them. Whoever came through the door would notice the progress he'd made, however meagre, and would move him and Fallon so far apart that all bets would be off.

Purkiss squeezed his eyelids shut against the sweat sting once again. He visualised the run-up to a long jump. Not just any long jump, but one that traversed a ravine, dark and bottomless. In his mind's eye he was loping up a grassy verge towards a small peak, the air cool and rarefied about him. As he approached the peak he picked up speed so that the lope turned into a sprint, and the nub of rock was coming on fast. He put everything into the final push, embracing the terror that leapt at him as his feet left the rock and cycled in the empty space over the terrible yawn of the chasm. Impossibly, defying the laws of physics, he was across and rolling and clear.

Fallon grunted something. Purkiss opened his eyes, disorientated for a moment. Looking down and around he saw he'd progressed an entire foot. Not bad.

'*Bastard.*'

'*Die*, damn you. *Die now.*'

It wasn't difficult for Purkiss to make his share of the shouting sound heartfelt.

They'd waited till Purkiss had got within two feet, his chair slightly to the side of Fallon's, before letting rip: nonsensical bellows alternating with profane curses. In the midst of it Fallon leaned forward as far as he could and tried an experimental butt. His forehead nudged Purkiss's nose.

The bootsteps came, then, at a dash, more than one pair, and in counterpoint to their rhythm the frantic jangling of keys. Purkiss glared into Fallon's eyes and gave a nod.

Fallon tilted his head back as if to sneeze and brought his face forward so that the frontal bones of his skull smashed into Purkiss's nose, snapping his head back against the chair. White light exploded up beneath his eyes, crowding out all sound and sight. Apart from the blood: there was a *lot* of blood, he was gratified to see. He flailed his head from side to side, flinging cords of gore-streaked mucus against the nearest wall and against the opening door.

As the first man stepped through, Purkiss threw his head back and arched his spine and rolled his eyes up and bit down on his tongue hard enough to draw more blood. He began to jerk his legs assymetrically.

Near his ear, one of the men yelled an oath involving somebody's mother. Purkiss felt hands grip his shoulders. He let the spasms ebb as the men, two of them, he thought, shouted in Russian that they needed to get him on the floor. The cords around his torso slackened and were unwound. He risked a glance and saw one of the men punch Fallon in the face, one-two, rocking his head to either side in turn. The man holding Purkiss tried to control his descent, but Purkiss let himself be dead weight and slipped through the man's grasp. He hit the floor, his head cracking audibly against the concrete. The man snarled at his companion to leave the bastard alone and come and help him.

Purkiss lay twitching on the floor, listening to the rising panic in the men's voices. He was wondering whether to void his bladder for added realism when one of the men said, 'Get him upstairs,' catching him under the arms while the other man took his feet. Only his wrists were fastened behind him now, no hood this time.

As they lugged him up the steps, the slumped Fallon and the basement receding through the doorway, Purkiss made his move.

Thirty-Four

The hangar echoed with the clang and scrape of tools, the footfalls of the men. They moved about, checking fluid levels, the pressure of the oxygen system, all things that had already been investigated but needed reviewing now that the move from the farm had taken place, in case there had been any changes in transit. Dobrynin with his technical knowledge took charge.

Venedikt walked slowly round the Black Hawk, keeping out of the men's way, gazing at the low-slung structure in something approaching rapture.

He hadn't pressed the arms dealer, the man of obscure nationality and ethnicity, on the detail of where he had procured the helicopter. It was none of Venedikt's concern. But the man had at one point spoken of a contact in Turkey, and Venedikt knew the Turkish Army was one of the international clients to whom the Sikorsky company exported its most famous chopper. Dobrynin had confirmed it was a basic UH-60A model, with the crucial modification of wing stubs.

Venedikt had examined the helicopter already, had twice seen it in flight when Leok, his pilot as well as driver, had taken it from the site of purchase to the farmhouse and again when he had taken off from the farmhouse en route to the current backup location. Now, with no pressing problems to distract him, Venedikt was able for the first time fully to appreciate its beauty, the terrible power that seemed contained in its silent length and beneath the canopy of its rotor like a demon trapped in an amulet, awaiting release.

The Black Hawk was far and away the more expensive of the two purchases he had made from the dealer, but if anything it was less important, less of a catch, than the other.

Leok, seated in the cockpit, conferred with Dobrynin, who stood alongside. Squatting and examining the front wheel was Lyuba. She'd been a helicopter pilot and mechanic in the unit, and had come recommended to Venedikt on this basis. She had, he acknowledged, delivered them the prize of Fallon, even if inadvertently. She was to be afforded the honour of being included in the final leg of the operation. The *mission*. The word was better, gave a sense of the purpose driving their plans.

There had been those among his men – and he counted Lyuba as one of his *men* – who'd wanted Fallon and Purkiss despatched with a bullet each. It was their *bodies* that were necessary, they'd argued. But bullet wounds would raise suspicions. Far better to allow the two men to perish in the conflagration that was to follow. Venedikt had prevailed, of course. None of the arguments had been meant as serious challenges to his authority. But he understood the fury of his men. Purkiss had reduced their numbers to the current rump of a dozen. It was natural that vengeance should be sought.

Vengeance would be theirs, he'd assured them. All they could do themselves was kill the man, but far worse was the fate that history would inflict upon Purkiss: the death of his very name under the curses of a thousand million spitting tongues, day after day, for ever.

*

Purkiss waited until the man at his legs paused to adjust his grip, then flexed his knees and his hips, the sudden movement pulling his shins free from the man's arms. He pistoned his legs so that both his feet caught the man full in the abdomen just below the ribcage, the force of the kick driving the man backwards and upwards. His head cracked against the frame at the top of the low doorway hard enough that flakes of plaster broke adrift. The impact against the man's torso had pushed Purkiss back against the man holding him under the arms. The man stumbled back against the steps. Purkiss landed on him and jerked his head backwards, trying to connect his skull with the man's face, but missed. The man recovered quickly, writhing out from underneath. Purkiss twisted his head round and got his teeth into the man's right ankle above his low-topped boot. He clamped his jaws tight around a mouthful of choking sock and yielding flesh.

The man yelled and jerked his leg loose, the movement making him lose his balance. Still on his back, Purkiss braced his feet on one of the steps and heaved back and up, launching his head into the man's exposed groin. With a shriek the man fell on his backside. Purkiss turned and found his feet. The man was already trying to stand but Purkiss brought a knee up under his chin and heard teeth gnash and shatter. The man sprawled and slid down a step before coming to rest.

Wrists still fastened behind his back, Purkiss squatted beside the man. With the fingers of his right hand he grabbed the grip of the pistol protruding from the man's belt and prised the gun out. As the man he'd kicked down the steps rose in the doorway below, weaving, his own pistol out and aimed, Purkiss turned side-on and fired twice.

The first shot went wide and the ricochet whined off the door jamb, making him half-duck. The second took the man in the chest, sending him back once more through the doorway. From below, he heard Fallon hiss, but there was no time to go back, they'd agreed on that. Purkiss crouched again and searched the pockets of the man sprawled on the steps, duckwalking awkwardly around him until his trussed hands found what they were looking for inside his jacket. A mobile phone.

Purkiss straightened and pushed the phone in his back pocket. He took the remaining stairs at a run, horribly aware that he had no sense of spatial orientation and had no idea what he would find at the top or which way he should head once there. Another door stood closed at the top in the left-hand wall. He pushed it open with his knee, didn't pause because there'd be no point, but charged through. He found himself in a narrow corridor, impersonally painted and uncarpeted – *he was in some kind of office building* – with no lighting of its own, but faint illumination coming from each end, a doorway limned in light to his left. To his right, a window looked out onto the exterior, swatches of rain flicking against the glass.

He ran at the window. Behind him came noise as the door opened and the shouting began. The window looked double glazed and wouldn't therefore yield in time. He glanced back over his shoulder where two figures were crowding into the corridor. He aimed backwards and fired a salvo, one of the men howling and twisting away. The other crouched and *was taking aim* and Purkiss fired again, dropping and rolling as the shots sang by and chipped into the wall. One of them hit the window and it starred and shattered. From the ground, Purkiss fired back, a low and sweeping volley. The man at the other end danced to keep his legs out of the way, ducked back inside the door. Purkiss was up and tucking his head as tightly as he could into his chest.

With as fast a run-up as he could achieve in such a short distance he launched himself at the jagged remains of the window and into the wet dark.

The shock of cold air and rain clutched at his breath. He landed hard on his shoulder and rolled, keeping the momentum going, tumbling over and over down a soggy slope of dirt and gravel, resisting the screaming urge to stop and look back. Somewhere far off he heard shouting again and the firing started. Dimly he registered that the bullets were relatively low-velocity because he heard the *crump* of the shots before the stinging whine as they sang past him.

When the ground stopped sloping and ran level he rolled once more and peered around at a crouch, taking a moment to aim, and releasing three shots at the window he had come through. It was almost hidden behind the hump of the ground he'd rolled down but he saw a figure twitch away. He kept low, below the hump, and ran along the edge of it, away from the building, which he saw was a broad two-storey office block of some kind.

The squall was surging again, sheets of rain lashing and cracking at the mercy of a puckish wind. Ahead of him was a concrete wall that enclosed the property. On the other side of it was a field. He reached the wall and tried to leap it, but without the use of his hands it was impossible. He fell back, gasping.

Purkiss looked back. From this distance the building he had vacated suddenly had a context, slotting in among the other parts like a piece from a jigsaw puzzle. On the other side of the building was a row of large, squat, oblong structures that receded away, floodlights illuminating the nearest one. A series of hangars.

He was in an airfield, and a largely disused one by the look of it. Off to the left, far behind the office block and the hangars, an assortment of aircraft shells sat and rusted, their incomplete, gutted state visible even in the silhouettes that were all that was visible of them against the night sky. To the right, disappearing into the shadows thrown by the floodlights, was what looked like a runway.

Figures were emerging from around the building, three, four, their shouts carrying faintly through the rain, their faltering gaits suggesting they didn't know exactly where he was. He strained eyes and ears for the first evidence of dogs, but there was none. Purkiss thanked Kendrick silently. He'd disposed of all of them back at the farm.

On either side of him the wall stretched as far as he could see. The other side wasn't visible from this close to the wall, but on his approach down the slope he'd seen the flat field stretching some distance before clusters of trees began to appear. Purkiss scrambled along the base of the wall to his right, where it was darker, and peered at an approaching shape. A shed of some kind.

It was dilapidated, and the wooden door gave easily despite the awkwardness with which he was forced to pull at it, tearing around the padlock. Inside, tools and mechanical equipment mouldered, red with rust. He found a hacksaw that still showed some silver in its blade. Squinting over his shoulder, he clamped its handle in a vice on the edge of a workbench and began to rub the plastic tie around his wrists rapidly against the teeth, feeling the serrations bite through his flesh. His arms sprang free and he flexed them, revelling for an instant in the sensation. Then he picked up the pistol again – another SIG Sauer, perhaps standard issue with this outfit – and looked out through the door. He saw the figures, blurred through the rain, running towards the wall further back in the direction he'd come from. He stepped out, tested the door of the shed with both hands, and with a sharp tug wrenched it off its hinges.

He lugged the door over to the wall and propped it at an angle, thankful that it reached the top and that the holes punched in it by time and neglect looked as if they would serve as footholes. Instead of running up it, he headed off along the base of the wall on the other side of the shed, the way he'd been going.

His wrists were sticky, the blood black in the darkness. He thought, hysterical laughter rising and threatening to erupt: *you'll need a tetanus shot*.

They'd left him his watch, a sports model. He pressed the button for the backlight, saw the time. Five forty-nine.

Two hours to go.

Thirty-Five

The first sharp noise had been equivocal, a far-off echo like something falling, and none of his men reacted so Venedikt disregarded it. The second could not have been interpreted as anything other than a gunshot, muffled to some extent by the intervening walls and the rain, but unmistakeable in character. It was followed rapidly by a volley of gunfire.

Venedikt was already running toward the doors of the hangar when Dobrynin began to move. Venedikt shouted, 'Stay here,'beckoned with his fingers to two of the others – he needed Dobrynin and Lyuba unharmed – and drew his gun as he ran. The shots had come from inside somewhere. The office building was the most likely choice.

He saw it immediately, the broken window in the office building with the glass on the outside. As he approached, one of the men, Raskov, appeared in the frame and gasped, 'One of them's loose, Purkiss, he's armed.' Venedikt didn't pause to ask if the man was hit, if any of the others were down, just set off at a sprint down the slope in the direction of the far boundary of the airfield.

The cloud cover was absolute. The absence of starlight together with the haze of rain made Venedikt falter, so that the other three men, the evidently uninjured Raskov and the two from the hangar, caught up with him. There was no point blundering into an ambush.

'Spread out,' he said. They spaced themselves ten feet apart, began to make their way across the sodden dirt and grass towards the wall. He took out his phone and hit the key for Dobrynin's number, wanting to tell him to send somebody into the office to make sure Fallon was still secure in the basement. There was no signal. This was something he hadn't planned for, the poor phone reception at the backup base, made worse by the weather.

Raskov found it, the shed door propped against the wall. On Venedikt's signal he scrambled up it and peered over.

'No sign.'

Venedikt said, 'Was he injured?'

'I don't think so. Not badly enough that he couldn't run, and he wasn't leaking blood.'

If Venedikt had been on his own he would have put his hand to his forehead, roared even. The loss of Purkiss in itself wasn't disastrous. He hadn't been a factor in the original plan and it could proceed without him. But although he wouldn't know where he was, and would find it extremely difficult to flag down transport to take him the eighty kilometres back into Tallinn at this hour of the morning, he still had over two hours to alert the authorities to the presence of a disused airfield somewhere out of town. By process of elimination Venedikt and his men would be found, eventually.

Two hours. Was it long enough?

The more men he dispatched to look for Purkiss the more likely he was to find him, but the higher the attrition rate was likely to be. For a moment he considered taking the Black Hawk up over the field to hunt for the man. He dismissed the idea. It was tempting fate, using his prize piece of equipment for a purpose it hadn't been intended for.

He made his decision. He, Lyuba, Dobrynin and Leok, the core personnel for the remainder of the mission, would remain at the hangar and proceed as before. The rest of his men would find Purkiss.

*

The wall led him away from the office building and the hangars. Purkiss followed it, stopping only to make out the vague shapes and sounds of men clustering where he'd propped the makeshift ladder. He satisfied himself that they weren't continuing their search along the wall, that they assumed as he'd hoped that he'd gone over to the other side.

When he reached the corner of the wall where it bent rightwards, and judged he was far enough away that it was unlikely sound would carry, he stopped again and took out the phone he'd lifted from the man on the basement steps. The signal icon had a defiant slash across it. When he tried to dial Elle's number a low repeated tone confirmed that he was out of range.

Purkiss took deep breaths through his mouth – his nose was swollen closed and he was afraid that the slightest attempt to force air through it would unplug a geyser – and prepared himself for what he was going to do. The treatment by Kuznetsov's men after his capture, the effect of seeing Fallon again, the head butt to his face, the escape, all contributed to the overpowering nausea that churned in his stomach. It would make matters easier.

He bent over near to the wall, put two fingers down his throat, and did it as quietly as he could. After two or three dry heaves it came, clots and ropes of swallowed blood mainly, but also the remnants of the sandwiches Elle had made. Bile stung his throat and his stoppered nose, and his eyes streamed. When he was sure he was finished he wiped away the tears and knelt. With his fingers he began to probe, disgust twisting his face.

He found the SIM card immediately, even in the dark, had in fact felt its sharp edges as it came up. He wiped it on his shirt tails until it felt as clean as it was likely to get. He didn't know how long a card could be exposed to stomach acids before it was rendered useless, but he supposed his education was about to be furthered. He swapped the card for the one in the phone. It was a long shot. Abby was no longer around to access the website from which she was tracking him, and he didn't know if Elle had the facilities to hack the site or in some other way locate the phone that held his SIM. He didn't know if Elle was even still alive, come to that.

From his corner he watched a figure detach itself from the group at the wall and move rapidly back up towards the buildings. The tableau was eerily still for a few moments, the fossil aircraft separating Purkiss from the hangars which brooded like great ancient megaliths in the gloom. Purkiss didn't have a clear view of the area between the floodlit hangar and the office building, but he saw the odd flicker of movement there. In time, two figures appeared and ran down the slope to join the others at the wall. He watched them clamber over. Five, then, on the other side. How many did that leave in the buildings?

He was at the back of the hangars, and none of the office windows were lit on this side of the building. He took a breath and began making his way back towards the structures, between the hulks of the abandoned planes, the SIG Sauer in his hand.

*

A scream jerked him awake. He cried out with pain and fought to keep himself upright, looking about in panic before orientation settled in.

The Jacobin was at the kitchen table, had dozed off slumped across it. Six fifteen. He'd been out for three quarters of an hour. He hadn't intended to fall asleep but it had done some good, he could feel it.

The scream had come from the television on the wall. It hadn't been a scream, rather a shout from a female reporter at a crowd scene, somewhere along the coast road on the way to the War Memorial. The rain seemed to have dwindled. Through the window the Jacobin saw smudges of grey beginning to streak the darkness.

The reporter pattered away: *perhaps the easing of the rain is significant in other ways*. Just as the choice of eight o'clock – sunrise – for the timing of the handshake was no coincidence. The Jacobin appreciated the power of symbolism, but as far as he was concerned this was nothing more than sentimental claptrap.

Against every sinew that was screaming for him to stay where he was, the Jacobin forced himself to stand and stretch, the agony making itself felt almost everywhere in his body. A hacking cough brought fresh stabs of pain. He filled a glass with water and drank and refilled and drank again, spilling the contents down his chin and on to his rank shirt front.

He had two options. Do nothing, let the situation play itself out, and face the bittersweet consequences: the re-establishment of the old roles, the old and righteous opposition of East and West, but – the bitter part – with West clearly in the wrong from the outset, its agents demonstrably responsible for the rekindling of hostilities.

Or, the second option, take the only course that would simultaneously ensure that the assassination proceeded as planned and absolve SIS of all responsibility for it: be there at the scene, and clean up the evidence afterwards. Remove the bodies, even if it meant killing Kuznetsov and every one of his crew in order to do so.

Option two was less realistic than it had been before he'd fallen asleep. What he'd gained in strength he'd lost in time wasted. Six twenty-one. In forty minutes the helicopter would be taking off. One hour after that, the hit would take place. The Jacobin had little more than an hour and a half to commandeer suitable transport and get to the site. And then – what? Kuznetsov was going to have backup. It was part of the plan. Eight, ten guns to deal with.

The Jacobin leant against the back of the kitchen chair, a compromise between enduring the pain and weariness and the siren trap of sitting down again. It was then that he noticed on the table the open laptop, the one that had belonged to the girl. Out of no more than idle curiosity he reached over and swiped the mousepad to bring up the screen from its sleep.

He allowed himself to sit down this time, staring at the screen. He had left open the tracking website. Instead of the message *no signal detected*, he saw a softly pulsing beacon on an ill-defined background that resembled a grid.

So Purkiss had taken his phone, or at least his SIM card, in with him after all. And either he'd been out of detectable range earlier for some reason and had now been placed somewhere where the signal could be picked up again, or – more likely – he'd found a way to get the SIM into a new handset. Which meant he was on the loose.

The Jacobin pulled the laptop towards him, all discomfort forgotten, and began to hit the keys.

*

The rear of the hangar wasn't floodlit and Purkiss hugged the wall in the dark. Through the concrete he heard a muffle of sounds, the occasional clash of metal.

When it became clear he wasn't going to be able to make out any speech he sidled along to one of the corners and glanced round. There was nobody in the space between this hangar and the next. He moved quickly down the length of the

356

structure towards the front. Halfway along was a small metal door, a Braille pattern of rust across its surface. He touched the handle and pushed it down with exquisite slowness, pausing as its unoiled surfaces emitted a tiny screech and controlling the movement even more finely. He gave the door the lightest of tugs. It yielded, though there was a squeal from the hinges. He froze, listening, but the sound had been drowned by the noises from inside.

He put an eye to the crack he had made. The angle allowed him to see the front left corner of the hangar. The large doors at the front stood open and the light from the floods was spilling in, though the interior had its own brilliant source of illumination. Somebody crossed the path of his vision. He flinched. The glimpse had been momentary, but it looked like Lyuba Ilkun, the woman from the nightclub.

Purkiss left the door ajar an inch, eased himself further down the wall towards the front of the hangar. As he got nearer to the light, voices began to emerge from the foam of sound. Low men's voices, the vowels pronounced far back in the throat in the Russian manner. At the corner he caught a glimpse of a figure stepping out into the dazzle of the floodlights. He drew back, not before he'd recognised the broad back and shoulders, the greater than average height. It was the man he'd seen getting into the four-wheel drive on the coast road. Kuznetsov.

He looked again. The big man was standing with arms folded, gazing up at the night. The temptation was strong. One shot, and he wouldn't see or hear it coming. It would be the end for Purkiss, of course, would bring all Kuznetsov's men down on him. More importantly, it might not be enough to put a stop to whatever was planned, if there were others lined up to take over the leadership role.

Kuznetsov turned his head a fraction. Purkiss ducked back, breathing as shallowly as he could through his mouth, his nose still swollen shut. From around the corner he heard murmurings. He realised Kuznetsov had been joined by another man. The voice was familiar, and after a moment he fitted a face to it. Dobrynin, the man with the mutilated hand from the Rodina offices. He could just make out the conversation.

'All done. Everything's checked, everything's secure.' Dobrynin.

'Good.' Kuznetsov's voice was lower. 'We need to clear up the mess inside.'

'I'll do it with Leok and Ilkun.'

'We'll all do it.'

By *the mess inside* Purkiss presumed he meant the body of the man he'd shot on the steps. He pressed himself closer to the wall. A few seconds later he heard several sets of feet and the rolling metallic grind of the hangar doors being pulled closed. After an age the job was completed. The footsteps seemed to be receding. Glancing round the corner, he saw four of them making their way towards the office building: Kuznetsov, Dobrynin, Ilkun and a man he didn't recognise. Leok, he assumed.

Purkiss slipped back along the wall to the side door and peered through the crack. The lights were still on in the hangar, but the interior was dimmer now that the doors had been closed against the floodlights outside.

He pushed the door further, having to force it, wincing at the jagged sound. He squeezed through the gap, covering right and left quickly with the SIG Sauer. There was no movement within, no sign of life, but he noticed this on an instinctual, animal level, because what caught his attention was the centrepiece, all sixty feet of it, the span of its rotors almost as great.

And he knew what they were planning to do.

Thirty-Six

Google Earth identified the location as an airfield, some eighty kilometres outside Tallinn along the coast to the west. A quick further search revealed that it was disused. It made sense.

If Purkiss had got free, he could still put a stop to the mission. This meant that sitting in the flat and waiting fatalistically for Kuznetsov to pull off the operation was no longer an option. The Jacobin had to stop Purkiss. Everything else, all his worries about Kuznetsov contriving to implicate SIS in the plan, had to come second.

The wet smell of the city was bracing as the Jacobin loped out to the car. Over to the east, the faintest shading on the horizon was beginning to colour the darkness. The Jacobin placed the laptop on the seat beside him. There was of course no way of maintaining the connection while he drove, which meant he wouldn't be able to see if the signal from the phone moved. It had remained stationary all the while he had been pinning down the location of the airfield, so perhaps Purkiss was holed up somewhere.

361

Eighty kilometres, in half an hour. It was possible.

The man whom Purkiss had winged, Yuri, disappointed and disgusted Venedikt. Slumped against the wall at the far end of the corridor, legs splayed and shirttails wadded against the wound in his chest to staunch the flow, he gazed up at Venedikt. His pained eyes at first seemed to show respect, understanding, but when Venedikt drew his gun and gripped the man's shoulder with his free hand and murmured, 'Your sacrifice will be remembered,' Yuri had begun to blubber and thrash. The shot hadn't been a clean one, clipping his head eccentrically so that one side of it was blown asunder. His legs continued jerking for several beats.

Beside Venedikt, Lyuba swallowed drily but stayed silent, as did Dobrynin and Leok. They knew there was no time to tend to a man with such injuries, and no justification for the risk involved in delivering him to hospital and the authorities. Yuri himself should have known that.

While Leok and Lyuba dragged the body into one of the offices, Venedikt and Dobrynin descended to the basement. The man Purkiss had overpowered on the steps, Tattar, stood guard over the bound man in the chair. Tattar straightened as Kuznetsov entered. Having suffered the humiliation of losing the other prisoner as well as his phone and his gun, he was not about to add sullenness or self pity to his list of offences.

The Englishman, Fallon, stared up at Kuznetsov through the one eye he was at least partly able to open. He was almost unrecognisable, plums blooming above his cheekbones, lips engorged to resemble twin kidneys.

'What is the plan? With Purkiss, now that he has escaped?'

The Englishman didn't react, not even to brace himself for a blow. Kuznetsov shook his head.

'It doesn't matter.' He motioned with his fingers and Dobrynin produced a boxcutter and cut the cords, grabbing Fallon as he toppled forward. He swiped the blade across the ties at his ankles and hauled him to a standing position. The Englishman staggered at once, his feet twisting beneath him. Dobrynin hooked an arm across Fallon's back. Kuznetsov stepped aside and Dobrynin half-dragged, half-walked the Englishman towards the steps.

*

The space was small and cramped and Purkiss was bent so that his knees were almost against his chin, his feet pressed against the box that occupied half of the interior of the bench. There would be far more room if he just took the box out but it would be noticed and would immediately give him away. The bench he assumed was for troops to sit on during transport. Its seat doubled as a lid for an interior that could be used for storage, thus economising on space.

He knew something about helicopters, including the Black Hawk, but not enough to call himself an expert. He was aware, however, that the stub wings at the top of the fuselage were significant. Designed to carry extra fuel tanks, they were equally useful for supporting ordnance. And what he saw on the stub closer to him when he stepped nearer was certainly not a fuel tank.

It was a missile, the length of a man, perhaps a foot in diameter, its phallic shaft surmounted with a silver head. Four squared-off wings radiated around the shaft towards the back. Quickly he peered around it at all the visible surfaces, but there were no markings. He ducked round to the other side of the helicopter and saw a featureless metal rod attached to the other stub, similar in length and width, but a plain cylindrical shape, unadorned by wings or head. A dummy, he suspected. A counterweight, without any other function.

One missile. Which meant there was something special about it.

He called up the camera facility on the phone he'd taken, and snapped the helicopter and the missile from as many angles as he could manage. He tried calling up an internet connection. There was still no signal. From some distance away a sound rocked the night. He tensed and crouched, almost dropping the phone. A gunshot. Had they decided to kill Fallon?

In the corners of the hangar were old pieces of machinery, rows of collapsed shelving, a sea of canvas tarpaulins. He could easily have found somewhere to hide, but Purkiss knew there was only one course of action worth considering. He pulled open the door of the helicopter and stepped inside.

It was more spacious than he was expecting. He remembered the Black Hawk took three or four crew members, two pilots and one or two crew chiefs, and could carry around a dozen additional troops. He wondered how many would be coming on board on this trip.

Once inside the bench compartment he lay curled with the SIG Sauer in one hand and the phone in the other. He waited, the rasp of his breath sounding so loudly in his ears he imagined he felt the helicopter tremble.

*

Dobrynin and Leok dragged the stumbling Englishman across the gravel towards the hangar, Venedikt following behind. They hadn't bothered hooding the man this time. Instead of going with them all the way into the hangar, Venedikt veered off down the slope towards the wall which separated them from the field beyond. Bobbing in the field were dots of torchlight.

He made his way to the shed door that served as a ladder and climbed to the top of the wall. He cupped his hands round his mouth and called, long and loud. One of the lights detached itself from the invisible string, began heading toward him. It was Raskov.

'No sign, sir.'

'There are trees over there.'

'Yes. We've looked. Ditches, too, a network of them, which you can't see so well from here. If he's lying low in one of them it could take us forever.'

After a moment's pondering Venedikt came to a decision. 'All right. Tattar's operational, I'll send him over to help. You bring one of the men and get ready to leave for the boat. The rest stay here and continue the search.'

'If we don't find him in time…' Raskov's tone wasn't defeatist, just curious.

'We have to find him, but if it's not before…. the *event*, it won't be disastrous. There's no cell phone reception, so he won't be able to summon help. If he has taken cover he'll have to stay there, he can't risk an open dash across the fields with four men looking for him, especially as it'll be getting light soon. Find him if we can, but as long as we can keep him pinned down until we've done what we're going to do, it'll be enough.'

*

His men had rolled open the doors of the hangar and inside Venedikt looked at his watch. Six forty-five. He itched to be at the location early, but recognised that the longer they were in the air, the greater the risk of their attracting unwanted attention. The Black Hawk had fuel enough for eight hundred kilometres of flight, plus the auxiliary tank. Eight hundred kilometres was nearly ten times the distance they would be travelling, especially now that the journey was going to be one way only.

Once again he was inwardly proud of his decisiveness. He strode over to the door of the helicopter. In the cabin the Englishman, Fallon, was seated on one of the benches, trying to keep his head from lolling. Lyuba was securing his feet together once more. She glanced up at his face. Venedikt saw in her eyes a hate so keen it almost made him grimace. A woman betrayed, if not exactly spurned.

Leok was seated in the pilot's seat, Dobrynin standing by Lyuba, awaiting instructions. Venedikt made sure he looked each of them in the face in turn.

'We go now.'

As they took their positions and a crackle of tension and excitement began to connect them in its web, he grabbed each one by the shoulder and squeezed.

His people. Together they were going to change history.

*

Through the lid of the coffin – Purkiss couldn't help thinking of it as such – the words were indistinct. He knew from the heavy creak above him that someone was sitting on the seat above him. His face was inches from the wood. Claustrophobia began to grip him and he smothered it.

Something was pushing beneath him. After a moment he realised it was the movement of the fuselage below. He gained a sense of directional motion as the helicopter rolled forward, had an impression even of a change in the timbre of the sounds penetrating the box he was in, as the chopper emerged from the hangar into the expanse of the early morning. For want of something more productive to do he checked the phone. Still no signal.

Another noise began to seep through, one accompanied by a tactile dimension. A rhythmic sweeping thud was followed in each beat by a gentle but distinct shake in the body of the helicopter. The rotor was starting up.

The throb of the blades gathered pace until a steady state was reached. Then there was the pressing of the base of the cavity he was lying in against his side, as the machine began to rise and they became airborne.

Seven oh three.

Thirty-Seven

The reporter had to raise her voice against the background surge, enthusiasm infecting her tone as she delivered more platitudes.

A real sense of camaraderie...

A feeling that the past is being let go...

This momentous day will be imprinted on our memories for years to come...

The Jacobin heard, yet didn't hear. He was staring at the sky, where the shape, black against the lightening ceiling of cloud, was rising, buoyed by the thrumming of its rotors.

He pulled over quickly beside a hedge, killed the engine to get rid of the exhaust fumes. He peered upwards. The helicopter had stopped ascending and hung, raptor-like, before swinging away to the north.

He'd thought he would be too late. In a sense he was, because the helicopter had taken off before he'd got there. But didn't that suggest Purkiss himself had failed to stop it? The Jacobin reached for his phone, into which he'd copied the web address of the tracking site. No internet connection.

A car was emerging in the distance through the gates of the airfield. It stopped beyond the gates and a man got out and closed them behind the car. The Jacobin started the engine of his car again. It wouldn't do to be noticed sitting in a stationary vehicle this close to the airfield. Nor would it be a good idea to turn round immediately and drive away, in sight of the car. The Jacobin continued along the road that ran past the airfield.

As he approached the other car, which was heading towards him, he glanced at its occupants, as one would naturally do when passing another vehicle on such an empty road. Three of them. Although none was familiar, he recognised the type. Kuznetsov's people, soldiers by background, grim faced. They wouldn't recognise him, had never met him before. No sign of Purkiss in the car. They would be the backup, the Jacobin assumed. The crew who were to meet the chopper out at sea.

To follow them, even at a distance, would invite suspicion, and if they turned on him the odds were hardly in his favour, not just numerically. He punched the address of a location he knew on the coast into the car's satellite navigation system. It directed him to continue the way he was heading. The Jacobin put his foot down, glancing every now and again at the display on his phone.

*

Through the windows of the cabin the sky was changing almost perceptibly to slate. Below, a light ground fog blurred the details of the fields and the sparse network of roads between them. The weather didn't matter greatly, Venedikt reflected. The handshake would take place in anything short of a hurricane.

He sat on the bench facing Fallon, forcing himself not to prowl about the cabin. Dobrynin was leaning into the cockpit and asking something of Leok and Lyuba, the pilot and co-pilot. Dobrynin was as excited, as moved as he was, Venedikt knew. He was simply more reserved in his personality and therefore didn't let it show.

Two missiles would have been ideal, one as backup for the other. The finances wouldn't have been a problem. The haul from the hijacking of the bank vans would have stretched to a second one. Availability was the stumbling block, as the arms dealer had told him. The missile was one of the most sought-after pieces of weaponry in the world, and therefore the most closely guarded.

Still, one would be enough.

The dealer had offered Venedikt a selection of warheads. After consulting Dobrynin, he'd gone for the Penetration/Blast/Fragmentation warhead rather than the High Explosive Anti-Tank round. There was no armour to be penetrated, and the PBF had bunker-busting capability and in terms of destructive power over a wider area it was the surer option. The War

Memorial would be destroyed, of course. Had it not been for the context, Venedikt would have baulked at this. But the symbolic power of such an outrage... it was almost as important that the Memorial fall as that the President be sacrificed.

The window was a wide one. The handshake was scheduled to take place at eight a.m. precisely. Even if there were a delay – Venedikt doubted it would take place ahead of time, these things never did – he had a radio link to the memorial site to guide him. The handshake would last a good few minutes for the benefit of the world's cameras. Then the two leaders would step up to their podiums and deliver their respective speeches of hope. Perhaps twenty, thirty minutes in total. The missile travelled at a velocity of one hundred and fifty metres per second. Over ten kilometres, that amounted to a little more than one minute from firing to impact.

A wide window, indeed.

The Black Hawk was capable of a speed just under three hundred kilometres per hour. There was no reason to hurry, and Leok and Lyuba kept it at well below a third of the maximum velocity. Beyond the smudged rim of the horizon, past the fields and the treetops, Venedikt began to catch the glitter and shift of the sea.

*

Encased in his crowded coffin, aware of the pressing down of at least one human body on the lid, Purkiss felt the claustrophobia ram its suffocating fist down his throat. All that stopped him from crying out, pounding on the wood inches from his face, was the knowledge of what would follow.

Instead he concentrated on his phone, staring at the backlit blue face as though by force of will he could summon a signal into being. By his watch they had been airborne for ten minutes. Assuming they were heading out to sea, as he suspected, they would by his estimate still be over land, and certainly potentially in range of a phone mast.

It was ingenious, he had to admit it, now that he understood what they were going to do. Purkiss was no expert on missile systems but he remembered reading something about the new Israeli development, a missile that could reach its target at a range of fifteen miles without the target's having to be in sight of the person operating the launcher. The exclusion zone for air traffic around the War Memorial had a radius of ten kilometres, Elle had said. Fifteen miles was twenty-five kilometres. There'd be plenty to spare.

He blinked, moved the phone an inch back from his face to make sure of what he thought he'd seen. A single bar had crept into the upper left hand corner of the screen. Weak, but a signal.

He had already composed the text message a few minutes earlier. He pressed "send". As he waited, the words that he assumed to be Estonian for "sending message" flashing at the top of the screen, their pulse almost mocking in its languor – *don't get your hopes up, friend* – he reread the message.

It's Purkiss. I'm hidden on board a Black Hawk heading out over the sea. They plan to use a long-range missile to make the hit. They have Fallon prisoner. I believe they have him on board & intend to leave his body in the wreckage of the chopper so it looks like SIS was responsible. You have to alert the authorities & they need to find us & shoot us down.

A smiley face filled the screen. *Message sent.*

*

The handset made a tiny chirrup. The Jacobin grabbed it off the seat and stared at it, negotiating the bends in the country lane with one hand on the wheel. The signal had been reestablished. Purkiss was on the radar again.

Instead of the stationary pulse centred in the airfield that the Jacobin had been expecting, the beacon was on the move, crossing fields, moving steadily across boundaries such as walls and streams. Purkiss was in the helicopter.

Three possibilities. One, Kuznetsov had him prisoner on board the chopper as planned, and had for some bizarre reason allowed him to keep his phone. Two, Purkiss had command of the

374

machine and was either flying it himself – virtually impossible – or forcing Kuznetsov's pilots to take it to some unknown destination. Or, three, Purkiss had stowed away on it.

Whichever was correct, there was only one course of action to take. He dropped the phone back on the seat, seized the wheel, and gunned the engine.

*

As a schoolboy Purkiss had developed the involuntary habit of waking seconds before his alarm went off in the mornings. He would lie paralysed by the lingering grip of sleep, anticipation of the blare from the clock radio rising in his chest to a peak of terror. He felt that way now, eyes on the tiny screen, fist slick around the handset, waiting for the reply.

Fallon, I got you in the end, he thought bleakly. It was too late to hear what the man had promised to tell him. He should have pressed him harder while they were imprisoned together in the basement. But he suspected it was all bluff. Fallon had no stunning revelations to offer. It was more likely to be a last-ditch torrent of blather to try to achieve absolution for his crimes.

It would be quick, Purkiss supposed. The Estonian security forces would scramble fighter jets with air-to-air missiles. There would be no messing about with close-combat artillery, no opportunity for Kuznetsov and his crew to go down in a blaze of defiance. Boxed in his coffin, Purkiss wouldn't hear the end coming. All of which assumed that Elle had got his text message and could persuade the authorities quickly enough of the seriousness of the threat. It assumed that the air force could locate the Black Hawk in time, before Kuznetsov and his crew discovered that Purkiss had raised the alarm and took evasive action.

The reply came then. Purkiss didn't register the words on the screen, was unaware of anything but the tone that heralded the arrival of the text, loud as a blast in the confined space, a double *ting* sound like the tapping of a spoon against the rim of an empty glass to gain an audience's attention before an after-dinner speech.

Didn't think of that, did you, forgot to mute it.

Purkiss knew it had been heard outside his hiding place too, because from beyond the lid he heard a muffled cry and a creak as the weight shifted on the lid.

Thirty-Eight

The man was a surly old walrus, moustache and fingers the same nicotine sienna. He stared through the haze from his rollup with eyes stewed in last night's booze.

'You're out early.'

'I wanted to get away from the crowds back in town.'

'You're not interested in the handshake?'

The Jacobin shrugged. 'Big deal. People make friends, they fall out again. Round it goes.'

The man was old enough to have been a child during the war. He gave half a laugh. 'Isn't that the truth.' He sat up straight on his stool, dropping ash on the newspaper spread on the counter before him. 'What can I do for you?'

The Jacobin told him: something fast. He took out his wallet and fanned the notes. Money no object.

The old man squinted through the smoke, nodded. 'Got just the thing. Come on.'

It bobbed among the small collection at the jetty, dull white in the morning gloom, a Finnish make, not brand new but well cared for.

'Handles exceptionally well, and I can't say that for some of these other buckets,' the old man said. 'Inboard motor, as you can see. Maximum speed a hundred and ten knots.'

Back in the office the Jacobin exchanged keys for cash. The old man eyed him. 'You all right? You look like you've had a rough night.'

'Touch of asthma. The morning cold always makes it play up. I'll be fine.'

'Good, because I want my boat back.'

The Jacobin accepted the man's offer of a waxed jacket to go over his suit. He climbed aboard. He wasn't an experienced speedboater, but the controls were easy enough to grasp. The engine started smoothly, its low rumble comforting beneath his thighs.

'Keep clear of town,' called the old man. 'They'll torpedo you if you get too close.'

The Jacobin nosed away from the jetty. Ahead the grey sea stirred, annoyed by this new intrusion.

*

Venedikt glanced sharply across at Dobrynin and saw he too had heard it. Some sort of sharp clinking of metal. He tensed, muscles bunching, hand moving to the pistol at his hip.

Across from them the Englishman, Fallon, arched his back sideways, his lumpish clotted face twisted in a grimace. Through lips of rubber he muttered: 'Seatbelt.'

'What's the matter? You want it on?' Venedikt laughed. 'Afraid you might hurt yourself if we stop suddenly?'

'Digging into my back.'

Dobrynin strode across the cabin and pulled Fallon forward by his collar. He fumbled at the small of his back and cast free the ends of the seatbelt. Venedikt relaxed. It was the movement of the parts of the buckle that had made the chinking noise. Fallon heaved his bottom up and down a few times, taking advantage of the marginal improvement in his comfort, until Venedikt said, 'Stop that.'

Up ahead in the cockpit, Leok and Lyuba were exchanging low remarks. The Black Hawk was proceeding northwards, keeping well clear of the no-fly zone, before it began its eastward turn and, at the end, its full swing to face back towards the shore.

Seven twenty-seven.

*

Inside the bench Purkiss cringed, breath held, readying his fists and his legs to emerge doing as much damage as he could before they cut him down. Instead of being raised, the lid creaked and bore down harder as if the weight on it were increasing. He heard, distinctly, Fallon's voice. It sounded like he said *seatbelt* in Russian.

Then another voice, further but still close, Kuznetsov's this time. Something about Fallon's not hurting himself.

Then a series of thumps on the lid. He recoiled at each one. A bark from Kuznetsov.

Silence followed.

Slowly, controlling the sound, Purkiss exhaled. Fallon too had heard the tone made by the arriving text message, had recognised what it was. Had realised Purkiss was on board the aircraft, and had covered it up. Unbelievable reflexes, in his beaten-up condition.

Purkiss found the "mute" button and pressed it. He read the message while his heartbeat slowed to normal.

Working on a GPS fix on your phone at the moment. So Fallon not working with Kuznetsov, then. Kendrick asks what sort of missile?

Two pieces of good news, then. They were both alive, Elle and Kendrick, and they had access to tracking technology, which meant the chopper would be easier to locate.

He typed back: *Fallon apparently also trying to stop Kuznetsov. One missile that I could see, five to six feet long, wings, no markings. I suspect of Israeli origin, non-line-of-sight.* He hesitated, added: *Any sign of Teague?* before deciding this was irrelevant for the moment. He deleted it and wrote instead, *Have you alerted the security forces?*

An age passed, during which he heard nothing more than the steady drone of the Black Hawk's twin engines. He checked his watch.

Seven thirty-eight. At the very least they might be able to evacuate the area around the War Memorial in time.

The screen lit up, silently this time. *Kendrick says probably right about the missile, if so it'll have a tank- or bunker-busting warhead, v. messy. Got a fix on you with the tracker.*

He waited for a follow-up message. When one didn't come, he thumbed in: *Have you told the security forces?*

In a moment: *No. We're coming to get you ourselves.*

Purkiss closed his eyes, hard, until the stars began to flare redly behind the lids. He sent a reply.

There's no time. This chopper has to be shot down.

And immediately back: *No.*

God *damn* them, both of them. He resisted the urge to crush the handset in his fist.

*

The signal on his phone was struggling to stay alive. It didn't matter any more, because the Jacobin saw it, distant enough that it seemed to be hovering but actually moving away from him, several knots away to the northeast.

He kept up the speed, but eased the wheel to the left so that he was heading due north in parallel with the course of the helicopter, the sharp stern of the boat slicing a thin furrow through the water's flesh. Far on the horizon to the west was a large ship, a freighter of some sort, making its early morning way towards Helsinki. Otherwise there was no traffic, the sea brooding alone under the brightening sky. In another six weeks the sea would go to sleep for the winter, frozen over until as late as next April.

It was time to make his decision. If Purkiss was hidden on board the Black Hawk, the Jacobin had to alert Kuznetsov in some way, and the only way to do so would be to approach and try to attract his attention and hope he was recognised from up in the air. If on the other hand Kuznetsov had Purkiss captive, then all the Jacobin could do was to wait for the hit to proceed, then try to persuade Kuznetsov not to use Purkiss's and Fallon's bodies as means to scapegoat SIS. Or perhaps retrieve the bodies from the wreckage himself.

The Jacobin was fairly certain Kuznetsov wouldn't try to kill him. The man knew the Jacobin had insurance, in the form of a document to be opened by lawyers in the event of his death or disappearance, spilling the beans on the whole operation, which would negate any use of Purkiss and Fallon as scapegoats.

The Black Hawk was tilting slightly to the right, eastwards, drifting inwards at the beginning of the circling movement that would wheel it to face the shore at the beginning of the final phase. Its crew would be looking out for the backup boat – and, yes, there it was, a bigger and noisier craft than the Jacobin's, steaming from the southeast some distance behind the Jacobin.

The backup crew. They would be able to provide access to Kuznetsov. The Jacobin began his own turn, to bring his boat across the path of the larger vessel.

*

Dobrynin tapped Venedikt's arm and nodded at the window. Venedikt turned and craned, saw the boat approaching far below, its occupants unidentifiable at this distance. Venedikt knew them to be Raskov and two of the other men. There would be additional room on board for the four of them: himself, Dobrynin, Lyuba and Leok, assuming they all made it out alive.

It was going to be impossible to land the helicopter on the water. They had agreed that Leok and Lyuba would bring them as close to the surface as they dared, and then Venedikt and Dobrynin would leave the craft, with pilot and copilot following. The Black Hawk would rapidly spin out of control and would hit the surface. It was then that they would be in the most danger from the rotor blades and the wild bulk of the machine. Once aboard the boat, they would leave the Black Hawk and its remaining passenger – Fallon – to the mercies of the sea and of the fighter jets that would descend on it like wasps.

Venedikt strained his eyes. A smaller vessel, a speed boat, was veering towards Raskov's, not heading directly at it but moving to head it off. There was a solitary figure aboard. Through the dim light and the spray from the boat's passage Venedikt couldn't make out who it was. It was his turn to touch Dobrynin's arm and point. Dobrynin got a pair of binoculars from a knapsack and peered thorugh them. He passed them to Venedikt, eyebrows raised.

Venedikt sharpened the image. The Englishman. What did he think he was doing?

An enormous cheer, loud enough to be heard above the chop of the rotors, drew his attention. He looked round. Dobrynin had turned up the portable radio he'd brought on board. The sounds from the War Memorial indicated that the convoy bearing the two presidents had arrived.

He turned back, picked up his phone and thumbed in Raskov's number, saw movement on board the approaching boat as the man answered.

'That speed boat approaching you,' said Venedikt. 'He's friendly, I think. See what he wants. Don't attack him unless he attacks you first.'

'Understood.'

Seven fifty. In ten minutes' time it would be done.

*

Still he heard only Kuznetsov's voice, the words unclear. The tinny patter of radio sound he identified as constant background cheering, like that at a sports match. Purkiss assumed they had the radio on and were using it to monitor events at the site of the meeting.

Close by his ear, through the wood, came two distinct sounds. Taps, rather than creaks.

He held his breath again, waiting.

Just as he decided he'd misheard, they came again.

Two. Fallon was signalling him. Two men, obviously excluding the flight crew.

He didn't dare tap back to indicate he'd understood.

It was useful information. Even if he didn't know the precise locations of the two men, having a clear idea of the number of one's opponents always improved confidence and speed. He'd have surprise on his side, too. The problem was, paradoxically, Fallon. He was seated directly above Purkiss, no doubt still bound. With his weight bearing down, Purkiss had no way of lifting the lid of the bench.

Another bluff was needed, another faked seizure or faint of some kind similar to the one Purkiss himself had pulled off in the basement. If Fallon managed to slide off the bench onto the floor of the cabin, Purkiss would be able to emerge quickly enough that he might get the drop on Kuznetsov and the other man. But he had no way of communicating this to Fallon, no way of knowing if Fallon might think of it himself.

The screen of the phone, nearly forgotten on the periphery of his vision, lit up, jolting him.

We see you.

Elle and Kendrick. And suddenly he knew what they had to do.

Thirty-Nine

The Jacobin stood at the wheel of the boat, his free hand raised in a gesture of non-aggression. The men in the approaching boat were watching him with curiosity rather than hostility. He glanced across and up at the distant helicopter, now side-on as it swung in its long arc to face the shore, and raised his hand in that direction. Kuznetsov would have spotted him, notified the men in the boat.

A hundred metres or so separated him from the boat. He let go of the wheel and cupped his hands around his mouth, called, 'You have to warn Kuznetsov. Tell him Purkiss is on board the helicopter.'

His voice came out more weakly than he'd expected. The rumble of the water and the larger boat's engine drowned him out. One of the men on the boat cupped a hand to his ear and shook his head. Frustrated, the Jacobin sat and applied acceleration.

His engine was racing more noisily than it should have, until he realised the noise wasn't coming from his boat but from another, a similar size to his, approaching from the south. The men in the larger boat were beginning to shout and point.

The Jacobin felt the tilt of disorientation: no fleet of military vehicles, just a speed boat like his own, with what looked like a two-man crew. Through eyes filmed with fatigue and pain and salt air he focused on the faces behind the arc of windscreen. One was a woman's, Elle's.

*

Through the front cockpit windows between Lyuba and Leok, Venedikt saw the lights of the city, awake for several hours by now, ten kilometres away. From the east, sunlight was leaking through the cloud cover and spilling glittering tendrils across the surface of the water. The sea below the helicopter was roiling, bewildered and furious at the sudden conjunction of three interlopers.

Venedikt had been distracted by the Englishman's approach and hadn't noticed the advance of the second speed boat until Lyuba had called out. He'd taken his eyes away from the binoculars, then immediately reapplied them. The woman was steering while the man, Purkiss's crony, had lifted his assault rifle over the top of the windscreen. In the larger boat the men were already hefting their own weapons into position across the back rail of the craft.

It took Venedikt a moment to realise that Purkiss's man was levelling his rifle not at

Raskov and his men in the boat, but upwards at the Black Hawk.

The helicopter was perhaps sixty metres above the surface of the sea, the approaching speed boat almost half a kilometre distant. It meant that the Black Hawk was at the limit of the AK-74's effective range, but Venedikt flinched as the characteristic clatter of the rifle cut through the *whap* of the rotors even at this distance and tiny streaks of noise whispered past the fuselage. Leok banked the chopper to the left and upwards. Venedikt struggled to keep his feet, gripping the back of the pilot's seat while with his other hand he swung the binoculars. He saw that Raskov and his men had opened fire themselves, no longer caring about the range now that the Black Hawk had come under fire. Crazily, Purkiss's man wasn't returning their fire, but was still aiming at the Black Hawk, now impossibly beyond reach, a modern Don Quixote tilting at his own particular windmill.

In his ear Dobrynin yelled, 'Now.' Venedikt looked at his watch. Seven fifty-eight.

He stepped forward into the cockpit, shouldered Ilkun aside, and crouched at the controls.

*

Close as he was to the engines, Purkiss couldn't at first be certain that he was hearing the remote noise of automatic fire. Above him, Fallon

389

thumped hard several times on the lid of the bench and he knew it was happening.

He felt the Black Hawk veer and yaw, felt rather than heard the ping of something off the undercarriage. Kendrick had hit it, he thought, even though he was probably too far away to do any damage. With the swinging of the chopper came a sudden creak in the bench lid and the thump of a body hitting the floor. Purkiss knew it was Fallon.

He released the breath he'd drawn and exploded upwards, flinging the lid up and out. He registered shock on the face turned towards him. A familiar one, Dobrynin, the man with the claw hand with whom he'd had such an urbane discussion in his office just the previous afternoon. Purkiss had the SIG Sauer up and levelled. He fired twice, catching Dobrynin in the chest with both shots, slamming him back against the partition that separated the cabin from the back of the pilot's seat. At Purkiss's feet Fallon rolled and gasped, hands fastened behind him. Purkiss stepped over him.

In the cockpit Kuznetsov squatted at some sort of apparatus that looked like it had been added to the basic design of the craft. A launcher. *The* launcher. Kuznetsov glanced round. Purkiss raised the pistol.

The chopper rolled then, to the right, almost through ninety degrees. Purkiss was flung off his feet and crashed against the cabin door. The world tipped as the helicopter was righted again, and somebody came charging through into the cabin. Not Kuznetsov but Lyuba Ilkun.

Her foot pistoned into Purkiss's abdomen. He doubled and twisted to protect against another blow, but she was reaching past him for the release on the door. The blast of air was torrential and terrible in its cold suddenness. She shouted and the craft gave a jerk again, *expert handling by the pilot*, he had to admit in a detached, crazy way.

Then he was tumbling through the gap out into the grey whipping void, away from Ilkun's triumphant, yelling face.

*

The Jacobin pulled on the wheel, taking the boat acutely to the right, away from the melee ahead. Kuznetsov's men were answering Kendrick with artillery of their own. It appeared he had given up on his ambition of bringing down the Black Hawk, was ducking low beneath the screen of the speed boat while Elle held it steady, no longer accelerating, keeping a distance. The cacophony was unbearable, a hammering magnified by the immense body of water beneath it.

The Jacobin paid little attention to the gun battle. He was looking up at the helicopter. Something was happening there. It had shaken and twitched even after it had stopped being fired upon. He didn't think it had been seriously hit, so why the acrobatics? The missile hadn't been fired yet.

His watch said three minutes past eight. There was time, but it was running out.

*

Lyuba yelled, 'He's gone.' Venedikt let out an inarticulate grunt of acknowledgement. Nothing was going to stop them now, nothing.

He huddled over the launcher and studied the screen where the co-ordinates had been pre-programmed. The missile was designed for use against tanks. As such, the gunner had the ability to reprogramme the co-ordinates after launch, as the target moved. There was no such need in this case because the target was stationary.

Beside him, Leok had tilted the Black Hawk's nose upwards to provide lift for the missile once it had been fired so as to counteract the pull of gravity during its flight. Venedikt raised his head, sighted for the last time across the expanse of water towards the distant city lights, seeming to hear the roaring of the crowds across the kilometres and the walls of noise in between. It sounded like destiny calling.

He lowered his gaze to the launcher.

*

Purkiss fell, and with him fell Claire, her body sliding to the floor from Fallon's grasp, and Abby, flung tumbling by the seam of gunfire.

He was cold, colder than he'd ever been before. He could see they were cold too, and lonely in death. He reached out to them, flung his arms to catch them. He felt unimaginable pain, but only in one arm.

He opened his eyes. The pain was in his left forearm just above the wrist where it had struck the lower lip of the doorway. Blood from the lacerated skin sleeved his arm almost to the elbow. There was no deformity, no suggestion of a break. His fingers gripped the edge.

He hung swinging beneath the helicopter, the roar of its engines trying to shake him off, its undercarriage immense at this angle. The wind whipped up by the rotors was furious. He felt as if the machine were trying to prise his left shoulder out of its socket.

He didn't look down. To do so would be to be lost. The chopper was tilted very slightly to its left which meant that he couldn't see up through the open doorway. He knew that at any minute Ilkun was going to close the door. His fingers would be pared loose. It would be the end.

Purkiss clenched his teeth, swung his other arm up and round so that his right hand gripped the edge of the doorway. For an instant the air beneath him took on the solid, springy character of a trampoline. He pulled upwards. His torso made it over the lip of the doorway.

Ilkun was reaching for the door. He heaved himself so that his centre of gravity was on the right side of the doorway, got an arm around her legs. Using his knees as a fulcrum, he rose.

He sent her over his left shoulder with almost balletic grace, through the open door. Her enraged shout dwindled into the storm of noise behind and below him as the sea received her.

*

In a corner of the cabin Fallon had hauled himself into a sitting position and was trying to stand, handicapped by his secured wrists. Purkiss charged forward into the cockpit. Kuznetsov was hunched over the launcher.

Purkiss moved in, but Kuznetsov half-turned and the gun in his hand fired. Purkiss ducked away. The bullet sang past into the cabin. He kicked at Kuznetsov's wrist, caught it. The gun spun in the air. Purkiss caught it and followed up by grabbing Kuznetsov by the collar and hauling his bulk backwards. The man didn't resist as much as Purkiss had expected.

He caught a glimpse of the big man's face. He was smiling. His lips moved.

'It's done.'

Purkiss stared through the front window of the cockpit, saw the smoky contrail of the shape that was streaking away, and understood he was too late.

The missile was launched.

Forty

Keeping the speedboat circling, the Jacobin watched the sky, saw Purkiss dangling from the doorway like a marionette with all but one of its strings cut, saw the chopper tip nose-up in the firing position, then watched Purkiss haul himself back inside the aircraft. An instant later a woman's body tumbled flailing, cracked against the water's surface.

The smaller speed boat was veering away. The small-arms fire had stopped and one of the men in the larger boat was levelling something heavy propped across his shoulder.

The grenade left the launcher with a sucking sound. A second later the rear of the speed boat exploded, a black and orange ball splitting the grey of the water, the roar eclipsing even the after-effect of the gunfire. The Jacobin saw the man, Kendrick, lifted cartwheeling into the air to plunge amongst the debris. He couldn't see Elle. The fibreglass front of the speedboat spun drunkenly before the waves claimed it.

From above, layered on top of the bulky sound of the explosion, came a *whoosh* and a prolonged hiss. The Black Hawk rocked slightly as the missile erupted from its cylinder on the stub wing.

The Jacobin stared off in the direction of the city, imagining he could see the small, deadly tube winging its way.

*

From where he lay, Venedikt could see Fallon trying to stand by shuffling his back up against the wall, every slight change in position of the helicopter thwarting his efforts and sending him sliding to the floor again. Venedikt's hand drifted in front of his face. He was surprised to see it spade-like with gore. He raised his head, looked down himself. Something was on his chest. Bloodied rags. No, they *were* his chest. Ah, yes. The other Englishman, Purkiss, had shot him. After he had launched the missile.

After. Not before. It meant he had triumphed.

Beyond the wound that was his chest, beyond his splayed feet, he saw movement in the cockpit: Leok, keeping control of the craft, unsure what to do now, and someone else – Purkiss – squatting in the copilot's seat. Venedikt felt no pain, so he was surprised at the rage that soared within him, having believed all strong feeling to be lost to him now.

He called a command to Leok but it went unheard. Venedikt's other hand came up to his face, clenching his phone. He punched at a number, missed, tried again.

'Raskov.'

Venedikt said: 'It's done. You –'

'We saw it, sir. My heartfelt congratulations –'

'Shut up. Shoot the helicopter down.'

'But you –'

'Do it. I'm dead anyway.'

'Sir –'

'*Now*.'

*

The tremor in his hands was threatening to spread to his whole body. He gripped the two curved handles on either side of the launcher to suppress it. Beside him the pilot was pulling the machine into a turn, glancing across at him.

Purkiss stared at the screen. It showed a point-of-view moving image of the surface of the sea, the quality slightly grainy and with the occasional split-second freeze and jerk of imperfect reception. In the centre of the image was a set of crosshairs.

Purkiss knew he was seeing the view from the nose of the missile in flight, relayed back to the launcher by optical fibre. Because of the movement over the sea, the missile seemed to be travelling slowly, until an aircraft of some sort disappeared with shocking speed above and to the left of the field of vision. The crosshairs dropped slightly and the spread of the city came into view. Purkiss understood that the trajectory had adjusted downwards like that of a plane coming in to land. In the corner of the screen separate sets of figures flashed by. Distance to target: 5000 metres, dropping at the rate of 150 metres per second. Time until impact: thirty seconds. Twenty-nine. Twenty-eight.

He seized the handles and twisted. Incredibly, the image changed, the shore on the horizon tilting away vertiginously as the missile swooped.

Then something hit the helicopter, a great fist out of the sky, and the handles were wrenched out of his grasp. He was thrown against the cockpit door. Across from him the pilot was yelling and hauling desperately at the controls.

Through the windows the world was spinning, the Black Hawk turning in a drunken pirouette, trailing black smoke from its tail, part of which, Purkiss noticed, had disappeared. *Something hit the back, something big*. He ignored it and lunged for the handles of the launcher. The missile had righted its course once more and the shore was rushing at the screen, terrifyingly close. As the chopper spun he pulled at the handles once more. Again the image changed.

One thousand metres to target.

Time to impact nine seconds. Eight.

The screen showed a stretch of the shore wild with rocks, spume geysering up over it, no shapes resembling human beings. As if it would help his aim, Purkiss roared through gritted teeth.

The rocks flung themselves to fill the screen. Then the screen went blank.

As the cockpit windows reached the part of the arc that took them past the shore, he saw for an instant the eruption, water soaring skyward like the pictures he'd seen of World War Two naval battles in the Pacific. By the time the heavy *crump* reached them the chopper had already spun through a hundred and eighty degrees.

Beside him the pilot was shouting, some sort of prayer or hymn in Estonian, his hands no longer attempting to control the aircraft. Purkiss left him and clambered back into the cabin. He stepped over Kuznetsov who lay glassy-eyed, dead.

On the floor Fallon slumped against the bench. 'What…'

'It missed.'

Fallon closed his eyes. Purkiss squatted to hook his arm around his back. He saw the blood: not the old, semi-dried stuff from his beatings but fresh, bright gouts, pulsing through a ragged tear in Fallon's trousers near his groin.

The stray bullet, the one Kuznetsov had fired at Purkiss just before he'd got him away from the launcher. It looked like it had hit the femoral artery.

'Get out,' rasped Fallon.

'You're coming with me –'

'For God's sake… it's about to go down.'

His lips were moving and Purkiss wanted to shake speech out of him but all he heard was something like 'Ask v–'. Then Fallon lolled forward.

Through the cabin window Purkiss saw the sea in an impossible place, standing parallel to the glass. He rolled and scrabbled at the release handle of the door beneath him, dropped out like a hanged man through a trapdoor and managed to turn himself into a diving position so that when he hit the water it wasn't side-on.

The shock of the impact, the cold, stoppered his breath. He plunged and crawled, kicking frantically, staying as deep as he dared while putting as much distance as he could between him and what was going to happen. When he found himself surfacing again, his head broke free into a terrific wall of sound as, behind him, the Black Hawk smashed into the boat. Almost before he had time to duck his head under again, the engines of both craft went up.

Beneath the water the explosions punched his body. Looking up, he saw a sheet of flame soar across the surface, black spinning fragments of debris swoop like bats. He crawled about, compressed by the cold, not wanting to emerge in the middle of a slick of burning fuel, until the blurred surface took on a grey hue once more. He burst clear, sucking in chestfuls of oily air.

From his position just above the surface the surrounding sea was barely recognisable as such. Wreckage, much of it still aflame, was strewn as far as he could see, like the contents of a night's ashtrays dumped in a toilet bowl. Coils of dark yellow smoke rose and flattened shroud-like overhead.

Ten feet away, one arm hooked around a remnant of hull, his face streaked with smoke, drifted the bull-necked man from so many earlier encounters. His free arm was extended across the fragment from the boat, and he was sighting down a handgun, teeth clenched.

Purkiss had jammed the gun he'd taken from Kuznetsov into his belt. He felt for it now, treading water, and got hold of the grip. It was too late, the man's finger was already bearing down on the trigger. At such close range he couldn't miss.

The man's face burst outwards, so unexpectedly that it took Purkiss an instant to realise he had to duck, head beneath the water again, because the man had been shot from behind by something high-velocity and his entire face had become an exit wound. When it sounded safe he lifted his face to the air again. The bull-necked man had rolled off the piece of hull, his head trailing a bloody slick.

Beyond him, Kendrick sprawled belly-down on his own makeshift raft of hull, looking absurdly like an armed body boarder..

'Told you,' he called. 'These Soviet guns. Reliable as hell in all weather.'

Purkiss turned his head, feeling groggy with the movement. A short distance behind Kendrick, also buoyed by a scrap of debris, was Elle, hair plastered across her white face. He wanted to swim over to them – they were fifty feet away, no more – but suddenly he lacked the strength.

In the far distance, towards the shore, sound was rising. Purkiss thought he could see airborne shapes through the smoke and the gloom.

All he could do was tread water and call across one word: 'Done.'

'Better be,' Kendrick answered. 'Ammo's out.'

Because of the ringing in his ears from the cacophony of the last half hour, Purkiss didn't hear the engine until the speed boat was up close, and he turned and saw the keel hurtling across the water straight at his head.

Forty-One

From his position circling a couple of hundred metres away, the Jacobin had cursed, out loud, at the ineptitude of the man on the boat. Instead of striking the engines or the cockpit, the grenade from his launcher had blasted off the Black Hawk's tail rotor. The damage would ultimately prove fatal, but it would be a slow death, and Purkiss would have time to abort the strike as long as the controls remained intact. Seconds later, the explosion in the distance confirmed the Jacobin's fears. He couldn't see it, but the hiss of water that followed it meant that the target had been missed.

When it became clear the chopper was going to land on the boat, the Jacobin had taken evasive action, speeding further out across the sea. By the time he'd circled back, he'd begun to believe Purkiss hadn't made it out alive. But there he was, head dwarfed by the bobbing debris, and there were his friends, too.

The Jacobin felt no disappointment, only emptiness. That, and a professional's urge to salvage what was possible from the situation, always with the future in mind. To clean up. On the horizon the cavalry was stirring, an awe-inspiring flotilla by the sound of it. It meant he had to work quickly.

*

With no time to turn and dive, Purkiss shoved his hands upwards against the water, the movement pushing him down. He ducked his head at the same time, resisting the urge to keep his eyes lifted to the arrowing point of the advancing keel. Once down as far as he could go he tipped on to his back to avoid the deadly churning of the propellors. He recoiled as they chewed the water inches from his face.

By the time he opened his eyes the hull had almost disappeared. He remained submerged, fire in his chest. In a moment he saw the dark shape loom into view again, turning for another pass.

He timed his move precisely so that he was rising to emerge on the side of the hull just as it passed overhead, before it could pick up enough speed to elude his grasp. His hands shot out of the water before his head did and he caught two fingers in a steel ring on the side, some sort of anchor for rigging. Although he felt as though his fingers were being wrenched out of their sockets he hung on, used his grip as a brace to swing his other hand up. He seized the rim of the boat, launched himself out of the water like a gymnast on a bar, and dropped hard into the boat. He was on his haunches, shuddering with the effort and above all the unimaginable cold.

Purkiss rose to stand, thigh muscles screaming, and faced the boat's skipper. Then he gave in and let himself drop into a sitting position, because he wasn't prepared for this. It was too much on top of everything else.

The cliché left his mouth like a breath.

'It's you.'

*

The Jacobin pressed home the advantage then, his surprise cancelled out by Purkiss's own. As Purkiss dropped his hand to the gun tucked in his belt, the Jacobin kicked out sideways. His shoe caught Purkiss high in the chest. Purkiss rocked back on his haunches.

The Jacobin let go of the wheel and moved in with feet flailing, a berserker's fury driving him, but even so he knew he was weakening and so did Purkiss, who was himself sapped. The Jacobin used gravity to aid him, dropping on to Purkiss with an elbow aimed at his throat. Purkiss rolled and took it on the shoulder, stood and brought a knee into the Jacobin's chest – *just there* – and his scream of pain was barely a wheeze. He rolled in turn and started to rise. Purkiss aimed a kick at his face which would have sent him overboard with his skull shattered, but the Jacobin was skilled in countering this particular move. He slapped the foot aside and caught the ankle and flipped it upwards. Purkiss lost his balance, landed heavily on the floor of the boat, hitting his head.

The Jacobin brought a foot up for the killing stamp onto Purkiss's exposed neck. Purkiss swiped the Jacobin's leg out from under him and it was his turn to land hard. Purkiss had slid to the other end of the boat and had the gun out.

And it was over.

*

'You should have let them put the chest drain in. You'd be in better shape.'

Purkiss's words sounded to him thick. Before his eyes swam two men, two boats.

'I did.' Between words Rossiter gave a little start, like a hiccup. He sat against the wheel of the now-drifting boat, both hands pressed against the left side of his chest. Much as Purkiss had seen him in the flat, after the stabbing.

'I had the drain, gave it half an hour. Then got them to remove it and discharged myself.'

'Because you had my friend, Abby, stowed away.'

'In the boot of my car, yes.'

A beat passed. Purkiss felt a flare of panic. Had he passed out for a while? But to the south, the mass of approaching traffic had advanced only slightly.

So many questions. 'Where's Teague?'

'Dead, in the bathroom in my flat.'

'He was on to you.'

'Yes.' He broke off, gasping, his voice softer afterwards. 'I surprised him in my flat, as I told you. But he was there looking for incriminating evidence.'

'You've failed.'

'I have.'

Purkiss didn't ask the obvious question. *Why did you do it?* He found he didn't care. Gingerly, to stop his vision blurring further, he craned round. The speed boat had covered more distance than he'd realised. Kendrick and Elle were specks in the water.

Rossiter said something. Purkiss said, 'What?' partly because he'd only half heard, partly because he had difficulty believing what he had heard.

'You can't take me in.'

'You're asking me to let you go.'

'Of course not.' He broke off, waxen, breath coming in hissing jerks between his teeth. 'You have to kill me.'

Purkiss waited.

'Kill me and dump me. *Quickly.*'

'Why?'

'The Service can't be implicated in any of this.'

Purkiss coughed a laugh. 'Bit late for that.'

'It doesn't have to be. Work with Elle, come up with a narrative. It was all Kuznetsov's doing. The Service wasn't involved at all.'

'The Service *wasn't* involved. You're not Service. You're a traitor.'

'It won't be seen that way.' Despite the pain in his voice he was managing to put urgency in it. 'The Service will be tainted. It'll damage our standing. Weaken us irrevocably.'

'*Our. Us.*' Purkiss shook his head. 'You really are something else, Rossiter.'

'Kill me.'

'No.'

'You'd like to.'

'More than anything else.'

Another beat. Then Rossiter said, 'I can make you.'

*

The first of the helicopters had arrived and were circling above the carnage like crows over roadkill, the gusts from their rotors ruffling the water. Without being asked, Rossiter had reached across from where he was slumped and given the engine some throttle to move the boat further away.

'Claire – your Claire – was mine.'

For a moment Purkiss misunderstood, thought he was hearing soap opera dialogue.

'Best agent I ever had. Bright, ruthless, utterly loyal. A master of subterfuge.'

Purkiss listened, the gun weighing down his hand.

'You know what I'm getting at, don't you.' Rossiter seemed to grin, but it was a grimace as he shifted position. 'She was the one who carried out the hit on the Iranian, Asgari. She told you she was investigating Fallon. Other way round. He was investigating her.'

Rossiter's voice was dwindling, the rushing blood in Purkiss's temples drowning it out.

'I was running her. Recruited her a couple of years after she joined the Service. She had passion, she had commitment. As you well know, John.'

One of the helicopters was taking an interest in them now that others had joined the scene. The crackle of radio static cut the air.

'Fallon was on to her, but he wasn't sure of my identity. Knew there was someone running her, of course, and I was on his list to be investigated. But there were several others, and he began with the people he was certain of. Claire was one of them.'

Purkiss hadn't checked the magazine, wasn't sure how many bullets were left. *Focus on that, focus on anything but what he's saying.*

'She loved you, John. Thought you'd be an ideal recruit, wanted to approach you eventually, open up to you about what we were doing. I agreed with her. You'd have done us proud. But for now, I advised her to keep her activities from you. It was her idea, a masterstroke, to make you believe Fallon was the one needing investigation.

It got you on her side against him, allowed her to gain the benefit of your skills.'

He was remembering what Fallon had said, in the basement.

'Fallon was searching your flat that night when she came home and surprised him. She was a fighter, John, you know that. He did what he had to.'

Fallon had said, and Purkiss had thought he was quibbling self-exculpatingly over semantics, that he'd killed her but not murdered her.

'It was self defence. She could well have killed him that night.'

A searchlight cut through the haze of slatey smoke, pinning them. Purkiss stood, the boat rocking even as it stayed stationary. He raised the gun.

'It isn't true. None of it.'

'But it is true.'

'No it isn't. But this is for suggesting it is,' said Purkiss.

He fired twice, three times.

Forty-Two

He leaned on the rail, watching a freighter lumber its way through the black water. To the left the river curved away from the bleak Essex marshes towards the sea.

The tang of cigarette smoke was what he noticed first. He didn't turn, not even when he was joined at the rail a few feet to his right. For once Vale had let him choose the meeting place. Purkiss didn't know why he'd decided on this spot. Claire had liked the Thames. Perhaps that was it.

They stood in silence for a minute, the raw October wind coming down the estuary off the North Sea, bringing with it creaking gulls and the stench of decomposing fish. Vale lit another cigarette and pitched the match into the reeds. Purkiss watched it stick headlong in the mud.

'You'll have worked it out, I imagine.' Had Vale's voice become coarser since he'd last heard it? He glanced across and yes, the man appeared to have aged, though it was barely two weeks since he'd last seen him.

'Fallon was your man all along. From before he killed Claire.'

Vale took a long drag, spoke on the exhale. 'He was my first agent, the first one I ran after leaving the Service. The original Ratcatcher, if you will. I'd set him on the trail of whomever it was that was co-ordinating the hits on Asgari the Iranian and others. He discovered Claire was involved. Obviously she wasn't the ringleader.'

'And he agreed to take the fall for Claire's death, accept a murder conviction, to keep his cover intact. With the promise that he'd be out in a few years.'

'Correct. We had credible intelligence that the Jacobin was operating in Tallinn –'

'The Jacobin?'

Vale waved his cigarette hand. 'Fallon's nickname for the ringleader, Rossiter as it turned out. You know what a French Revolution buff Fallon was. Burke's *Reflections* and all that.' He drew on the butt again. 'Rather apt, I suppose, "The Jacobin". A fanatic, committed to the destruction of the enemy, blind to all else.'

'Sounds like you had a fair amount of affection for Fallon.'

Vale sighed. 'Yes, I did care for him. He was a brilliant agent, a brilliant man. You liked him as well, you must admit. Before... well, before.'

'So after he went to gaol, you needed me as – what? Filler?'

'Far from it. I needed a replacement for him. You were the best there was.'

'And once he was out, I'd step back into the shadows?'

'*No.*' It was the first time Vale had raised his voice. 'I couldn't run you two as a team, naturally. But you'd be my agents, both superb, each with his own unique talents for particular situations.'

Purkiss watched the water fowl for a while.

'Seppo and Fallon were sharing the flat in Tallinn.'

'Yes. Seppo was mainly a backup man. Fallon knew the Jacobin was one of the three, Rossiter, Teague or Klavan. He penetrated Kuznetsov's crew by getting in with that woman. Then he went missing. I couldn't very well just send you in to rescue him. You'd never have gone. So I had to create the legend that Seppo had only recently spotted him in the city, that he'd been released from prison without my knowledge.'

'And when I told you later I was refusing to pull out, broke off contact with you –'

'I didn't exactly tear myself apart trying to persuade you otherwise, no.' Vale made a sound as dry as the leaves in his cigarette. 'I must admit, I was worried you'd get suspicious then.'

*

Vale had moved quickly in the aftermath of the downing of the Black Hawk, working with the Embassy in Tallinn, securing the release of Purkiss and Elle and Kendrick. Purkiss himself had been patched up with fair speed. The other two spent several days in hospital with hypothermia before flying back to London. In the meantime, the remaining members of Kuznetsov's crew had been identified and either apprehended or subjected to the sort of manhunt that was mounted by the security forces of a country the size of Estonia perhaps once in a generation. Christopher Teague's body had been found in Rossiter's bathtub, neck broken, hand still clasped around the paperknife he'd used to stab Rossiter.

Abby's body had been flown home. Purkiss had wanted to speak to her distraught, bewildered parents in Bolton, but Vale had stopped him. The Official Secrets Act applied, and Purkiss had to remain in the shadows. He and Kendrick would attend her funeral, though, no doubt keeping back in the rain while the small crowd of family and friends stood bowed and shaking in the churchyard afterwards.

Purkiss spent more time with Vale in those first days than he had for months previously, yet they hadn't talked properly before today. In his head Purkiss had played out today's inevitable encounter in all the forms he could imagine it taking. He hadn't been prepared for *this*, this bald stating of facts, this utter absence of affect.

Vale flicked another spent match, this one far enough to draw the momentary attention of a gull before it dropped into the water. 'Think about what life would have been like if you'd known about Claire from the start. Think of the last four years. Bitterness, self-loathing at having been taken in by her... all the things you're experiencing now. You wouldn't have gained anything by finding out earlier. But you would have lost four years.'

Purkiss swallowed, and for a moment thought his throat would stay closed permanently. 'So the more years of your life you spend wallowing in delusion, the better?'

'Sometimes,' said Vale. 'Sometimes it's better not to know.'

They watched a cargo ship groan and blink its way down the river until it was out of sight. Purkiss said, 'What's happened to him?'

'Rossiter? Yes, you have a right to know if anyone does.' Vale rubbed his eye with the thumb of his cigarette hand. 'It's all very hush hush, no trial or anything. He's kept his mouth shut, so far. Everything's been tried, from the usual threats to an offer of full immunity.'

'Are you serious?'

'Oh, of course. That was always going to be an option. And no, I don't like it any more than you do. But in some ways it doesn't matter because you know what drives him. He'd never accept something like that. No, my bet is we'll never find out who else he was running, if there was anyone else. He'll rot in a cell for the rest of his days.'

'I've heard that before.' Purkiss looked away.

'You must have been tempted.'

In his mind's eye Purkiss saw Rossiter cowering, injured chest forgotten as his hands came up to protect his face, the shots chipping and splintering the boat around him. When the shooting stopped he lowered his hands and looked at Purkiss. In his eyes was defeat, and acceptance.

Purkiss straightened, walked along the railing away from Vale. He saw movement below, and stopped.

From behind him Vale said: 'So this is where you throw your badge and gun into the river.'

Down in the thicket of mud-smeared reeds something flopped wetly. A rodent of some sort.

'What's it to be?' Vale said.

Purkiss turned to look at him. 'What do you think?'

THE END

Acknowledgements

My thanks are due to Jon Elek, literary agent at A.P. Watt, for his enthusiasm, encouragement and editorial input. Thanks also to Stephen Hopkins for technical advice, Tony Buckley for pointing the way down some extremely interesting avenues, and Jane Dixon-Smith at JD Smith Design for the cover.

Finally, heartfelt thanks to my wife, Pippa, to whom this book is dedicated, for her love and forbearance.

19066413R00251